The feel
sent a
trickling

His musky scent invaded her nostrils, heightening her awareness of him.

"It's timing and precision," Quinn said, his voice a husky murmur beside her ear.

Piper shivered, amazed at the unprecedented sensations that rippled through her. Why was it, she wondered, that this man affected her on so many different levels when none of her suitors ever had?

When she cocked her arm, while his hand guided the motion to ensure the proper flick of her wrist, she could feel his muscled chest pressed against her back. His solid thighs were meshed against the backs of her legs. The whisper of his breath caused gooseflesh to pebble her skin. Piper had difficulty breathing.

Sweet mercy! All she really wanted to do was turn in his surrounding arms and help herself to a taste of him…!

* * *

The Ranger's Woman
Harlequin Historical #748—April 2005

Praise for Carol Finch

"Carol Finch is known for her lightning-fast,
roller-coaster-ride adventure romances that are
brimming over with a large cast of characters
and dozens of perilous escapades."
—*Romantic Times*

Praise for previous titles

Texas Bride
"Finch delivers another well-paced western with likable,
realistic characters, a well-crafted backdrop and
just enough history and sensual tension to
satisfy western and romance readers."
—*Romantic Times*

Call of the White Wolf
"The wholesome goodness of the characters…
will touch your heart and soul."
—*Rendezvous*

"A love story that aims straight for the heart
and never misses."
—*Romantic Times*

**DON'T MISS THESE OTHER
TITLES AVAILABLE NOW:**

#747 THE VISCOUNT
Lyn Stone

#749 THE BETROTHAL
Terri Brisbin, Joanne Rock and Miranda Jarrett

#750 ABBIE'S OUTLAW
Victoria Bylin

CAROL FINCH

THE RANGER'S WOMAN

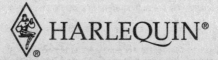

HARLEQUIN®

TORONTO • NEW YORK • LONDON
AMSTERDAM • PARIS • SYDNEY • HAMBURG
STOCKHOLM • ATHENS • TOKYO • MILAN • MADRID
PRAGUE • WARSAW • BUDAPEST • AUCKLAND

If you purchased this book without a cover you should be aware that this book is stolen property. It was reported as "unsold and destroyed" to the publisher, and neither the author nor the publisher has received any payment for this "stripped book."

ISBN 0-373-29348-8

THE RANGER'S WOMAN

Copyright © 2005 by Connie Feddersen

All rights reserved. Except for use in any review, the reproduction or utilization of this work in whole or in part in any form by any electronic, mechanical or other means, now known or hereafter invented, including xerography, photocopying and recording, or in any information storage or retrieval system, is forbidden without the written permission of the publisher, Harlequin Enterprises Limited, 225 Duncan Mill Road, Don Mills, Ontario, Canada M3B 3K9.

All characters in this book have no existence outside the imagination of the author and have no relation whatsoever to anyone bearing the same name or names. They are not even distantly inspired by any individual known or unknown to the author, and all incidents are pure invention.

This edition published by arrangement with Harlequin Books S.A.

® and TM are trademarks of the publisher. Trademarks indicated with ® are registered in the United States Patent and Trademark Office, the Canadian Trade Marks Office and in other countries.

www.eHarlequin.com

Printed in U.S.A.

Please address questions and book requests to:
Harlequin Reader Service
U.S.: 3010 Walden Ave., P.O. Box 1325, Buffalo, NY 14269
Canadian: P.O. Box 609, Fort Erie, Ont. L2A 5X3

This book is dedicated to my husband, Ed, and our children, Kurt, Jill, Christie, Shawnna, Jon and Jeff. And to our grandchildren, Livia, Blake, Kennedy and Brooklynn. Hugs and kisses!

Chapter One

~~~~~~~~~~~

Southwest Texas, June 1877

What the devil am I doing, Piper Sullivan asked herself as she stepped up into the stagecoach to endure more endless hours of being bounced and jostled in her arduous journey westward. Thus far, she had encountered six unruly and offensive individuals during her exhausting trip from Galveston to Fort Stockton. And the rugged-looking traveler who sank down across from her had all the markings of further trouble. He looked unapproachable. And as disagreeable as the meal she had ingested at lunch.

Piper pegged the man as a shiftless gambler, judging by his style of dress and the well-used pistols that hung low on his hips. She watched him sprawl inelegantly on the seat across from her. His long, muscular legs straddled her feet to accommodate his six-foot-four-inch frame.

The solemn expression in his golden eyes assured

Piper that this was not a man who was teeming with charm and warmth. And worse, he kept staring at her. *Through* her was more like it, as if he was probing beneath her outward appearance to reveal the fact that she was an *imposter.*

Piper had carefully disguised herself as an aging widow, complete with a thick concealing veil, gloves, cane and padded black gown that made her appear thirty pounds heavier. Unfortunately, she didn't feel as well protected as she would have preferred when her companion kept appraising her astutely.

Piper thought it was ironic that for the first time in her life she *wanted* people to take her at face value and not probe deeper to discover who she was on the inside. But to her way of thinking, the *lack* of association with anyone during this trip was important. She also decided that making a *bad* first impression would help to protect her from trouble.

As she'd done with the others, Piper made a point to alienate her companion by getting in her bluff, right from the start. "Staring is considered rude where I come from," Piper declared as she squirmed uncomfortably on the hard seat.

The man never changed expression and he didn't move, which annoyed her because he still had her feet trapped between his long legs and she felt pinned in. That was not what she needed while battling the sour stomach caused by her midday meal.

"Would you mind giving me my own space," she requested. "I paid for *half* of these meager accommodations, after all."

When he whipped his head around his long dark hair scraped the collar of his jacket. His square jaw—that sported three days' growth of stubble—clenched. His thick brows swooped down as he leveled an intense stare on her.

As stares went, this one was quite unnerving. But Piper had squared off against her domineering father enough times during her twenty years of existence to learn how to hold her ground. This rough-edged rascal was *not* going to intimidate her.

"You've got a complaint?" he drawled in challenge.

She nodded curtly. "Indeed I do."

He made a stabbing gesture toward the ceiling. "Then ride up top with the guard and driver if you don't like the company or the cramped space."

His smirking voice was like gravel and grit and it set her teeth on edge. Was he purposely trying to annoy her? That was supposed to be *her* role to protect her identity.

Piper didn't think *he* was putting on an act.

Resigned to an unpleasant journey with her disagreeable companion, she occupied her time by glancing out the window to pan the miles of rolling range that seemed to stretch out forever. And as she recalled her father's unacceptable decree that she would soon wed a man he had handpicked for her, she stiffened her resolve. Traveling cross-country—for four endless days—with one offensive male companion after another was far better than marrying a man who inspired no respect and affection.

Piper had given up on finding the kind of love her older sister had discovered. Of all the men her father had thrust in her direction since she turned sixteen, none of them interested her. She was tired of being told that she was too strong-willed and spirited and that she needed to change her ways to become a suitable wife for some dandy. In addition, she had given up trying to be someone she wasn't, just to appease her father. Neither did she want her life decided for her without having a say in the matter.

Brace up, Piper. Your sister is waiting at the end of the trail and so is your new life. You just have to ride through hell to get there, is all.

When a cloud of smoke rolled over her, then swept out the window, Piper choked for breath. She glared at her inconsiderate companion who had lit his cigar.

"In case you haven't heard it is not considered good manners to smoke in front of women," she pointed out.

Undaunted, he took another draw on the cigar, then blew smoke rings that drifted toward her. She swallowed a chuckle when he tossed her a defiant smile. Having a man challenge her rather than fawn and pamper her was a refreshing change.

However, she had to remain in character. It wouldn't do to let the ornery gambler know that he amused her. Her whole objective was to make sure he wanted very little association with her.

Determined to be as cantankerous as he was, she shot out her hand to grab his cheroot. After she tossed it out the window she waited to see how he would react.

He glared at her. No surprise there.

"That was an expensive cheroot," he muttered at her.

"And you were being purposely rude. Now we're even." She nudged the calf of his right leg with the heel of her shoe. "And move your feet, *please*. I will not stay cramped for hours because you refuse to stay in your half of the space."

Grudgingly, her companion shifted his shoulder against the corner of the seat and stretched his legs diagonally to grant her a fraction more space.

"Thank you," she said aloofly.

"*Please* tell me that you're getting off at the next stage stop," he grumbled.

"Ah, that I could be so lucky." She made a big production of flicking imaginary ashes off her sleeve. "But no. I'm bound for Fort Davis."

The news didn't appear to please him. He just kept staring intently at her.

"And you, sonny? Where are you headed?" she asked, hoping to divert his attention so he would stop evaluating her so closely.

His massive shoulders lifted and dropped lackadaisically. "Haven't decided. I'll stop for a drink and a game of poker whenever the mood strikes."

She studied him for a long moment. "Do you find it rewarding to live a life of no obligations or commitments, drifting from one dusty frontier town to the next?"

He flashed her an one-eyed squint. "It's a living."

When he narrowed those unnerving amber eyes at her, she resolved to let him know she intended to stand her ground and that she was not a woman who could be pushed around or easily intimidated.

Having been raised in polite society, constantly told

to guard her tongue and to cater to the powerful and elite, she found it amazingly gratifying using her disguise as a curmudgeon to speak her mind. And she had learned the knack from the best, she reminded herself. In fact, her former instructor at finishing school was the inspiration for her disguise and her imperious demeanor. The old battle-ax had given Piper fits for years.

"Gambling is not much of a living, as I see it," she replied. "Fleecing folks for profit is hardly what I would call respectable. A man should strive to make something of himself, not squander his life on cigars, card games and loose women."

"This is going to be a helluva long ride through rough country, lady," he told her gruffly. "Try to keep your nagging and lectures to a minimum because you're liable to tick me off."

"I thought I already had," she said, biting back a mischievous snicker.

"Trust me, that's the very last thing you should want to do, especially since this stretch of road has been plagued by outlaws. I might not be inclined to defend your honor if I'm so fed up with you that I'm ready to let the thieves have right at you."

She chuckled from behind her dark veil. "If you are trying to frighten me into submission then you have wasted your breath. At my advanced age, I do not feel the need to kowtow to anyone, you and prospective desperadoes included."

She poked the end of her cane into his sternum, pushing him back against the seat. "Trust *me,* mister, you don't want to get on my bad side, either."

He stared at the black cane that poked his chest. "You have a good side?"

"Not much left of it these days," she said, then resettled her cane beside her.

"Not much left of mine, either, so don't push it."

He grabbed the hat beside his hip and pulled it low on his forehead. He closed those penetrating amber eyes that reminded her of a mountain lion's.

Piper smiled in satisfaction when the gambler settled in for what she supposed was a nap. But he didn't fool her into thinking that he was sleeping. No doubt, this pantherlike man was merely lying in wait.

Shifting sideways, Piper struck the same pose as the gambler and tried to catch a much-needed nap to soothe her churning stomach. The monotony of the overland trip was wearing her down. She wanted nothing more than to be reunited with her sister, Penelope, at Fort Davis, without losing the money and valuables she carried to make her new start in life. Learning that this area was crawling with thieves did nothing to reassure her.

The thought prompted Piper to push her reticule protectively beneath her hip before she closed her eyes and nodded off.

From beneath half-mast eyelids Quinn Callahan appraised the crotchety old hag who had finally dozed off. She was swathed in yards of black fabric, her head and face concealed behind an oversize plumed hat that was draped with a heavy veil. He could easily imagine what the witch looked like—beady eyes, hooked nose and pointy chin. And plump as a grain-fed old hen.

Yet, there was something about the way she moved, the way she held herself, that didn't quite ring true. But Quinn reminded himself that he was cautious and suspicious by nature—and habit. It was difficult to grasp what there was about her that niggled him because he was too busy countering her taunting comments.

Which made him wonder if she was doing it to distract him. From what? He wasn't sure. But every time he stared overly long at her she dreamed up something to say that dragged his attention away from the way she looked and forced him to concentrate on her challenging remarks.

And then there was her grating, nasal voice that sounded so unpleasant to his ears. If he didn't know better he would swear she was purposely trying to alienate him. Just why was that? He didn't know the answer to that, either.

One thing that didn't escape his attention was how she had tucked her beaded purse protectively beside her after he mentioned the possibility of encountering outlaws. He was willing to bet she was carrying a great deal of money that would make her ripe for the picking.

Well, it didn't matter what this persnickety—and obviously wealthy—old widow was up to, Quinn told himself. He was a man on a mission. He had volunteered to pose as a shiftless gambler who boasted about his recent winnings to every stage agent and employee he met along the route from Fort Stockton.

And Quinn would bet his life savings that the gang he was after—that spoke in code and referred to themselves as the Knights of the Golden Circle—had spies working for the stage line.

That was the only logical explanation for the accurate targeting of passengers who carried valuables and cash.

Quinn had made the same monotonous ride back and forth to El Paso three times in the last two weeks, and had gained nothing for his exhausting efforts. Tired, impatient and cranky though he was, he vowed to make this trip a dozen more times, if need be. He wouldn't rest until he encountered the ruthless outlaws that had killed the one true friend he'd ever had. The attack had taken place six months earlier in a secluded canyon near Catoosa Gulch. He was going to become bait for the thieves so he could track them to their remote hideout.

His thoughts trailed off when the coach hit a deep rut and catapulted him against the ceiling. He braced himself as he watched the old woman tumble willy-nilly off the seat. She let loose with a shrill squawk when she sprawled atop his legs.

When he reached down to upright her she elbowed him out of the way and crawled onto the seat. "Keep your hands to yourself," she demanded huffily.

"I was only trying to help," he said defensively as he watched her fluff the dust off her gown and sink a little deeper into her corner of the coach.

"I've taken care of myself for years. Confounded conveyance coaches anyway," she grumbled before she craned her neck out the window to scan the area.

Quinn studied her discreetly as she leaned farther out to survey their surroundings—to check for the outlaws he had mentioned earlier, no doubt. He kept waiting for the breeze to lift that heavy veil so he could get a good look at her. But she withdrew before the air rushing past the speeding coach caught her veiled hat and sent it flying away.

"Well, thank God," she said with a relieved sigh. "About time we had a rest stop."

Quinn glanced outside to see the station a half mile ahead of them. He was more than ready to stretch his legs and boast of his supposed winnings to the stage line's hired help. He silently willed the nest of outlaws to attack so he could do what he had been sent here to do. As for the perplexing widow, he thought that having her wits scared out of her might improve her disposition.

He glanced at her again as the stage rolled to a stop, then decided that being frisked and robbed would probably make her more difficult to deal with than she was already.

Piper didn't wait for the gambler to exit the coach first so he could hand her down. She couldn't risk having him touch her more often than necessary without arousing his suspicion.

Leaning on her cane to remain in character, she watched three Mexican attendants stride from the corral, leading a fresh team of horses. Her gaze strayed reflexively to the gambler who emerged from the coach. His long shadow fell over her, eclipsing the afternoon sun. Despite her better judgment, she found herself oddly fascinated by his rugged appearance and the confident way he held himself. The comparison to a graceful mountain cat came to mind as she watched him saunter over to strike up a conversation in Spanish with one of the attendants.

Physically speaking, he was a rare specimen of brawn and muscle. Nothing like the gentleman dandies she was accustomed to. Not that she would ever be romantically interested in any of the suitors who treated her like a prize catch because of her wealth and affluence in polite society. Neither would she be interested in a man like this gambler, she assured herself sensibly.

Truth be told, Piper wasn't sure she wanted any man in her life at the moment. And maybe never. She had given up on the idea of love and romance because she had never found a man who inspired her affection, no one who was willing to accept her for who she was.

The whole objective of this long jaunt was to gain control of her own existence without some man trying to dictate, manipulate and use her for his ulterior purposes, she reminded herself.

Her gaze narrowed in concern while she watched the gambler fish two silver dollars from the pocket of his gold brocade vest, then roll them over his fingertips. He had told her no more than three hours ago that thieves lurked in this area. Yet here he was, flashing coins that caught the rapt attention of the stage attendants.

Piper surged forward, tapping her cane in agitation. She clutched the gambler's arm to draw him aside. "What the dickens are you doing?" she said with a quiet hiss. "Put those coins out of sight. You might as well send an engraved invitation to outlaws that you have money for the taking."

Quinn stared down at the old crone who stood only a few inches over five feet tall. Her mouth, he decided, was bigger than she was and she never hesitated in using it. "Where did you get the idea that anything I do is your business?"

Her head snapped up and he knew instinctively that she was glowering at him. "*Your* carelessness and lack of discretion might affect *me*. Can't you find something else to do besides flaunt your money?"

Quinn did exactly that. He pulled another cigar from his vest and lit it up. When he blew smoke over the top of that ridiculous-looking plumed hat she grew exasperated and tramped off. Her cane beat a sharp staccato on the trodden path.

"A relative of yours, gringo?" one of the stage attendants asked as his gaze followed the old battle-ax until she disappeared around the corner of the adobe station.

Quinn chuckled. "Not hardly. We just met. I'm hoping it will be a short acquaintance."

To ensure that the attendants knew he carried valuables as well as money, he retrieved the expensive gold pocket watch to check the time. He also flashed the diamond ring he wore on his pinky finger. He noted the interest he had drawn from one of the Mexicans—the same man he remembered from his previous jaunts along this route. He took note of the fact that the man was wearing the same patterned red bandana around his neck that another attendant had been wearing at one of the relay stations.

Quinn frowned curiously as he ambled toward the barn to stretch his legs. As he recollected, at least one attendant at every stage stop between here and El Paso wore similar bandanas. Coincidence? He didn't think so. He wouldn't be surprised to learn that was how the ring of far-flung spies identified each other.

Quinn derailed from his train of thought when he heard a wild feminine shriek. Instinctively, he took off at a dead run. When he rounded the corner of the building he saw the widow plastered against the wall, staring at the mutt that bounded around her. When she jabbed her cane forward, the mutt gnawed on the end of it.

"Get away, you beast," she said, scowling.

"Are you talking to me?" Quinn had to ask.

"No, this mongrel." She jerked back the cane and the oversize pup approached her.

Quinn barked a laugh when the dog reared up on its hind legs and planted its saucer-size front paws on her bosom. "He's not attacking. For some reason the pup likes you."

That in itself surprised him because the old harridan seemed to go out of her way to ensure folks took a wide berth around her. He was still trying to figure out why.

"Get down!" she ordered the mutt. "And behave yourself. I have dealt with enough bad manners for one day."

To his disbelief, the mutt sank down obediently on its haunches and stared adoringly at her. The dog was obviously so starved for affection that he was ready to align himself with the devil's sister.

"That's much better," she cooed at the pup.

Quinn frowned, bemused by the abrupt change in her voice. His curiosity doubled when she reached down to scratch behind the pup's floppy ear—the other one stood straight up. Whining, the mutt rolled onto his back, paws stuck in the air, so she could scratch his belly.

"Wonders never cease," he murmured as he left the

hag with her new friend—the first and last she would likely make during this trip—to get something to eat.

Piper waited until the gambler rounded the corner before she sank to her knees to give the pup another affectionate pat. The dog had startled her when he came bounding up from nowhere to pounce zealously at her. She had expected to be attacked, but from the looks of this scrawny creature all he wanted was food and affection.

"Come along, dog," she encouraged as she got to her feet. "If this meal is as unappetizing to the palate as the one I had for lunch then you can have my portion."

The pup bounded onto all fours and trailed along behind her—until the station manager gave him a kick in the flanks when he tried to walk inside. "Get out and stay out, you fleabag."

Piper whacked her cane against the man's shins before he could give the poor pup another painful kick. "Leave him alone!" While the barrel-bellied man glowered at her, she surveyed the shadowy dining area, listening to the buzzing of flies, noting the table still had food stuck to it from previous meals. "You may bring my meal outside and don't be stingy with the portions. In fact, I'll have *two* plates for supper," she insisted as she plucked a coin from her reticule then handed it to the proprietor.

Leaving the man staring after her, Piper spun on her heels and hobbled off.

The pup followed devotedly behind her.

"That old lady sure is full of spit and vinegar, ain't she?" the manager said to Quinn.

"Seems to be," he murmured absently as he watched

her move more swiftly than he might have expected of someone in her declining years.

The proprietor dipped up several cups of beans and sloshed them on the tin plates. "Here," he said. "You take these out to the witch and tell her not to waste food on that mutt because he's slated for execution. He showed up here two days ago and keeps trying to chase the horses for entertainment. I won't put up with that. These horses have to stay in tip-top shape to pull the coaches."

Carrying two platters of greasy beans, stale bread and a chunk of meat he couldn't identify because it was burned to a crisp, Quinn strode over to the shade tree where the dragon lady had plunked down, her faithful mutt by her side.

"Don't get too attached to the mutt," Quinn cautioned as he handed her one plate and set the other one on the grass for the dog. "The manager is talking extermination. This could be the mutt's last meal."

Quinn started when the woman suddenly bounded to her feet with considerable speed and agility.

She thrust her plate back at him. "We'll just see about that! Extermination indeed!"

And off she went, leaving Quinn to watch the mutt slurp up the beans, then devour the bread in two gulps. A moment later the crone approached, carrying another plate of beans. In disbelief, Quinn watched her set a second plate between the mutt's oversize front paws.

"No one is going to turn you into tomorrow's main course," she told the dog in that nasal voice that reminded Quinn of someone raking fingernails across a blackboard. "Your miserable life just got better, dog. Wish I could say the same for mine."

Quinn rolled his eyes when the woman plunked down to pat the mutt's head while he gobbled the second helping of food. What was wrong with this woman? She could be civil and caring to a scroungy mutt, but she wanted nothing to do with him?

Well, what else was new? he asked himself as he handed her the supper plate, then walked off to take his meal indoors. He had been fighting for respect and acceptance for most of his life and never got it. He had been fighting, period. Hell, it was all he knew.

Since when did you start brooding over the hand fate dealt you, Callahan? You just play your cards the best you can and consider yourself lucky. Your life could be worse. You've already seen the worst humanity can rain down on each other. Just right the wrong and see to it that justice gets served.

Chapter Two

This poor dog was not going to be rejected and cast off the same way her father had turned his back on her older sister, Piper decided as the gambler walked off. Indeed, part of the objective of this trip was to see that her sister received rightful compensation. She was here to ensure that at least one of Roarke Sullivan's loud decrees didn't stick. If Roarke hadn't realized it yet, he would soon discover that he had lost control over *both* his daughters.

Resolved of purpose, Piper made sure the mutt was well fed and bathed and approached the waiting coach. When she alighted inside the gambler squinted at her.

"About time. We're ten minutes behind schedule."

The crooked smile that came and went in the blink of an eye suggested that he was purposely taunting her. Piper rose to the occasion. "Can't imagine that it would matter much to a man who has no particular place to go

and has no pressing engagement when he gets there."
She shoved his long muscled legs sideways with her
heel to grant her half the floor space.

She snapped her fingers at the mutt that stared hopefully up at her. "Well? Are you coming or not?" When
she patted the space beside her on the seat the dog
launched himself inside, his wet tail banging against the
opened door.

"You are kidding," the gambler said in astonishment
as he watched the pup turn a tight circle, then plunk
down next to her. "You both smell like wet dog."

"I have heard that cleanliness is next to godliness,"
she countered.

He smirked. "Didn't know God categorized folks by
how often they bathed."

"Perhaps not but I didn't want the mutt to offend you
when he climbed aboard with me. I certainly wasn't
going to leave him behind to die."

"You're all heart, ma'am."

"Likewise, I'm sure."

Piper hated to admit it, but she actually enjoyed their
banter. Thus far, the other male passengers had let her
be after one or two of her pointed remarks. But this gambler gave as good as he got. Plus, he hadn't tried to im-
press her with polished manners and premeditated
charm. Not that he had any to spare, of course. The fact
that she found this man intriguing and physically appealing astounded her.

"By the way, what is your name? I see no reason for
me to keep referring to you as the no-account gambler,"
she teased.

"Cal."

"Cal what?"

"Just Cal. Short and sweet."

"Short, yes," she said, chuckling. "But I'm not so sure about sweet."

When he leaned toward her the mutt jerked up his head. But Cal didn't seem the least bit alarmed that the dog had become protective of her. She rather suspected that he was trying to get a better look at her through the dark veil.

He tossed her a mocking grin. "What should I call you besides the nagging old hag?"

"Agatha Stewart," she said without missing a beat.

"Agatha," he repeated, rolling the name off his tongue. "Somehow that fits you. So…are you going west to *torment* anyone in particular?"

She snickered in amusement. "Just my sister. Luckily we are a great deal alike," she replied, wondering why she was daring to spend so much time conversing with Cal. She knew she would be better off if they traveled in silence. But she had to admit that she was curious about him and wanted to get to know him better. "Do you have family somewhere, *Calvin?*"

His dark brows flattened and he frowned at her. "The name is just plain Cal."

"So you say," she said with a dismissive flick of her gloved hand. "Where does your kin call home?"

Something flickered in his eyes that made Piper think she had accidentally hit an exposed nerve. When he settled himself deeper into the seat and folded his arms over his broad chest, as if closing himself off from her, she stared bemusedly at him.

"I don't have kin, Agatha."

"I'm sorry. I didn't mean to pry," she murmured sincerely.

He shrugged. "Forget it." A moment later a lopsided smile crossed his sensuous lips—and confound it, she was annoyed with herself for noticing. "I'm sure you just couldn't help yourself. Meddling probably comes naturally."

Piper was enormously affected by his smile because it altered his entire appearance and changed her perception of him. For the first time in their association she sensed hidden warmth in him, a flicker of humanity. Maybe he wasn't as much of a good-for-nothing as she had first thought.

He *had* tried to upright her when the bouncing coach sent her plummeting onto the floorboards. He had also been the only one to rush to her rescue when the oversize mutt had startled her. Plus, he had carted out food to her for supper.

He was not without a few saving graces, she realized.

"I hail from Galveston," she said conversationally, careful to keep the nasal twang in her voice. "My family is disgustingly rich and I have been pampered and spoiled my whole life. Extenuating circumstances, which I won't bore you with, have made me wary and cynical."

"Then we are the perfect traveling companions," he replied. "We may seem like exact opposites, but I suspect we are very much alike." He nodded his head toward the pup sleeping contentedly beside her. "Like the mutt, I've been kicked around, cursed, ridiculed and rejected most of my life. I'm a mite cynical and suspicious myself, but for entirely different reasons. So…are we about done with the idle chitchat, Agatha? It's not one of my best talents."

"I do believe we are done with the chitchat," she said as she settled back on the seat.

His previous comment about leading a hard life aroused her curiosity. But Piper cautioned herself not to become overly intrigued by a man who was never going to be more than a temporary footnote in this chapter of her life.

"I could use some shut-eye," he mumbled.

That said, he pulled down his Stetson hat, swung his muscled legs up on the seat and settled in for a nap.

Left with nothing to do—a hazard of lengthy overland coach travel—Piper stared out the window. She surveyed the rugged mountains that rose in the distance, admiring the looming peaks that were swathed in the red-and-purple hues of the sunset.

When the coach hit a bump in the road, she braced herself against the window frame, then patted the mutt's head when he stirred beside her. Piper noticed that Cal simply shifted on the seat and braced his feet to counter the jarring motion of the coach. This time it looked as if he were actually sleeping rather than faking it.

Piper decided she might as well catch a nap, too. What else was there to do besides contemplate the man across from her? She had thought about him entirely too much already.

Somewhere around midnight, the coach ground to a halt and Quinn groaned tiredly. Having traveled this route recently he knew they had reached the isolated trading post that rented upstairs rooms to passengers. He stretched his arms and worked the kinks from his back. An amused smile quirked his lips when he noticed Agatha had conked out and lay at an uncomfortable angle on the seat. The dog had curled up between her bent knees and her outflung right arm.

Damn if Quinn could figure out why that mutt was so devoted to the old woman.

Well, yes, he could, come to think of it. Persnickety and outspoken though she could be, she seemed to have a soft spot for strays. She had defended the mutt's right to survival against anyone who dared to cross her. It was encouraging to know that beneath Agatha's prickly armor of defense beat a kind and caring heart.

He doubted, however, that she wanted many people to know that because it would destroy the standoffish air she tried to project. But *why* she wanted to keep people at arm's length he couldn't figure out. Of course, there were several things about Agatha that puzzled him, he reminded himself.

Quinn reached over to nudge her shoulder, which seemed to be strangely well padded. He wondered if it was her insulation against the rough coach ride from Galveston. "Agatha," he murmured. "Wake up. There's a cot with your name on it at this trading post."

Her quiet moan surprised him. It sounded nothing like the grating voice he was accustomed to hearing from her. Frowning, he studied her in the dim lantern light that sprayed through the window. Yep, there was definitely something about this old hag that didn't quite add up.

The thought turned to a flash of pain when she came awake with a start and accidentally banged her head into his chin when she pushed herself upright. His teeth snapped together so quickly that he bit his tongue.

"Oh, sorry, Calvin. Where are we? What's going on? Are we being robbed?" she demanded in an unfamiliar voice.

"No, we've just stopped for the night," he said, studying her suspiciously.

Abruptly, she became the old woman he thought he knew. Her voice changed, and so did her manner. Her image shifted before his eyes as she clutched her cane, then tapped him on the shoulder with it.

"You climb down first. I'll be behind you when I get my wits together."

And so he climbed down. He also waited beside the coach—just in case she stumbled and needed a hand down. The dog bailed out first and trotted off to the nearest scrub bush. Then Agatha's plumed hat and veil came into view. For a split second Quinn thought he caught sight of her face in the light, but she ducked her head so quickly that he couldn't tell what she looked like.

Having been warned off previously, he didn't offer to take her hand, but he waited nearby in case she found herself in need of his support. He watched as she carefully extended her foot to the step. She anchored her hands on the door frame, then stepped down beside him.

"Nice place." She smirked as she scanned the shabby stone and timber trading post that had been built at the base of the rugged mountains. "I've heard this part of Texas referred to as Hell's Fringe. It seems to fit."

"At least the place is reasonably clean," he reported as he fell into step beside her. He flashed her a wry grin. "It even has a tub upstairs for those of us who need to bathe. Naturally, I'll want to spiffy up so I won't offend you."

She burst out with a hee-hee-hee, much to his amazement. "Oh, come now, Calvin, surely you know me well enough by now to realize that I would have insisted that you ride up top with the driver and guard if I found you offensive."

Curiosity got the better of him as they entered the crude trading post. "Let me guess, you ousted someone during the first leg of your journey. Forced them up to the luggage rack, did you?"

"Of course I did. The two heathens reeked of whiskey and turned offensively obnoxious. The stench was so overpowering that it made my eyes water. If I were younger *I* would have climbed atop the coach to avoid them."

"It might help if you discarded that thick veil," Quinn suggested. "It probably traps in smoke and foul aromas."

"And expose this horribly disfigured face of mine?" she scoffed. "Trust me, Calvin, this veil is for your convenience and protection as much as mine."

When the proprietor—who, according to the wooden plaque on the counter was named Ike—objected to the mutt following Agatha inside, she chastised the mammoth of a man. It wasn't until she offered a silver dollar to pay for the mutt, that the proprietor backed off.

"Okay, lady, but keep that mangy animal off the bed," Ike insisted harshly.

"Deal. But I just bathed him. He is as clean as the rest

of us. And certainly much easier to get along with," she said with a disgruntled sniff.

She plucked the key from his beefy hand and swept off, her cane thumping rhythmically against the floor and the steps as she disappeared from sight.

"Feisty old witch," Ike muttered after her.

"Hey, leave her alone." Quinn slammed his mouth shut, wondering why he was defending Agatha.

Apparently, Ike was wondering the same thing because he blinked at him in surprise. "That your granny or something?" he asked as he handed over the room key.

"No, but if I had one I'd want her to be just as full of sass and spunk as Agatha. She doesn't take any guff and she doesn't let anyone push her around. You gotta admire that about her."

"Do I?" Ike pocketed the extra dollar. "Don't see why I should. I get paid the same for meek and complacent customers, ya know."

Quinn waited for the guard to haul in their luggage, and then carried his and Agatha's belongings upstairs. When he knocked on her door, she opened it only slightly to determine who had arrived.

"Thank you, Calvin. You are turning out to be more considerate and sociable than I first thought." She grabbed the handle of her oversize bag and dragged it into her room. "Well, good night. Don't forget to check for bedbugs."

"I'll do that," he said before he turned and walked away.

Piper waited until she heard his door click shut before she peeled off her veiled hat. She unpinned her long, silver-blond hair and shook it loose, letting it tumble down her back in springy curls. She breathed a long-awaited sigh of relief when she stepped from the cumbersome gown. No wonder she was so tired, she mused as she draped the heavily padded garment over a nearby chair. She wasn't accustomed to carrying around this extra weight night and day.

She smiled fondly when the mutt plopped down at her bare feet. "Too bad you aren't a man," she said. "You, I would enjoy dealing with on a regular basis. Loyal, devoted and true-blue. Unlike most men I've met."

On that thought, Piper stretched out in bed and promptly fell asleep, thankful not to be bouncing around in that dreadful coach and have her stomach churning constantly.

At dawn, Quinn headed down to the spring-fed creek to bathe and change into a clean set of clothes. He'd heard Agatha thumping down the hall earlier, requesting that Ike prepare her bath, so he granted her the luxury of the tub while he sought out more primitive accommodations.

After snooping around the barn, Quinn noticed a new hireling—a thin, wiry white man who wore a bright red bandana, which was tied in exactly the same place on his left shoulder as the attendant he had encountered the previous afternoon. Pulling the silver dollars from his pocket, Quinn wandered over to strike up a conversation while he rolled the coins over his fingertips. He also boasted about the big jackpot he had won at the gaming tables in Fort Stockton.

As he strolled off, he asked himself how a ring of

spies might discreetly communicate their information about prospective targets when they were miles apart. Frowning pensively, he circled the coach that waited unattended while the guard and driver ate breakfast.

"Bingo," Quinn murmured when he noticed the red bandana wrapped around the handle of the strongbox. Not only was he carrying the tempting bait of extra money, but also there must be valuable loot in the strongbox. Plus, the potential profit of whatever Agatha was carrying in her reticule.

When he heard voices he veered away from the back of the coach. His anticipation mounting, he predicted that he would finally hit pay dirt during the next leg of the trip. His only concern was how Agatha was going to react if this stage was held up. He could visualize her squaring off against the bandits and trying to protect the money she obviously carried.

If the stage were indeed robbed he would have to caution her to be careful what she said and did.

Amused, he watched Agatha toddle outside to set down a plate of food for the mutt. Agatha paid no attention to Ike who towered over her, complaining that he didn't want the dog eating off "people" plates.

"Stop fussing at me, Ike. All I'm doing is keeping this poor dog from starving to death. It won't hurt you to give the plate a good scrubbing."

Quinn bit back a grin when Agatha flounced off and Ike sent a rude gesture flying behind her. Scowling, Ike lurched around and lumbered back into the trading post. Quinn had to agree that Ike was making a mountain out of a molehill and that Agatha was right. His plate had dried food caked on it and it could have used a good scrubbing.

"What are you smiling about this morning?" Agatha asked as she came toward him.

He opened the door of the coach for her. "I enjoy watching you set folks straight, as long as it isn't me," he said dryly.

When she climbed in, he caught a whiff of her appealing perfume. It reminded him of the wild lilac bushes that grew around his childhood home.

And that was about the only fond memory he had retained from childhood.

Well, no sense dredging that up, he told himself while he waited for the pup to bound into the coach. His life hadn't been a fairy tale. So what? He had learned a long time ago to *endure*. As far as he could tell that's what life was about.

"Are you getting in, Calvin, or do you plan to stand there woolgathering? And where are the driver and guard?" She looked him up and down, then said, "You look nice this morning in that colorful red vest."

"Thanks," he said, startled by the unexpected compliment.

As if on cue, the driver and burly guard scurried outside. For a moment Quinn appraised the shaggy-haired guard, wondering if he might be in on the robberies. He would make sure to keep a close eye on the man if they were held up so he could watch how he reacted.

Three hours later, as the coach bounced over the rock-strewn path that wound through a mountain pass, an eerie sensation skittered down Quinn's spine. He jerked to attention to survey the looming granite walls that rose on each side of the narrow pass.

Soon, came the instinctive voice inside his head. He could almost feel danger looming in the distance, having dealt with it so often in the past.

He glanced at Agatha, who was carrying on a one-sided conversation with the mutt. "I've got a bad feeling."

Her head snapped up and she tensed. "About what?"

"All my instincts tell me trouble is lurking. Do yourself a favor and don't provoke the bandits if we get held up."

"What?" she squawked, glancing this way and that. "Hell and damnation, this is just what I *don't* need!"

Sure enough, she clutched protectively at her reticule again. Yep, she had something valuable with her, he predicted. If he could see her face, he knew it would be skewed up with alarm and anxiety.

Her hand shot out toward him. "Give me one of your six-shooters. I'm not going down without a fight."

Quinn shook his head. "You shoot and they shoot back. Believe me, you would not like getting shot."

"You speak from experience?"

He nodded grimly. "Yeah, it ain't much fun. It would make you cross and cranky."

She snorted at that.

"Okay, a lot more cross and cranky," he amended wryly.

She poked her head out the window to study the towering stone precipices, and then she twisted around on the seat so that her shoulder and face were turned away from him.

"What are you doing?" he questioned, bemused.

Her head swiveled around, the thick veil swinging across the collar of her gown. "I'm unloading, of course."

He saw her tuck something down the front of her gown. "If you don't think bandits won't frisk you because of your gender and age, think again. You might as well accept the fact that no one gets by untouched."

"And you're an expert, are you? Don't tell me you supplement your lack of funds at the card table by holding up stages and banks."

"No, but—"

Quinn's voice dried up when he heard the first gunshot echoing off the rock walls, and then felt the coach lurch into a swifter speed.

"Oh, my God," Agatha wailed as she grabbed hold of the window frame to prevent being launched into his lap. "This is going to spoil everything!"

He noticed the absence of the nasal tone in her voice again, but he didn't have time to dwell on it. He poked his head out the window to watch six masked riders descend from an elevated trail. Sure as shootin', their faces were concealed by the same patterned red bandanas.

"It's about damn time," he said to himself. "Finally, some results."

"What did you say?"

"Nothing—"

The coach caromed around a sharp bend in the road, flinging him sideways. Agatha screeched, a high-pitched sound that nearly burst his eardrums—and sent the frightened mutt up in howls. When the coach rocked wildly on its springs Agatha was flung on top of Quinn before he could upright himself. He barely had time to register the fact that she felt as soft as a feather pillow before she planted her hands on his chest and shoved herself away.

Quinn peered out the window to see two riders thundering beside the coach. A moment later, the stage skidded to a halt.

"Hands up!" one of the masked bandits roared at the driver. "And you there, throw down that shotgun."

"Ohmigod, ohmigod," Agatha chanted as she laid a shaky hand over her bosom.

While the driver and guard were being disarmed, Quinn unfastened his holsters and laid them on the seat.

"I never would have taken you for a coward." Agatha's voice was harsh with disappointment. "You aren't even going to put up a fight, are you?"

The condemnation of her words rolled off him like rain off a canvas tent. "No, I'm not. Money comes and goes. I might have the nine lives of a cat, but I've used up about half of them already. I don't intend to expend another one of them today. Since you probably don't have too many to spare yourself, I suggest you act complacent for a change."

"When *my* money goes it's gone for good," she grumbled.

"Be quiet," he said, making a slashing gesture with his hand. "I'm thinking."

"Well, think fast, Calvin. We are in serious trouble here!" she muttered.

Although the outlaws wore bandanas to conceal their faces, Quinn made note of the ringleader's bushy eyebrows and beady eyes that were shaded by his wide-brimmed sombrero.

Quinn quickly memorized the appearance of the outlaws' horses, saddles, boots and spurs for future identification. When he brought these murdering bastards to justice he damn well intended to point an accusing finger at each and every one of them.

"Step down from the coach," one of the men ordered gruffly. "And hurry up about it."

Piper's heart was pounding so hard that she swore it was about to crack a rib. She sat there second-guessing herself, wishing she had devised a better way to transport the money and valuables she had with her. Although she had tried to consider and plan for every risk involved on this cross-country trip, she had no way to forward the money she needed to make her fresh new start. Now she faced being robbed!

She cast Cal a panicky glance. For the life of her she couldn't imagine how Cal could remain so calm and unruffled. It was as if he was sitting there staring out the window, taking mental photographs. What was the point of that? They would never see their money, valuables or these banditos again.

"I'll go out first," he said quietly. "This time you're going to let me help you down, like it or not." He stared grimly at her. "If you misstep and go tumbling down it might set off a chain reaction and all hell might break loose. Do *not* purposely get them riled up. Understand?"

Piper nodded jerkily, then watched Cal unfold his muscular frame from the seat and move slowly down the step. She had called him a coward, but she realized now that he was nothing of the kind. What she saw in his facial expression was utter fearlessness and coiled control. For all his projected casualness, you would have thought these bandits aiming their pistols at his chest were inviting him out to a Sunday picnic.

Her breath jammed in her chest when the suspicious thought that Cal might somehow be involved in this holdup hit her like a slap in the face. He had predicted this possibility earlier, she recalled. Plus, he hadn't seemed the least bit alarmed by approaching bandits. Also, if she had heard the odd comment he'd made earlier correctly, she would swear that he was *expecting* this robbery.

Piper stiffened in outrage. That sneaky sidewinder! He would probably laugh himself silly while he retrieved the money she had crammed down the front of her padded dress. Well, they would see how long and hard he laughed when she grabbed her cane and hit him squarely in the crotch. Then he would be singing a different tune…and in a higher key!

Chapter Three

Roarke Sullivan pelted down the street of Galveston, hell-bent on his crusade to mount a patrol of capable men to track down his runaway daughter. Of course, he had a pretty good idea where Piper was bound. She had been pestering him for months to retract his decree that Penelope would be forever forbidden from acquiring her share of the Sullivan fortune.

Now, five days after Piper's disappearance—and he had only received word an hour ago that she had not returned to her position as teaching assistant for the summer session at Miss Johnson's Finishing School for Women—Roarke had to move quickly. He didn't know how many days it would take his unruly, independent-minded daughter to travel across Texas, but she had to be somewhere close to her destination by now.

Roarke veered into the city marshal's office to throw some weight around. Well known in this city, he expected his request to be met immediately.

"I need a posse to track down my daughter," he said without preamble. "I'm putting you in charge, Drake. After all, I'm partly responsible for seeing to it that you were elected to this position."

"Your daughter?" William Drake parroted as he drew his feet off the edge of the desk and bounded upright. "Which daughter would that be?"

"The only one I still claim," Roarke said, and scowled. "I suspect she is headed to Fort Davis. My guess is that she took the train as far as the rails run then hopped a stage. She's probably traveling under an assumed name so I can't track her easily. I want you to notify law officials as far west as the telegraph lines run and order the formation of a posse."

He loomed over the marshal who was a good six inches shorter and fifty pounds lighter. "I want reliable, responsible lawmen. Not two-bit gunslingers with the morals of hounds. I want Piper returned in the same condition she left and her fiancé-to-be damn well does, too!"

His voice boomed across the office and reverberated off the walls. "I am offering a five-hundred-dollar bonus for each posse member that escorts Piper safely back to me. There is another five hundred in it for you if you make the necessary arrangements."

William Drake snatched up his hat. "Yes, Mr. Sullivan, I'll get right on it."

"I want Texas Rangers." Roarke decided in afterthought. "Never mind about a posse."

Drake fidgeted with the dingy hat that he had clamped in his hands. "Well, sir, that is not exactly the Rangers' forte. They are frontier fighters, ya know."

"They've been known to track down and rescue kidnap victims taken by Indians, haven't they?"

"Yes, sir, but your daughter wasn't exactly kidnapped, was she?"

Roarke flung his arm in an expansive gesture. "A technicality. We will quibble about that later. Just send the telegram to Ranger headquarters in Austin. I'll add another five hundred to your bonus."

When the marshal scuttled off, Roarke expelled an agitated sigh. "Confounded, headstrong female."

He glared at the visual image that popped to mind. Piper had become as contrary as a mule after he had sent Penelope away without his blessing. And Roarke had paid the schoolmistress plenty of extra money to bring Piper under thumb for him.

Waste of time and money, he fumed as he wheeled around to stalk back down the street to his own office. He could buy, sell and ship merchandise at home and abroad by signing his name to contracts. But damn it, he couldn't control that impetuous girl of his at all. He had money galore and barrels of influence and prestige. But what good did it do when he couldn't handle one pint-size female who was the last heir to his vast fortune?

Damnation, he had found Piper the perfect fiancé, too. John Foster hailed from a distinguished family. He had been groomed to take over his father's merchant business since the age of fifteen. This was to be an exceptional match, the merging of two influential families among the crème de la crème of Galveston society.

Until Piper had defied his wishes and left without notice.

Roarke growled in annoyance as he shouldered his way through his office door. Piper could run, but she couldn't hide from him, he thought confidently.

Scowling mutinously, Piper eased a foot onto the narrow step to confront the desperadoes. She wanted to bite Cal's offered hand instead of grabbing hold of it for support. And there was that cool, unflinching stare of his again—the one that indicated that he was nowhere near as rattled and upset as she was.

He *should have been*, damn his black soul. He *had* to be in on this!

"Ah, the black widow," one of the bandits said in stilted English. "We heard you were on board."

She shot Cal a murderous glare—not that he could see the fire in her eyes. Too bad about that. Now where could these men have heard about her, if not from this no-good, backstabbing gambler?

To her astonishment Cal tossed her a warning glance and discreetly squeezed her hand before he released it.

Now she was completely confused.

"You first, gringo," the thief wearing fancy silver spurs demanded. "Empty your pockets."

Cal accommodated by slowly reaching into the pocket of his breeches to retrieve a hefty roll of bank notes, then pulled off his diamond-studded ring.

"Don't stop on my account," Silver Spurs taunted as he raised his pearl-handled Colt and aimed it at Cal's head. "What else ya got that's of any worth?"

Cal fished into his vest pocket for the expensive watch and a handful of silver dollars. "That's all I have," he said. "You've wiped me out until someone takes pity and grubstakes me for another poker game."

Silver Spurs gestured his head—which was concealed by the bandana mask and a wide-brimmed sombrero—to the two hombres riding a roan and a buckskin gelding. "Loot the strongbox while Granny hands over her valuables."

"I have nothing valuable except sixty years of wit and wisdom," she insisted.

Silver Spurs snorted. "You'll have to do better than that, crone. Now hand over your money and valuables before I lose my patience."

Quinn flinched when the old woman huddled closely behind him and commenced yowling about how she was so terrified that she was about to have a seizure.

"Don't let them hurt me, Cal!" she shrieked.

"Nobody will be biting any bullets if you cooperate, lady," Silver Spurs snapped. "Now hurry it up."

Quinn tried not to show his surprise when he felt Agatha tug on the waistband of his breeches, then drop something down the back of his pants. Then she shuffled sideways to step into clear view of the four outlaws holding them at gunpoint.

"I told you I didn't have much money," she gritted out as she opened her beaded reticule. She waved one lone coin in Silver Spur's masked face. "See? Only one lousy dollar. And if the fright you have given me over one measly coin becomes the death of me, I swear I will come back to haunt you."

"Agatha…" Quinn muttered warningly.

"What? Just because I'm down to my last dollar and

he's taking it from me doesn't mean I have to like it. And shame on all of you!" she shouted at the gang at large.

"Agatha—" he began again.

"Scaring an old woman to death like this," she harrumphed. "If you don't cease your wicked ways you will all wind up in the seventh circle of hell!"

"Will you please shut up!" Quinn growled, but quietly.

"Fine. I'm shutting up—" Her voice broke off when a shotgun blast erupted from behind the coach, startling the team of horses.

"Hey, boss, come look what we found," one of the thieves called out a moment later.

Silver Spurs gestured his pistol toward the coach. "You two get back inside, pronto."

Quinn grabbed Agatha's hand, but she pushed him ahead of her. No doubt, she intended to block the outlaws' view so they wouldn't notice the bulge in the seat of his breeches.

"Some watchdog you turned out to be." Agatha scowled at the pup that was sprawled out on the seat.

Quinn heard the cackles of delight coming from the back of the stage. Obviously the booty in the strongbox had pacified the bandits.

Six gunshots erupted simultaneously and the stage lurched forward. Harnesses jangled. Horses whinnied. Another round of gunfire sent the team lunging off at a swift pace.

Quinn thrust his head out the window, noting the driver and guard—their arms held high—had been left afoot.

The bandits split up and headed for the hills.

"Damn it to hell," he muttered as the runaway coach

careened around a sharp curve, hurling Agatha against the window frame.

Flinging open the door, Quinn tried to twist around to grab the luggage rail atop the coach. Agatha pulled him off balance and he sprawled backward on the floorboards. Snarling, he stared up at that veil-covered face. He was tempted to rip off that concealing getup so he could give her the full benefit of his irritated glare.

"What is the matter with you, woman?"

"You are not bailing out on me," she snapped brusquely. "You are in on this scheme, aren't you?"

He stared at her in disbelief. "Where did you get the idea that I'm part of that outlaw gang?"

"You *knew* we were about to be robbed," she hurled in accusation.

"That's because I have good instincts."

She scoffed at that and tilted her head to a challenging angle.

"I wasn't bailing out on you," he insisted as he lurched to his knees. "In case you haven't noticed, no one is guiding this coach. Unless you want to plunge off a cliff I need to climb onto the driver's seat and get control of the horses."

"Fine, but not until I have my money and valuables back!"

Grumbling, Quinn rolled onto one hip and dug out the heavy pouch that she had stashed on him for safekeeping. "There. Happy now?"

She bobbed her head a couple of times and clutched the leather pouch to her ample bosom.

Muttering at the woman's obsession with her worldly

possessions, Quinn plunked onto the seat and hurriedly strapped on his holsters. He couldn't track those desperadoes until he stopped this stage and grabbed one of the horses. Agatha, insisting on retrieving her precious valuables, had cost him several minutes he didn't have to spare. Those bandits could be miles away before he went after them.

Clamping a hand on the luggage rack again, Quinn leaned out to survey the road ahead of them. "Son of a bitch!"

He recoiled the instant before the opened door crashed into an outcropping of rock on the narrow trail. The door was ripped off its hinges and it shattered to pieces against the stone wall beside them.

Quinn collapsed on the seat and gripped the window frames on either side of him. He stared solemnly at the old harridan. "Agatha, if you're a religious woman, I suggest you start praying. Now."

"Why?" Her voice was wild with alarm.

He nodded his ruffled head toward the open doorway. "Take a look for yourself."

She grabbed the window frame and peeked out. "Good God!" she howled in dismay.

"My sentiments exactly. And it's been nice knowing you...sort of."

The mountain pass they were traveling at breakneck speed had opened into a yawning canyon where the ledge plunged at least a hundred feet straight down. It would take only one wheel dropping off that unprotected curve in the road to send the coach plummeting off the cliff. No way could Quinn scramble atop the stage to gain control of the horses on such a dangerous bend of the road. All he could do was hold on for dear life and encourage Agatha to do the same.

The coach jostled and rocked on its springs. Fallen rock must have littered the path because the stage bounced violently. He and Agatha were simultaneously launched upward and tossed off balance.

The pup howled and cartwheeled onto the floorboards.

Timber cracked and shattered. Quinn had the sickening feeling that the front left wheel had broken into bits beneath them because the coach spun wildly, then tilted to a precarious angle.

"We're going to die!" Agatha squawked as the swaying coach sent her lurching headfirst into his lap.

Quinn let go with one hand to grab hold of the nape of her gown, then jerked her up beside him. He felt the horses' momentum swinging the wrecked coach into a hapless skid. It rocked sideways, teetered off balance for a few unnerving seconds...and then *wham!*

The coach crashed onto its side, hurling the occupants against the opposite wall. Quinn made a wild grab for Agatha when she toppled over him toward the broken door. There was nothing beneath the opening except a wide expanse of nothingness, a craggy tumble of rocks on the mountainside and a swift-moving stream riddled with white-capped rapids.

Agatha screamed bloody murder as she dropped through the opening, held aloft only by Quinn's death grip on the neck of her gown.

Dust rolled around the confines of the coach, filling his eyes. Agatha's terrified screams blasted his ears and his pulse hammered so hard in his chest that he could barely draw breath.

One false move, one careless shift of weight and the coach would be taking the short way down the mountain.

Quinn kept a stranglehold on Agatha while her legs churned to find solid footing. He could have told her she was wasting energy because there was nothing but air beneath her.

Carefully, he inched his legs farther apart without shifting to a position that would alter the perilous balance of the coach. Quinn hauled in a steadying breath. He had been in dozens of hair-raising scrapes through the years. But this one tested his mettle to the limits.

If he tried to save himself it meant that he had to release his hold on Agatha. Pain in the patoot that she could be at times, he didn't relish the idea of watching her body bounce from one outcropping of stone to another until she hit rock bottom.

He really wished he could see her face, wondered if she had made peace with the world…just in case. But there was that damn veil standing between him and this cantankerous old crone that he found himself liking for reasons he was at a loss to figure out.

Quinn kept remembering the sound of her grating voice hurling curses at Silver Spurs, vowing to come back and haunt him in the afterlife. He figured if his tenuous grasp on Agatha slipped, she would be cursing *him* all the way down the mountain. That was one ghost he wouldn't want breathing down his neck till the end of his days.

He swore colorfully when he heard the shoulder

seam of her gown rip loose and saw her drop a quick six inches. She was staring death in the face. Knowing her, she would have something mean and nasty to say about that, too.

Gritting his teeth, Quinn tried to figure out how in the hell he and Agatha were going to get out of this mess alive.

Chapter Four

"Stop thrashing about and grab hold of my arm!"

Piper stared up at the rock-solid man who stood between her and certain death. *She* was terrified and was having difficulty drawing breath, but *Cal* was his usual calm and collected self. It amazed her that nothing seemed to faze him.

But of course, *he* wasn't the one hanging on by the thread of his torn shoulder seam. And honestly, considering how she had needled him the past two days she was surprised he didn't just let her go with a feigned smile of apology.

"Hurry up, Agatha," he demanded. "The horses are going to start shifting any second and this coach might topple off the edge and shatter to pieces. There won't be a damn thing for us to hold on to if that happens."

Piper eased the strap of her reticule up her arm, then clamped her free hand on his forearm and tried to heave herself up as if he were a human rope.

"Stop!" Cal growled when her mad scramble altered the precarious balance of the overturned coach. "No sudden moves. Understand? Just hang there and let me haul you up an inch at a time."

The mutt that was somewhere behind Cal suddenly appeared by his right shoulder. He whined and wagged his tail when he spotted her.

"Stay there, dog," she commanded as Cal lifted her another inch away from imminent death.

She heard the mutt's tail bang harder against the wall and realized his intentions *after* she made the crucial mistake of speaking directly to him. "No! Don't move!"

To her terror and dismay the dog bounded playfully around Cal to lick her veiled face and paw at her hat.

"Damn it, get back, mutt," Cal muttered as the coach rocked unsteadily.

Another stab of horror knifed through Piper when the dog's oversize paw connected with the side of her head, causing her plumed hat to shift sideways. When the mutt grabbed the feathers on her hat, as if they belonged to a bird that he was instinctively trying to shake the life out of, Piper shrieked.

Cal let go with his left hand that was braced against the window frame and pushed the dog out of the way. Piper's veiled hat was still clamped in the mutt's jaws as he tumbled helter-skelter inside the coach.

Sickening dread pooled in the pit of Piper's stomach when she found herself staring directly into Cal's shocked expression. She watched him appraise her without her protective disguise. She could see disbelief, condemnation and suspicion gathering in those golden eyes as he registered the fact that she wasn't who she pretended to be.

She decided, right there and then, that it was not a good idea to shock the person who held your life in the balance. Cal was so stunned that she felt his hand loosen on her arm momentarily, causing her to drop a quick two inches before he regathered his composure and clamped a fierce hold on her.

"I thought there was something peculiar about you that didn't add up," he said, then scowled down at her.

"I can explain," she squeaked, then glanced down at the empty space beneath her. "Oh, God!" She thrashed in attempt to find footing.

"Hold still!" Cal barked at her. The expression on his face was thunderous.

Piper froze in midair. Her heart pounded inside her chest and she reminded herself to breathe.

"I know this looks bad," she chirped. "But please don't let me go. And if I die, promise me that you will take my money and jewels to my sister at Fort Davis."

"I already have one last request to fulfill," he muttered. "I don't need another one."

"Then at least tell Penelope what happened."

"Fine. I'll do that. But in the meantime here's what we're going to do. On the count of three I'm going to throw myself backward and you're going to lurch forward and grab hold of me. And get hold of that mutt with your free hand if you can. Ready?"

Piper wasn't sure she would ever be ready because if this plan didn't work she was a goner. He might be, too.

"One, two, three—"

Quinn threw himself backward with enough force to drag Agatha—who had turned out to be an exceedingly attractive young con artist—through the opening. The team of horses shifted uneasily, dragging the coach a little farther off the edge of the cliff. Quinn shoved the woman sideways to counterbalance the teetering coach. Then he vaulted to his feet.

"Get up and make it quick!" he told the imposter when she didn't react swiftly enough to suit him.

Using the heel of his hand he popped open the door that was above him. He heaved himself up to sit atop the overturned stage, then thrust his hand back inside to grab Agatha—and he was dying to find out who she really was. Well, not dying to find out, he amended. That was a bad choice of words, considering they had come within a hairbreadth of catapulting into the hereafter.

To Quinn's surprise and exasperation, she tossed the squirming dog to him. Frankly, it astounded him that she placed the mutt's safety above her own. Then he reminded himself that she had saved the mutt from extermination and had gotten attached to him.

Quinn hooked his arm under the mutt's belly, then set him aside. Then he clasped the woman's arm and towed her upward. For the space of a moment, while they were face-to-face, he tumbled into the depths of eyes so blue that they gleamed like silver in the sunlight. Quinn glanced away before the woman's astonishing beauty sidetracked him.

Whoever she was, she was the fraud who had teased and tormented him for two days. He wasn't wasting more time or sympathy on her either, he promised himself. But for damn certain he was going to find out *why* she was charading as a crone and *who* was the rightful owner of the money and pouch of valuables that she had with her.

She had to be up to no good, he thought cynically. Most of the folk he encountered were, after all.

When he set the woman to her knees beside him, he spun around and hopped off the coach. As he reached back to pull her to safety the dog leaped to the ground— and got right under his feet. Scowling, Quinn tripped backward and the woman landed on top of him, forcing his breath out in a whoosh.

Any other time he wouldn't object to having a beguiling woman sprawled on top of him. But not now and not this treacherous female. Muttering, Quinn hooked his arm around the woman's well-padded waist and sent her rolling to the ground beside him.

Launching himself to his feet, he darted to the back of the coach to hurriedly unstrap their luggage before the coach tumbled off the ledge.

And sure enough, he barely had time to set aside the satchels and his bedroll before the horses pranced impatiently and the stage flipped upside down. Quinn darted forward to remove the pin that kept the tongue of the coach secured to the team of horses. He grabbed the reins to prevent the horses from charging off when the coach plummeted down the side of the mountain.

Debris scattered everywhere as the coach struck one jagged outcropping of rock after another. Shattered pieces of the stage kerplopped in the stream and floated away.

Quinn stood there for a moment, studying the wreckage and counting himself damn lucky that he wasn't a part of it.

"As I said, I can explain…"

The woman's voice no longer held that nasal, grating pitch. Quinn rounded on her, feeling deceived and betrayed. He'd had more than enough of that in his line of work, without this sneaky female pulling the wool over his eyes.

"This better be good," he said, and smirked disrespectfully. "Posing as a persnickety old harridan who is probably carrying stolen money—and who knows what else—doesn't say much for your integrity, does it? I've dealt with several treacherous bandits in my day, but you're about as conniving as they come, *Agatha*." He spit out her name like a curse, which is exactly how he meant it.

"My name is Piper…uh…just Piper," she introduced herself.

"Another alias? Somehow I'm not surprised."

The fact that she refused to provide her last name made him all the more wary of her. He would bet his right arm that she was a fugitive from justice, traveling incognito and carrying stolen money.

Vowing that a pretty face wouldn't sway him—and she definitely had that going for her—Quinn stalked over to tether the horses. While Piper watched him curiously, he reversed direction to retrieve his satchel and bedroll.

"What are you going to do? Surely you don't intend to leave me in the middle of nowhere!" she howled at him.

"Surely I do," he said, refusing to be influenced by the

shocked expression on her beguiling features. "I'm tracking the outlaw gang that killed my best friend six months
ago in a canyon near here. You're on your own, lady."

She stamped her foot and glowered at him. Ah, that
feisty disposition wasn't just an act, he noticed. The
woman was teeming with indomitable spirit and fiery
temperament.

"Now, see here, Cal. You can't just ride off and leave
me here, knowing I'll probably die." She wagged her
finger in his face. "And if I do, I *will* come back to
haunt you. You can depend on it."

"I'm sure you will. But you'll have to get in line. I've
heard the same threat from a number of folks."

When she scurried after him, he stopped short and
then grunted uncomfortably when she slammed into
him. "Look, lady, I'm going to change into my usual attire before I grab a horse and ride out. I suggest you
change into something more practical for riding, unless
you want to hang around here waiting for the eastbound
coach to show up."

"And when will that be?"

"In a couple of days."

"A couple of *days?*" she wailed in frustration.

He watched her draw herself up and tilt her chin at
him. Quinn blinked when the image of Agatha-the-hag
superimposed itself on Piper. Scowling, he whipped
around, then strode off to change clothes, refusing to
give the lovely shyster another thought.

Piper watched Cal disappear from sight, then hurried
over to rummage through her luggage for appropriate
clothing. Knowing she would be living at an army gar-

rison, she had packed two pair of riding breeches and blouses.

Casting a cautious glance over her shoulder to ensure Cal wasn't spying on her, she tugged the padded gown down to her waist, then shrugged on her white blouse. Sparing another wary glance in the direction Cal had gone, she shoved the gown and petticoats past her knees, then snatched up her breeches and boots. When dressed, she crammed the padded gown, undergarments and valuables she had retrieved from Cal earlier into her satchel.

She staggered backward a few steps when Cal rounded the corner and stopped short to gape at her. He regarded her with the same astonished expression that she had trained on him. In the matter of a few minutes they had both altered their appearance drastically.

It took some getting used to.

Cal had cast off the flashy vest, white shirt and trousers. Now an Indian headband, decorated with beaded designs, held his long hair away from his face. Although he wore a white man's black shirt, his muscular legs were encased in buckskin breeches, leggings and moccasins.

An ammunition belt hung diagonally across his broad chest and the double holster rode low on his hips. He carried a bullwhip that was coiled over his left shoulder, and he had a sheathed dagger strapped to his right thigh.

Now who was the imposter? she wondered suspiciously. He didn't look to be a full-blood Indian, though the sun had darkened his complexion. But he definitely dressed like an Indian. Whoever or whatever this man was, she had the inescapable feeling that he wasn't the tumbleweed gambler that he had impersonated.

"Who *are* you?" Piper demanded when she finally recovered her powers of speech.

"Quinn Callahan," he replied as he gave her the once-over-thrice. "I'm a Texas Ranger."

His penetrating stare caused her to shift uneasily from one foot to the other. This was proof positive that her disguise had been a good idea. Thanks to her disguise, she hadn't had to deal with speculative male stares during her journey.

Whoever Callahan really was, she didn't believe for a moment that he was a Ranger. He looked more like a half-breed renegade to her. In addition, she wasn't sure she could trust him not to take advantage of her vulnerability while they were alone in the wilderness.

He looked her up and down once again. His expression was so unreadable that she couldn't figure out what he was thinking…or planning to do to her.

"I hope you're packing hardware, Piper," he said before he strode past her to retrieve a horse. "You won't last a half a day in this wilderness, especially dressed in that garb. That getup advertises every feminine asset you have. If you come across any other men of less moral fiber than I have then whatever righteous virtues you might have left will be gone by nightfall. Guaranteed."

"Which is why I relied on a disguise for my protection," she pointed out. "I am not a complete fool, you know. I am fully aware that men are not to be trusted. They *always* want something from a woman."

Quinn chastised himself for glancing over his shoulder to admire the appealing sight of this shapely female. She was right, he admitted to himself. He would like something from her, too, although he wouldn't allow himself to yield to the temptation.

He made it a policy to avoid devious women whenever possible.

But the damnable truth was that Piper was the most strikingly attractive woman he had ever laid eyes on. Plus, every time he stared too long at her he lost his train of thought. That was not good.

Everything male inside him had responded fiercely the instant he rounded the bend of the road—and saw *her* standing where Agatha Stewart should have been. Agatha he could have handled. *This* woman he wasn't so sure about. She was a distraction of the worst sort at the worst time.

"You don't look like a Ranger," she said doubtfully. "I want to see proof."

It wasn't the first time he had heard that demand. Quinn retrieved his sidearm from his left holster, then dug out the tarnished star that he only flashed about while making arrests. "This good enough for you? Or this…" He waved the small, leather-bound book in her face. "It's a fugitive list that gives the names and descriptions of wanted criminals. All Rangers carry them." He stared suspiciously at her. "I bet if I looked closely I could probably find *you* in it."

"I am not on anyone's wanted list. Well, except for perhaps—" She jerked up her head and glared at him. "Don't try to sidetrack me, Cal. The point is that you could have *stolen* that badge and that little black book."

"Right, just like *you* probably stole the money you're carrying. My guess is that you trussed yourself up like an overweight old widow to conceal your identity and throw lawmen off track. Then you hopped a stage for parts unknown," he countered. "Admit it, I'm right about you, aren't I?"

She stamped her foot in frustration again. "No, you couldn't be more wrong! I did not steal anything! And if you really are a Ranger then you should be more concerned about my welfare instead of threatening to abandon me!"

He tucked the silver star in his holster. "If you want sympathy and concern you're barking up the wrong tree, lady. I already have an important assignment, and you aren't it."

Quinn released one of the horses hooked to the team, then grabbed his knife to cut off a section of the reins to fashion a harness. He had brought along his own bridle, anticipating that he would have to confiscate a horse. But Piper needed a means to control her mount when she rode off—in the opposite direction that he was headed.

He flicked her a quick glance, noting that watching him create a makeshift harness had distracted her. He rather thought she looked impressed by his adaptability. Not that he cared what she thought of him, of course. The sooner he ditched her the happier he would be.

"Here." He thrust the reins at her. "This makeshift tack will get you to the next stage stop. You can catch the next westbound coach that comes through, if that's what you want to do. It makes no difference to me."

Leaving her holding the reins to the horse, Quinn

fished into his saddlebags to grab his bridle and bit. Then he strode over to pick out a horse for himself.

"I will pay you to escort me to the next station," she negotiated.

"With what? Stolen money?" He eased the bit into the horse's mouth and placed the bridle in proper position. "No thanks. I have more pressing things to do besides play nursemaid to an imposter and thief."

"I am not a thief!"

He derived tremendous pleasure in throwing her own words back in her face. "Fine, then *prove* it."

She stalked over to station herself in front of him, determined to gain his undivided attention. His betraying gaze dropped to her heaving bosom and he cursed himself soundly for being the least bit attracted to a woman who was far more trouble and frustration than she was worth.

"I didn't lie to you when I said I was bound for Fort Davis. I'm on my way to join my sister, Penelope. She is married to Captain Matthew Duncan. Part of the money and jewels I'm carrying are compensation for my sister."

Okay, so maybe he could believe that part since her last wish—while she was dangling off the cliff—was to contact her sister. But Quinn had been fed so many concocted and convoluted lies in his day that he had learned never to take anyone at his word until checking the story thoroughly. He had no way of knowing how or where she had acquired the money and valuables.

"My charade as an elderly crone was for my own protection," she repeated slowly and distinctly. "I am traveling without a chaperone and I was taking precautions so I wouldn't invite trouble from untrustworthy men. Surely you can understand that my disguise was a necessary deception."

She stared at him. "*Especially* since *you* were charading as a shiftless gambler." She arched a challenging brow. "Double standards, Calvin? Hmm?"

Well, she had him there. But that didn't change the fact that he had been traveling undercover on official business and now he had a ring of ruthless desperadoes to track down. He didn't have the time or inclination to deliver Piper Whoever-She-Was to her sister. He knew she wasn't being completely honest with him and he didn't trust her, so he wasn't going to bother with her.

Quinn figured Piper would be reasonably safe on the next leg of her westward journey. He couldn't give her a guarantee, of course, because this isolated area of rugged mountains was home and hideout to all sorts of predators.

The bandits that had held up the stage had headed north, but that didn't mean there weren't smaller groups of desperadoes prowling the area. If she was lucky she might reach the next relay station without encountering difficulty.

He frowned thoughtfully. He would give her a fifty-fifty chance. He glanced at her appealing physique. On second thought, that was probably too optimistic.

Cutting away another section of the long reins, Quinn secured the leather strap around her horse's girth, then tied her bulging satchel in place.

"I'll give you a step up," he offered, linking his fingers together to form an improvised stirrup.

She stared at him with those fascinating silver-blue eyes. "Perhaps we could compromise," she suggested, flashing him a charming smile.

It was difficult not to respond to her smile, but he managed. "I never compromise. You start making exceptions then that's all you get done. I was sent here to locate the outlaws' hideout in this wild tumble of mountains so a Ranger battalion can attack. That's exactly what I'm going to do."

"Then I'm going with you. Once you have pinpointed the hideout, you can escort me to Fort Davis."

He stared incredulously at her. The woman had gumption, he'd give her that. "Lady, I will be traveling across rugged terrain. *I'm* used to it. *You* aren't. By dark you will be whining and complaining and I have heard enough of that while you posed as Agatha Stewart. The answer is *no.*"

When she refused to accept the step up that he offered, he hooked his arm around her waist and swung her onto the horse. "You can't miss the relay station at Perdition Pass. It sits at the base of the canyon, directly beside the road. You can probably make it there a few hours after dark."

He handed her one of his Colts. "Keep your eyes peeled for varmints. These craggy peaks and valleys are known for panthers, wolves, rattlesnakes and a few other—" His voice dried up when she turned his own firearm on him.

Just went to show you that offering an ounce of kindness to anyone in this part of the country could get you shot, he mused cynically.

"In case you've already forgotten, I saved your life an hour ago," he muttered as he stared at the speaking end of his pistol, and then glared at her.

"You aren't finished saving my life yet, Callahan. I am going with you or you are going with me, but I'm *not* venturing off by myself. When my veiled hat went over the cliff with the coach I lost a vital part of my protective disguise. I do not intend to become the target of every scoundrel I might encounter." She poked him in the chest with his pistol. "*You* chose which direction we're going first. But *we* are going together."

Quinn knew he could disarm this feisty female in the time it took to blink. But damn if he knew why he allowed her to keep the upper hand. Maybe it was because she was so impossibly attractive that he liked looking at her. Maybe it was the prospect of sending her off alone to be hurt—or worse—that got to him.

If she *did* meet with disaster he would probably feel guilty as hell about it.

He didn't have to be a fortune-teller to know that the kind of men who might cross her path would use and abuse her for their own lusty pleasure. And she was right. Trussing herself up in that padded black gown wouldn't do her much good if she didn't have the veiled hat to conceal her bewitching face.

"Well?" she demanded impatiently. "It's your call."

Piper was dismayed when he turned his back on her momentarily to retrieve his horse. He didn't even bother to look over his shoulder. Obviously he didn't believe she would gun him down. Which she wouldn't have.

That would have defeated her purpose of trying to hire a guide and protector.

Considering that she had never fired a weapon in her life, Piper didn't like her chances of making the long ride to the next stage station if she might have to confront predators of the four-legged and two-legged varieties alone. She had no idea what awaited her and that made her apprehensive and twitchy.

The only logical solution was to stick with the irascible Quinn Callahan. And if he was a Ranger then she was better off with him than riding west alone, wasn't she?

She watched Quinn fashion another strap to hold his saddlebags and bedroll in place before he hopped onto the horse. Then he leaned out to slap one of the spare horses on the rump, sending it galloping westward. The remaining horses followed suit and disappeared around the bend.

Piper extended the firearm to Quinn, butt first. "Here. I really hadn't planned to shoot you," she admitted.

"Nice to know," he mumbled as he holstered his Colt.

He trotted the horse right past her without saying another word. She gaped at him, pretty certain this hardhearted rascal was going to abandon her. She knew he didn't like her. He didn't trust her or believe her story, either. Damn him, he *was* going to leave her alone to face whatever calamity came her way.

Just when she had given up and decided that Quinn Callahan didn't have one smidgen of conscience or humanity in him, he halted his horse before he veered around the outcropping of rock. He stared grimly at her.

"Looks like we're stuck with each other," he said sourly. "Are you coming or not?"

Relief washed over her like a tidal wave. When she smiled gratefully at him he scowled. Clearly, he was not pleased with his decision to allow her to tag along on his mission.

"What made you change your mind?" she asked as she trotted her horse up beside him, then called to the mutt to join them.

"Must have been what's left of my conscience," he grumbled resentfully. "But I'm telling you here and now that if I give you an order, then I expect you to obey without question. No exceptions."

Piper bristled immediately. He sounded exactly like her domineering father who insisted that the world follow his master plan. No exceptions allowed.

He squinted at her and a ghost of a smile twitched his lips. "Figured you would have a problem with that." He nudged his mount eastward. "Regardless, if I tell you to duck then I want you to flatten yourself over your horse. If I tell you to ride hell-for-leather then you do it."

"For my own safety and protection," she murmured, then flashed him a smile. "I can do that."

Quinn scolded himself harshly when he felt himself melting beneath her radiant smile, which made her unique eyes sparkle like starlight. Damn it, he didn't want to be distracted or affected by this female that he was obligated to drag along with him. He predicted she was going to wilt like a delicate rose after scrabbling over this rough terrain for hours on end. Then what was he going to do with her?

Face it, Callahan. You are responsible for her welfare whether you like it or not.

Which he definitely did not.

He would have liked to think that she might have made the long jaunt to the next stage station without mishap. That was wishful thinking and he wouldn't want to bet her life on it, nuisance though she was to him.

Resigned to traveling at a slower pace to accommodate Piper, Quinn aimed his horse in the direction of the site where the robbery had occurred. He didn't hear a peep out of Piper, thank goodness, when he picked up the pace to compensate for lost time.

Commander Scott Butler hunkered over his desk at Ranger headquarters in Austin and frowned pensively at the telegram Lieutenant Cooper had handed to him. "Kidnapped female," he murmured. "Age twenty. Blond hair. Blue eyes. Likely traveling by train or stage." He glanced up at the lieutenant. "That's not much to go on."

"No, sir," Vance Cooper agreed. "All we know is that the girl's father thinks her abductor might be headed to the Fort Davis area. But there is no explanation as to *who* might have absconded with her and *why*."

"We have a battalion working out of Van Horn that might be able to begin a search," Butler commented, then frowned when he recognized the name of the man whose daughter was reported missing. "Good God! *Sullivan?* No doubt, the girl is being held for ransom and Roarke will be expected to spend half his fortune, in hopes of getting his child back."

"Sullivan, sir?" Vance Cooper repeated.

Butler nodded. "Extremely wealthy merchant from Galveston. Owns half the businesses in town and con-

trols a freighting company that ships all over the world."
He frowned pensively. "We'll start by requesting information at stage stations to find out if a woman was on board that matches this description."

"We have Callahan in the field," Cooper prompted. "He has been riding the stage back and forth between Fort Stockton and El Paso for two weeks, trying to locate the criminals that have been plaguing the area. Too bad we can't get word to him. He's the best tracker we've got."

Commander Butler readily agreed with that. He had worked with his share of frontier fighters during his thirty-four years of service with the Rangers. There were several standouts in the rare breed of men who policed this wild country. Quinn Callahan headed up that list. He was tough, resilient, intelligent—and about as affable as a grizzly.

Butler smiled wryly. Cal was a lone wolf who wasn't much for small talk and lacked polished social graces, but he was hell on outlaws. Cal had kept to himself until Taylor Briggs had befriended him and refused to be held at arm's length.

Honest to God, Butler never had figured out why two men who hailed from completely different walks of life had become as close as brothers. Taylor could have talked your leg off if you let him and Cal barely gave you the time of day unless it was important that you knew it.

Damn shame about Taylor Briggs, he mused. The man had been a credit to his battalion—until he had tried to follow Cal's practice of venturing off on his own to scout and track the desperadoes that had been robbing stages, banks and plundering ranches in southwest Texas.

"Have you received more information about the outlaws who decided to call themselves the Knights of the Golden Circle?" Butler questioned.

Cooper nodded his auburn head, his countenance grim. "The news isn't good, sir. One of our men has been interrogating a suspected member who has been jailed in San Antone. According to the report, the Knights aren't simply looting and plundering for personal gain. This outbreak of thievery is bait for a trap."

Butler's thick brows flattened. "What kind of trap?"

"Word is that a band of Mexicans have recently joined up with the Knights to sell stolen livestock over the border. The outlaws even disguise themselves as renegade Indians and depredate the frontier."

"Well, hell," Butler muttered.

"According to our informant, the plot is designed to draw the attention of our Ranger battalions," Cooper continued. "The gang leaders are bent on revenge and they intend to kill as many of our men as possible because we have been making their lives miserable and arresting members of their group."

When Cooper hesitated, Butler glanced up and scowled. "It gets worse?"

Cooper expelled an audible sigh. "We also have reason to believe that this organized ring is trying to bribe Rangers as informants and destroy our battalions from inside out."

Butler swore foully. "If there is one thing I can't tolerate it's a traitor among our ranks. I have seen a few Rangers go bad in my day and I have taken particular pleasure in punishing every Judas that betrays the frontier justice system for personal gain."

He pushed away from the desk and came to his feet. "Contact the battalion in San Antone and tell them to put the squeeze on our informant and convince him that he will be protected if he starts naming names."

"Yes, sir." Cooper gestured toward the telegram lying on the commander's desk. "Do you want to send out a troop to search for this high profile kidnap victim?"

Butler shook his head. "I plan to oversee this request personally because the region where the woman might have been taken is the same area Callahan is working. That place is a hotbed of trouble. We might be able to provide reinforcements for Cal, if he is able to locate the outlaws' stronghold. We can investigate the woman's kidnapping at the same time."

He glanced curiously at Vance. "Were you able to pass along the possibility of a death trap when you were in communication with Cal?"

"No, the telegram from our Ranger unit in San Antone arrived only an hour ago." Cooper came to attention. "Sir, I would like to volunteer for duty. I would bet my last dollar that Quinn Callahan gets some results. I would like to be on hand when we go up against those desperadoes."

Butler nodded agreeably. "I'll ask for four more volunteers and we'll ride out immediately. If Cal can sniff them out then we're going to let loose with all the firepower we can throw at those cutthroats." He stared solemnly at Cooper. "And it won't just be in the name of Texas justice. This will be for Taylor Briggs as well."

Chapter Five

When Quinn reached the site of the robbery he was relieved to note the driver and guard weren't lying in pools of their own blood. Apparently the two men had decided to hike the shorter distance to the stage station that sat on the east side of the mountains.

Quinn veered off the trodden path to follow the narrow trail that he had seen one group of desperadoes take when they made their getaway. He predicted he would find evidence that the outlaws had joined forces along this route. As anticipated, he noticed a menagerie of hoofprints coming and going along the trail.

"I'm curious about the combination of your style of clothing," Piper remarked as he led the way up a steep incline. "Any particular reason for it?"

He didn't bother to glance back at her. No need to torment himself more than necessary. She was too attractive and he wanted to consider her no more than an unwanted companion. Whatever else happened during this assignment, Quinn promised himself that he was *not* going to be physically or emotionally involved with this woman.

She was an inconvenience that would cause him frustrating delays and that was *all* she was to him.

"Well?" she prompted when he didn't respond immediately. "Aren't you going to speak to me unless you're spouting orders that I am to obey without question?"

"I told you that I'm not long on chitchat," he replied. "And yes, there's a reason for this style of clothing. This is who I am."

"Just who *are* you?" she asked interestedly. "I don't understand what you mean."

Not many people did, Quinn mused. But then, most folks weren't interested in getting to know him, just steered clear of him unless they required his fighting skills for protection. But *she* dared to dig deeper than surface appearances. He should have known this female was inquisitive. That mind of hers seemed to be buzzing constantly.

"I was captured by Kiowas when I was twelve," he confided. "I had to adapt to their style of dress because I had nothing else to wear."

Why am I telling her this? he wondered. Maybe because she *was* one of the few who had ever bothered to ask.

"I'm sorry. That must have been a terrifying experience for a child."

"It was no picnic, believe me," he muttered, then tamped down the bitter memories that he had buried beneath layers of ruthless self-discipline. "I hated the Ki-

owas for killing my father when he tried to protect me.
I hated them even more after I tried to escape their camp
and they staked me out to a tree for a week to punish
me and to make certain I didn't repeat the attempt."

Piper grimaced. She couldn't begin to imagine the
emotional turmoil Quinn had undergone as an impres-
sionable child. The fact that the warriors who had taken
his father's life had become his keepers must have left
him outraged, defiant and battling inner conflicts. How
had he coped with the tragedy?

She thought she knew the answer to that question. He
had buried the anger and grief deep inside him. But it
was still there. She could hear it in his gritty voice. But
she also knew that he was a master at concealing his
emotions because she had seen him do it several times
during their short acquaintance.

There had been times when his face had gone carefully blank and she had wondered if he felt any emotion at all. But it was there, simmering in places that he
refused to reveal to the world.

"How did you escape from the Kiowa camp?" she
asked curiously.

"I didn't. When I was fourteen they traded me to a
Comanche shaman who wanted an interpreter while he
and the chieftains were conducting powwows with the
army. Since I spoke English, Spanish and the dialects
of both tribes they needed me as a go-between."

Piper clamped her legs tightly to the horse's flanks
as they veered through a narrow passage that opened to
a sheer drop—exactly like the one she had found herself dangling over a few hours earlier.

When anxiety threatened to swamp her she closed her eyes and concentrated on carrying on her conversation with Quinn. "What were you supposed to interpret for the shaman and Comanche chiefs?" she asked, her voice wobbling noticeably.

"Worthless peace treaties," Quinn said, and snorted.

"The Comanche broke their promises?"

"No, the government did," he said. "The army sent a strike force to our winter encampment in the Sierra Diablo Mountains north of here. They practically annihilated the clan I was living with. Those who survived were rounded up and herded like cattle to Indian Territory."

Piper grimaced. This tale just kept getting worse. She felt ashamed of herself for harboring ill feelings toward her domineering father. They seemed trite and insignificant compared to the tragedy Quinn endured. Her trials and struggle for individuality hadn't been life-altering nightmares like Quinn's had been.

She doubted a hard-bitten man who had obviously built walls around his emotions would want her sympathy and compassion, but he had it, all the same.

"Anything else you think you need to know about me?" he asked flippantly.

"Yes." She was thoroughly intrigued with the story of his life, even though it was obvious that he was reluctant to discuss it. Honestly, she wasn't sure why he had confided in her. But she was glad he had. It helped her understand why he was the way he was. "Did the army take you back to your kinfolk after their attack on the winter encampment?"

The question earned her a disgruntled snort. "They

tried, but by then it had been seven years since my abduction. I had been thoroughly indoctrinated into the ways of the Kiowa and Comanche. My mother had died from complications of childbirth and I had no family left in Texas. But that didn't stop the army from taking me to San Antonio with their returning patrol."

She glanced up to note that his broad shoulders had stiffened and he sat rigidly on his horse. No doubt, whatever he was about to impart had not been a pleasant experience.

"When we rode into town, the whites mistook me for a half-breed prisoner. I found myself subjected to their curses and ridicule. Even when the lieutenant in command declared that I had been a captive, my own culture wanted nothing to do with me. According to the sneers and jeers, I had lived with the savages for so long that I was one of them."

Piper retracted every derogatory thought and comment she had made about him.

If he held a grudge against the world she figured he had every right to.

Her heart went out to Quinn, knowing his life had been one traumatic adjustment after another. Considering the way he had been treated in Indian and white cultures it was a wonder to Piper that he had allowed her to join up with him temporarily.

She imagined that he preferred to be alone and that he avoided civilization as much as possible. It also astonished her that he was out to save the world from brutal lawlessness when the world treated him like a social pariah.

"I enlisted with the Rangers after two years of serving as a guide for the army," he added belatedly. "With the Rangers, my worth and respectability is measured by my ability to handle myself in difficult situations. My past doesn't matter. All that matters is that I can hold my own in the middle of a firefight…watch your head."

The warning was a split second too late. Piper looked up—and rammed her forehead into the low outcropping of rock. The blow sent her reeling backward, startling her horse. When her mount tried to bolt past Quinn's horse on the one-lane trail she pinwheeled sideways, scraping her hip and shoulder before she landed in a tangled heap.

Stars exploded in front of her eyes and an instant headache pounded against her skull. The pup bounded up to lick her cheeks, but Piper pushed him away so she could prop herself upright and check herself for serious injury.

"You okay?" Quinn asked as he dismounted.

"Not very." Piper squinted against the pain as he hunkered down in front of her. His somber expression didn't give much away and she wondered if he even cared if she had very nearly knocked herself senseless and scraped a layer of skin off her hip, elbow and shoulder.

But at least he didn't say *I told you so.* For that she was grateful. He simply appraised the knot that she could feel swelling up on her forehead.

"My fault for not paying attention to where I was going," she murmured as she tried to gain her feet. Unfortunately, dizziness left her so wobbly that she had to brace her hand against the rough rock wall and sink back to her knees.

His hand clamped around her forearm to hoist her onto shaky legs. When they threatened to fold up beneath her Quinn slid his arm around her waist to support her. "You better ride with me until you get your bearings."

Piper was all in favor of that, particularly since she wasn't sure she could react quickly enough if she had to duck under another low-hanging shelf of rock. Plus, if she passed out she might keel over the ledge. She didn't want to risk that possibility again.

"Not much of a rider, I'd guess," he said as he shepherded her back to his horse.

"Unfortunately, no. My father insisted that proper ladies didn't need to know how to ride because we were supposed to be *driven* in the comfort of a carriage." She smiled impishly. "My sister and I did sneak off several times to ride horseback, but not as often as we would have liked to."

Quinn set her carefully on his horse then looked her over closely before he pulled himself up behind her. Her face was peaked and the knot on her head reminded him of a goose egg. Also, it hadn't taken him but a few minutes to realize that she was having difficulty riding bareback.

He could spot a tenderfoot a mile away and that's what she was. Stunningly attractive and spirited—and so far out of her element that it was laughable.

Just what he needed while tracking a gang of cutthroats, he mused sourly. The men responsible for his friend's death were miles ahead of him and here he was, playing bodyguard and nursemaid to a woman who didn't know beans about surviving in the wilderness. Con artist though she probably was, she was accustomed to moving in society, not battling inclement weather and unexpected dangers of the wilderness.

His thoughts flitted off when Piper settled herself more comfortably in front of him. Her shapely derriere wedged against his crotch and her thighs brushed the inside of his legs. Her back was pressed against his chest and he had to grit his teeth against the jolt of pleasure that her nearness evoked.

He resented the fact that the feel of her body gliding rhythmically against his got him all stirred up. He was on an important assignment, damn it. He was also trying to keep the promise Taylor Briggs had demanded with his last breath.

Get those sonsabitches for me, Cal. Every last one of 'em. Promise me that, Taylor had gasped before he collapsed, a victim of ambush.

Quinn had made a solemn vow that day. Now he was burdened with the prettiest female he had ever laid eyes on and she was the worst distraction he had ever encountered. Period.

"Is there some place I can get a drink?" she asked with a seesaw breath. "I don't feel well at all."

"Right. Sure," he grumbled.

The nearest watering hole was Sunset Springs. It was located about five miles out of the way, down the side of the mountain. While he catered to the needs of his injured companion—who felt so damn good nestled against him that it was making him crazy—the outlaws' trail was getting colder by the minute.

Hell's bells, could anything else go wrong with this assignment? Quinn knew better than to send that question winging heavenward, for fear it would sound like a challenge. He had plenty of those to deal with already.

"I'm really sorry to be such a burden," she mumbled. "But this bump on my head is making me queasy and my throat is as dry as a desert."

Quinn didn't want to feel sorry for her, didn't want to feel obliged to accommodate her. He had told her to watch her head, but her instinctive reactions obviously hadn't been tested and perfected as well as his had. Furthermore, he wasn't accustomed to having to issue warnings to the other Rangers he worked with on occasion. They were seasoned fighters and trackers who were attuned to their surroundings.

But not *this* female, he mused. She was a disaster waiting to happen—and if he weren't careful he would land right smack dab in the middle of it with her.

If he were lucky enough to locate the stronghold without being spotted, he might be able to spare the time to escort Piper to Fort Davis, then rejoin his battalion so they could lay siege to the outlaws' stronghold.

That was the best-case scenario. Which rarely ever happened in his line of work.

When Quinn reined toward the edge of the rocky cliff, forcing the horses to sidestep downhill, Piper stared warily at him, her face losing all color. "Where are we going?"

Another rush of pleasure shot through him when she plastered herself against him, as if seeking reassuring support while they sidestepped down the steep hillside.

Quinn battled tooth and nail to prevent his lusty response to the feel of her curvaceous body pressed to his.

"You said you needed a drink. My canteen is dry and the spring is tucked in a lower valley. The only way to reach it is to pick our way down the footpath to Sunset Springs."

Piper huddled against the solid wall of his chest, comforted by the feel of his arms holding her securely in place. She refused to glance sideways, knowing she wouldn't be comfortable peering over bluffs anytime soon without feeling as if she were about to plunge to her death.

"If you can hold out for an hour you'll have more water than Moses," Quinn assured her.

Frowning, she glanced back at him. "What has Moses got to do with this?"

"He had forty days and nights of rain, didn't he?"

Piper smiled. "No, that was Noah and his ark of animals," she corrected. "You have your stories mixed up."

Which was no surprise, considering his unusual upbringing.

A long hour later, feeling drained and light-headed, Piper glanced toward the spring-fed pool that glittered in the sunlight. A sense of relief rippled through her, overriding the nagging nausea and throbbing headache. The moment Quinn drew the horse to a halt she swung her right leg sideways and slid to the ground. Her legs buckled immediately.

If Quinn hadn't snaked out a hand to grab her by the nape of her blouse she would have collapsed. Steadying her with one hand, he dismounted, then propelled her to the edge of the inviting pool. Piper cupped her hands together to scoop up a sip of water.

Her thirst finally quenched, she splattered water on her face and neck. A sigh of pleasure tumbled from her lips while she bathed her face again and again.

When a shadow fell over her, she glanced up to see Quinn looming over her. There was a squint in his golden eyes and a questioning expression on his bronzed face.

"Can you handle a firearm?" he asked out of the blue.

"No. That was just a bluff earlier. I've never fired a pistol before."

"Figured as much." With practiced ease he slid the Colt from the holster and handed it to her. "You can stay here to rest while I scout ahead. Most likely I won't be back until dark. Varmints gather here to drink so keep your guard up and the pistol close at hand."

He showed her how to cock the trigger and informed her that there were five rounds in the chamber. "Use this weapon only if absolutely necessary," he cautioned. "Sound carries for miles in these stone valleys. We don't want to alert unwanted guests to the fact that we're here."

"That's it?" she chirped incredulously as he pivoted on his heels to amble toward his horse. "You're just going to leave me alone indefinitely?"

Piper was sorry to say that she had become shamefully dependent on him. Blast it, part of the reason for fleeing from her father was to establish her independence and regain her sense of self. Unfortunately, being held at gunpoint by bandits and dangling over a cliff had taken most of the starch out of her. Humiliating though it was to admit, she felt secure and comforted by Quinn's presence—even when she knew she was an unwanted inconvenience to him.

He gestured his head toward the mutt that was lapping water on the far side of the pool. "He'll be here to keep you company."

"That is hardly comforting, I—"

Her voice fizzled out when he walked off, towing his horse along behind him. The clatter of hooves against stone echoed around her, leaving her feeling more alone and isolated than she had been in her life.

Muttering at Quinn's insensitivity, she braced herself against a slab of stone and cursed inventively. Just when she began to feel kindly and sympathetic toward Callahan he turned as hard as the rocks she had propped herself against.

She asked herself which was worse, being abandoned and ignored by this hardhearted Ranger, or bored to tears by her would-be fiancé who yammered incessantly about the merchant business and his grand plans for his future.

Piper laid back her aching head and decided that once she got to where she was going she would refuse to rely on—or associate with—men unless absolutely necessary. Now all she had to do was emulate Quinn's impressive survival skills and she could become as much a free spirit as she wanted to be.

Quinn halted his horse on a flattop mesa, then fished his field glasses from the saddlebag. He was aggravated at himself for feeling guilty about dragging Piper on this arduous trek through the mountains.

Not to mention that she had suffered a painful injury—one that he might have prevented if he had been more attuned to her inability to function in the wilds. Plus, he had spent so much time trying to ignore the attraction he felt for her that he had forgotten to adequately warn her about the hazardous terrain.

Now, thanks to his lack of consideration, she had a nasty-looking bump on her forehead and she was battling nausea and exhaustion.

He shifted restlessly on his horse as he scanned the rocky terrain, looking for signs of the outlaw gang. It frustrated him that his mind kept trying to veer in two directions at once. Just when he thought he had focused absolute concentration on those murdering thieves, the image of Piper popped into his head.

If the sight of her in those form-fitting clothes wasn't hard enough on a man's senses, he had held her familiarly against him for an hour while he descended the winding trail to the spring. Now he knew her scent, knew the tantalizing feel of her body…and he wanted more.

Damn it, he did *not* need this right now! Did not want to be intrigued by this woman. He had never spent so many consecutive hours with a woman and he wasn't sure how to relate to her because his previous liaisons with women were of a brief, sexual nature.

Plus, he wasn't sure he trusted her to tell him the truth. The fact that she had refused to divulge her last name suggested that she was hiding something important from him. Quinn didn't like surprises and secrets.

They always spelled unexpected trouble. *Piper* was *trouble* and that heaping pouch of money and jewels made him suspicious.

To be fair though, he had to admit that he didn't trust anyone very much. Life had taught him that counting on anyone but himself was risky business. Taylor Briggs had been the exception. It was the first time in years that Quinn had taken anyone into his confidence. Taylor had never been judgmental or prejudiced. He had accepted Quinn for what he was—a man without strong ties or connections to family or one culture in particular.

A lone wolf prowling the frontier, ridding the area of the kind of injustice that tormented his past. That, according to Taylor Briggs. He had been the only man who had cared enough to find out what made Quinn tick and Quinn had come to understand what made Taylor the man he was. They had learned to think alike, to predict each other's actions in the face of battle. They had come to depend on each other to guard their backs when trouble descended on them.

His thoughts scattered when he noticed a thin flute of smoke rising above a craggy peak to the north. He put away his field glasses and nudged the horse across the mesa. The horse stumbled as they moved along the fingerlike arroyos that could provide cover—in case a lookout had been posted to take potshots at unwanted intruders.

Quinn dismounted to lead the horse through the labyrinth of ravines before he hiked up the steep slope to investigate. Sprawled on his belly, he peered over the ledge to see six men sitting around a small campfire.

There was barely enough daylight left to identify the group, but with the aid of his spyglass he noted the red bandanas around the men's necks and identified their horses.

Sure enough, these were the hombres who had robbed the stage. Quinn would have liked nothing better than to pick off these bastards one by one and send them to hell where they belonged. Unfortunately, that would defeat the purpose of his reconnaissance mission. He wanted to trap the entire nest of outlaws and remove the threat they posed to nearby ranches and communities.

His Kiowa and Comanche training had taught him to be deliberate and patient, to consider the advantage and disadvantage of each option. Unfortunately, the need to avenge Taylor's death made him eager to act.

If not for Piper, Quinn would camp out right where he was to keep a close eye on these scoundrels so they could lead him to their stronghold. Too bad he had to backtrack to Sunset Springs.

Scowling, he inched backward, then moved soundlessly down the slope to fetch his horse. He picked his way back to the secluded pool by the light of the full moon that glowed like a silver dollar in the cloudless night sky.

Piper was right where he had left her hours earlier, sprawled beside the spring, using her satchel as her pillow. His pistol was lying an arm's length away. But to his dismay he noticed that a sidewinder had crawled to the water's edge and lay across her knees. The pup was obviously off hunting and wasn't around to alert her to trouble.

Quinn reached for the bullwhip coiled over his shoulder. With practiced skill he popped the whip, catching the snake unaware. The lashing whip brought Piper straight up to stare wide-eyed at him. Wheeling, Quinn slung the snake that he had snared with the whip against the stone cliff.

Piper's shriek of alarm overrode the deadly hiss and rattle, but Quinn refused to let her distract him. He hurled his dagger, anchoring the snake to the sand gathered at the base of the cliff. With one swift slash he rendered the viper harmless.

Piper swallowed with a gulp while she studied the dark profile of the man who had appeared from nowhere to save her from a nasty bite. The sting of the whip against her leg had awakened her abruptly and she had nearly suffered heart seizure when she realized the serpent had used her for a pallet. Even now, the aftereffects of icy fear were thrumming through her quaking body. Lord, that was close!

Mutely, she watched Quinn behead the snake, as if he had performed the task a hundred times before. Which he probably had since this untamed wilderness was his domain.

"Thank you," she wheezed as she watched Quinn toss the scaly reptile onto the pile of wood and twigs that he had obviously picked up on his way back from wherever he had been for the past few hours.

"You should have been paying attention," he said darkly. "Snake bites are about as much fun as getting shot."

She stared distastefully at the snake. "Please don't tell me that's going to be our supper."

He glanced at her then smirked. "Okay. What do you want me to call it then?"

"I'm not hungry." Her stomach growled, making a liar of her.

"Well, *I* am." He dropped into a crouch, using his dagger to chop up the meat. "Gather up some stones. I'm going to teach you how to build a campfire that doesn't attract unwanted attention."

Piper did as she was told, then stacked the rocks according to his specific instructions. She constructed the semblance of a miniature chimney, then watched as he lit the fire. Only a narrow ribbon of smoke wafted in the breeze.

"This traps in the heat for cooking without giving away our location. Old Indian trick," he explained.

"I wish I had an instruction manual of old Indian tricks," she murmured wistfully. "I definitely need to brush up on my survival skills."

"We'll start with learning to handle a dagger," Quinn announced as he retrieved the knife from the sheath on his thigh.

Piper paid close attention while Quinn showed her how to hold the blade in her fingertips, cock her arm then snap her wrist. Her first attempt to hit a clump of grass near the spring left the dagger thunking on the ground and bouncing twice before it came to rest.

"Get yourself aligned with your target," Quinn instructed as he retrieved the knife.

He moved up behind her to position her shoulders. The feel of his lean fingers curled on her shoulders sent a tingle of pleasure trickling through her. When he situated himself directly behind her, surrounding her with his body as he guided her arm in the proper motion, her pulse kicked up. His musky scent invaded her nostrils, heightening her awareness of him.

"It's timing and precision," Quinn said, his voice a husky murmur beside her ear.

Piper shivered uncontrollably, amazed at the unprecedented sensations that rippled through her. Why was it, she wondered, that this man affected her on so many different levels when none of her suitors ever had?

When she cocked her arm, while his hand guided the motion to ensure the proper flick of her wrist, she could feel his muscled chest pressed against her back. His solid thighs were meshed against the back of her legs. The whisper of his breath caused goose flesh to pebble her skin. Awareness intensified and Piper had difficulty breathing normally.

Sweet mercy! she thought. It was impossible to concentrate on hurling the dagger when all she really wanted to do was turn in his surrounding arms and satisfy the feminine curiosity that was burgeoning inside her.

"Piper?"

His raspy voice vibrated through her while his masculine body remained so tormentingly close that it felt as if they were sharing the same skin. "Yes?" Was that her voice? It sounded rusty and completely unfamiliar to her ears.

"Hurl the dagger."

"Right." She inhaled a steadying breath and then caught another tantalizing whiff of him. Her senses reeled and desire burned through her. She felt herself easing instinctively closer to him, yearning to savor this moment for as long as it lasted. She liked the feel of him, liked the scent of him and she seemed to need something more.

And suddenly Quinn stepped away. The pleasure of being so close to him vanished in a heartbeat and disappointment overcame her. Her arm still cocked in midair, she glanced back at Quinn. He was staring at her with those glowing amber eyes and a muscle leaped in his clenched jaw. His hands were fisted at his sides and he had an odd expression on his face.

"Throw the damn dagger," he said through his teeth.

Piper dragged in a fortifying breath and asked herself why standing so close to her seemed to annoy him so much. Then she concentrated on her target and flung the dagger. She was amazed that the knife speared directly into the clump of grass because her hand was still shaking in the aftermath of the pleasurable sensations that had bombarded her.

"Keep practicing while I check on supper," he commanded before he wheeled around and walked away.

Piper retrieved the knife and practiced her newfound skills repeatedly. She kept flicking glances at Quinn at irregular intervals, wondering why he had been in such a rush to break physical contact with her. Did he find her that offensive? She didn't usually have that effect on men. It was disheartening to realize that she found him altogether irresistible and he wanted nothing to do with her.

Ten minutes later Piper rejoined Quinn and watched as he turned the skewered meat over the fire.

"I caught up with the outlaws earlier," he said, averting his gaze from her. "They made camp in Devil's Canyon. Damn appropriate, I'd say."

Piper smiled briefly. Quinn's manner of speech was short and to the point, unlike her would-be fiancé who yammered nonstop and imparted little in the way of information—except as it pertained to his favorite person. *His Truly.*

"How's your head feeling by now?"

"It still hurts. *Throbs* is more accurate."

"I thought it over and decided it was my fault you got hurt," he announced out of the blue.

Piper frowned, bemused. "*I'm* the one who didn't look where I was going. How can that possibly be your fault?"

He shrugged impossibly broad shoulders—and she wished she would stop noticing all his masculine attributes, stop longing for the feel of his muscular body pressed familiarly to hers. It was more than obvious that Quinn resented any close physical contact with her. The instruction with handling a dagger indicated that he didn't enjoy being close to her for too long at a time.

"I didn't take into account that you're a female," he went on to say.

The comment scattered Piper's wandering thoughts and got her dander up in one second flat. If he dared to talk down to her, dared to equate her gender with stupidity, the way her father had done on several occasions, she was going to use her new skills with the dagger on his throat!

Chapter Six

"Which means?" she baited, giving him enough rope to hang himself.

Something in her voice must have given away her indignation because he glanced at her, and she noticed the ghost of a grin that tugged at the corner of his mouth.

"Don't get all riled up, greenhorn. I only meant that you aren't conditioned to cope with life in the wilderness. You haven't perfected your skills or sharpened your instincts. But don't take it personally because most women never do."

"If that is supposed to make me feel better it doesn't," she mumbled.

"I should have taken that into account instead of assuming you were attuned to our surroundings." He gestured toward the meat sizzling in the fire. "Take the snake for example. No one taught you that cold-blooded vipers seek out warmth when the temperatures drop at night. It's a lesson you have to learn the hard way unless someone takes you under wing to teach you. I didn't prepare you."

Piper stared at the coiled whip that lay beside his moccasined feet. "Who taught you to be so effective with the whip?"

All expression vanished from his face, except for the flare of gold in his eyes. "I learned from the man who used it on me. To him, I was a half-breed, a savage."

Piper grimaced at the awful thought. Before she realized it she had moved toward Quinn. Her hand folded consolingly over the banded muscles of his forearm. "If I had been there I would have wanted to shoot him for what he did to you."

He was on his feet in a single bound, moving away from her as quickly as he had during the dagger-hurling lesson. Clearly he had an aversion to her touch and her offer of sympathy. Did he hate her that much? she wondered dejectedly. Did he resent her presence because she was a burden, a disruption in his mission?

Piper knew the answers to those questions. He didn't want her around for any reason, even for the reason most men wanted contact with women. He certainly didn't need her, for he was a man who didn't seem to need anyone or anything. To Quinn Callahan—survivor extraordinaire, seasoned fighter, dark angel of vengeance and long arm of justice—she was a bothersome nuisance who slowed him down.

She should have ridden west and taken her chances, she realized in retrospect. If she hadn't been an emotional wreck after her near-death experience on the cliff perhaps she wouldn't have become so dependent on him. But the truth was that she had been too much a coward to brave the wilds alone and face the unknown after having the wits scared clean out of her.

Now, Quinn was paying for the inconvenience of having a greenhorn female underfoot.

"I plan to pay you for every delay I've caused," she insisted determinedly. "Furthermore, you should track those desperadoes and leave me here. I'll make my way back to the stage route. *My* problems aren't yours and I'm sorry that I nagged you into bringing me with you when it is clear that I am completely out of my element and I am shamelessly unprepared to handle the difficulties of the wilderness."

He cocked his head and surveyed her for a pensive moment. "We are about as far out into the middle of nowhere as we can get and *now* you are ready to strike off on your own? What changed your mind?"

She dodged that probing stare that seemed to look straight into her, searching out her deepest secrets and hidden weaknesses. "For starters, you don't want me underfoot. I'm a burden to you. Because of me you had to backtrack instead of dogging the bandits' trail to their hideout. I'm costing you precious time. Plus, you don't trust me and you dislike me so much that when I touch you, for whatever reason, you can't get away from me fast enough to suit yourself."

"You've got that right," he mumbled sourly.

Fortunately, she had *mis*interpreted his reasons for not wanting her close, Quinn thought. Her touch, the feel of her lush body gliding erotically against his made his sap rise—to the extreme. Plus, she was intelligent, well educated, and she unwillingly intrigued him. However, they were about as far apart on the social pendulum as two people could get, which made him leery of getting emotionally attached to her.

In fact, he wasn't going to get emotionally attached to *anyone* ever again. He had allowed Taylor Briggs inside his protective barrier and losing his friend had become an unwanted reminder of the turmoil of his childhood.

Not feeling anything for anyone was easier.

Quinn had learned that the hard way.

Scowling at the impossible temptation this woman represented when he stared at her for more than five seconds, he snatched up his bedroll. He shook it out then placed it a safe distance from the pool that was a favorite watering hole for predators. The realization that there was only one pallet between them and they would have to share it had him grumbling all over again.

Hell, you'd think that fate had purposely tossed this stumbling block of a female at you, if only to test your resistance and restraint. Just what he needed, another difficult challenge. Personally, Quinn thought he had been tested quite enough in life. He wasn't an optimist who expected happiness, but extended periods *without* torment would be nice.

"Come sit over here and I'll bring supper when it's cooked," he said, gesturing toward the pallet.

While Piper sank down, he peeled off his shirt, then balanced on the rocks beside the pool to partially bathe himself. He cursed soundly when he heard her gasp and realized that he had unintentionally exposed the scars on his back to her. No doubt, the sight of his marred flesh repulsed her.

"I *definitely* want to shoot whoever did that to you," she muttered, surprising him. "Give me his name…and a gun."

That was not the reaction he had expected.

Quinn glanced over his shoulder and got lost in those silver-blue eyes that roamed unhindered over him. "Why do you care who did this?" he asked, bewildered.

"Because it's inhumane, for one thing! And regardless of the fact that you despise me and resent me for intruding into your life, I admire you. I am also impressed by your skills and abilities and I'm—" Her voice crackled and she jerked her blond head around to stare at the cliff overhead. "I'm dreadfully sorry you're stuck with me, Callahan. I *really* am."

Didn't like her? Hell, she was about as wrong as she could get on that count. He liked her *too* much, that was the problem. He liked the looks of her. Liked the sound of her voice. Liked her fiery spirit. He would never trust her, of course. But that didn't mean he was immune to her sweet scent, aroused by her shapely body and hypnotized by those unique eyes and her bewitching face.

When he heard her choked sob, he steeled himself against the instinctive need to gather her in his arms and comfort her. First off, he wasn't the comforting type. Didn't know beans about relating to people in general and women in particular. Secondly, he couldn't trust himself to stop after giving her a consoling pat on the shoulder.

Didn't trust *her.* Didn't trust *himself* with her. Hell of a dilemma, he mused in frustration.

"You about done blubbering?" he asked as he splashed water on his chest and then let it trickle over his shoulders and down his back. "I've never yet encountered a situation where crying solved a damn thing. A complete waste of emotion if you ask me."

"Well, no one asked you, you hard-hearted, rough-edged—oh!" she spouted from behind him. "Never in my life have I met anyone as difficult to deal with as you!"

He smiled wryly, knowing he had accomplished his purpose by goading her to anger. She'd gotten mad enough to cease crying. Good. He didn't want her to know how much her tears got to him.

Never let a man or woman expose your weaknesses, for they will prey on them. Quinn had learned that lesson from the shaman who had furthered his training in the ways of a warrior and also taught him to concoct the healing medicine potions used by the Comanche.

Quinn had just come to realize that Piper's tears crept beneath his defenses and made him feel vulnerable.

He made a mental note not to let it happen again.

He pivoted slightly to stare over his shoulder. He noticed Piper was glaring poison darts at him. "Feeling better now that you've turned your wrath on me?" he asked.

"No," she snapped. "I don't know which headache is worse. The one caused by the bump on my skull or the one I've got from dealing with *you*."

He shrugged into his shirt. "You insisted on coming along," he didn't fail to remind her. "I told you, no whining. The wilderness is unforgiving and you have to deal with that, like it or not."

"Unforgiving like you?" she hurled at him. "I swear

to goodness, Callahan, if opportunity presents itself and *you* bawl your head off in front of me, I will never let you hear the end of it!"

Quinn threw back his head and laughed at the absurd idea that he would reduce himself to tears. He had done that after he lost his father, after the Kiowa captured him. Then he had braced up and forced himself to forget about his white heritage because he had become an Indian for all intents and purposes in order to survive.

He hadn't cried in twenty-one years.

And he couldn't remember the last time he'd laughed.

It amazed him that this fiery female had evoked so many emotions from him during their short acquaintance. Which was reason enough to find the isolated hideout. Pronto. He couldn't afford to get attached to her because he intended to deliver her to Fort Davis so he could contact Commander Butler. He planned to lead the strike force to remove the criminal threat in the area.

That was his mission and this exasperating female was not going to get in his way.

Turning away from the spring, Quinn broke off two limbs from a scraggly juniper tree to serve as skewers for the meat. He gathered several chunks of rattlesnake steak then offered them to Piper who was still pouting resentfully because he had goaded her for bleeding useless tears.

"Thank you," she said in a voice that didn't sound the least bit grateful.

"You are welcome," he said just as insincerely.

He sank down on the far side of the pool to take his

own meal. Unfortunately, his betraying gaze kept darting to Piper. She had pulled the pins from her hair and the frothy mass of moonbeam-colored tendrils cascaded over her shoulders to curl enticingly against the full swells of her breasts.

The impulsive urge to run his fingers through those silky strands stunned him. Was he insane? *Not* touching her and *not* staring overly long at her were his objectives. And damnation, why did he have to be so aware of how alluringly attractive she was?

Ah, how he wished she were still charading as Witch Agatha. He could deal with that snippy crone more effectively than he could deal with Piper, golden-haired goddess of masculine fantasies.

He watched a smile light up her face when the mutt returned from wherever he had been for the past hour. She fed him some meat and he plopped down devotedly beside her. The pup was in dog heaven, savoring all the food and attention he could get.

"You gonna give that hound a name?" he questioned between bites.

She frowned thoughtfully as she stroked the mutt. "Nothing comes to mind."

"Why not call him Dog? That's what he is," Quinn suggested.

She shook her head. "He deserves better than that."

"Then come up with something better so he'll learn to come to heel when you call him. Nothing worse than an untrained dog or horse or—"

"Or woman?" she supplied. "I suspect that's how you like your women. They sit when they are told to sit.

They come to heel when ordered. No trouble. No nonsense. No fuss."

"It's easier than dealing with the likes of you." He smiled wryly. "If I asked you to come to heel you'd probably bite a chunk out of my ankle."

She paused from eating and stared consideringly at him. "This is how it's going to be between us for the duration, isn't it? Tormenting each other for spite?"

He bobbed his head. "Yep. Until I know exactly who you are and precisely what motivates you then we're destined to remain at odds. That's how I deal with suspicious characters."

"And just like that," she said, snapping her fingers, "if I divulge who I am, you will trust me immediately? You'll stop staring at me as if you expect me to bury a dagger in your back when you're not looking?" She scoffed at him. "Cynical as you are, I seriously doubt that, Callahan. I'm not sure you could bring yourself to like me, even if I *paid* you handsomely for it."

"Try me, Agatha or Piper or whoever you really are. What *is* your agenda?" He stared intently at her. "And try telling me the *truth* for once. The whole truth and nothing but."

"You want my life story? Fine." She propped herself against the stone wall and stretched her legs on the pallet. "I have one question though. When I tell you who I am and confide how much reward you might rake in if you return me to my home, will you be tempted to take it?"

"Maybe."

"Then I can't trust you, either." She fed the pup another bite of meat, then said, "Lucky."

He stared at her, befuddled. *"What?"*

"I'll name the mutt Lucky because he's lucky to be alive. Does that meet with your approval?"

His shoulders lifted and dropped nonchalantly. "Doesn't matter to me. He's not my dog. He's devoted to you. Can't imagine why though."

"I'm *trying* to get along with you and you are impossible," she erupted suddenly. "Stop badgering me!"

He watched her vault to her feet and storm toward him. He allowed her to loom over him, all fired up and huffy, because he liked knowing that he had the ability to ruffle her feathers. He also liked seeing the challenging glitter in her silver-blue eyes.

She fit somewhere in between the teasing camaraderie he had learned to share with Taylor and his natural desire to be intimate with a woman. In other words, she was a novel experience that simultaneously pleased and frustrated him to the point that he wasn't sure how to relate to her.

Furthermore, watching her lose her temper with him was better than being the object of her sympathy and watching her battle tears. Quinn was never going to pamper, cater to or fawn over this woman. He simply didn't have it in him and she needed to know that.

He and Piper were going to share an arduous journey through these rugged mountains and she was going to have to toughen up because he couldn't spend all his time wondering when she would burst into tears, when she would fall apart and tell him that she couldn't take anymore.

She had asked for this, he reminded himself. This ordeal would test her to the limits. It was high time she figured that out and realized that he wasn't going to mollycoddle her the way most men probably did.

"All right, Callahan," she seethed at him, her hands fisted on her shapely hips, her full breasts heaving with indignation. "So you've had a difficult life and don't give a tinker's damn about anyone. You're entitled, I agree. That doesn't mean my life hasn't been frustrating, even if I haven't faced the kind of hardships you've endured."

She glared at him good and hard and said, "But when you start treating me as if I count for nothing and my feelings are of no importance then you are too much like my father and you are standing on the last good nerve I have left today!"

Her rising voice echoed around the canyon and Quinn said, "Stop shouting before you draw unwanted attention. Those hombres over the ridge might decide to check it out. I know I would."

She dropped to her knees in front of him, wincing slightly when she landed on her scraped leg. She had regained the color in her cheeks—due to the anger she directed at him, he expected. He didn't flinch when she grabbed a fistful of his shirt and got right in his face to blow off steam.

"You want to know what motivates me? All you had to do was ask." Her unique eyes glittered with fiery temper and feisty spirit. "I want independence, freedom and the chance to make my own choices, *for once* in my life. And I'm not afraid to accept the consequences.

"For your information my father, Roarke Sullivan,

the reigning king of merchants in Texas, sees me as the extension of his will. He took over full responsibility of raising my sister and me after Mamma died of pneumonia eight years ago. He is infuriatingly domineering and he decided to marry me off so he could merge our family business with his closest competition. I objected so I lit out before he could drag me into a wedding I didn't want and find myself tied to a man I will never love."

"Sullivan?" His eyes popped. "Holy hell! You are an heiress. Even *I*'ve heard of the Sullivans of Galveston."

"Fabulously wealthy. The envy of society's upper crust," she said distastefully. "But I have no wish to marry John Almighty Foster and pose as the empty-headed trophy on his arm, the belle of the ball that he expects me to be."

Quinn chuckled, trying to picture Piper as the dutiful, submissive wife. The image didn't fit her assertive, spirited personality.

"For years my father has tried to browbeat me by siccing a teacher on me who was everything you met in Agatha Stewart," she confided. "According to Miss Johnson, I could never do anything quite right. I was too willful, too headstrong, too much of a free spirit to stay in my rightful place. She tried to make me docile and subservient, because that's what Papa thought a woman should be when she took a husband."

Quinn swallowed down a smile, thinking that this Miss Johnson person had been given a daunting task. Taming Piper, who had more sass, spunk and determination than any woman he had ever encountered, was as useless as beating your head against a brick wall.

Altering Piper's natural temperament would be as much of a waste of time as trying to mold him into a socially accepted gentleman.

"My father wanted a puppet he could control," she went on bitterly. "But he didn't get it with my older sister, because she dared to take control of her own life when she married Captain Matthew Duncan, who is now stationed at Fort Davis. Papa gave up on Penny completely. He tried even harder to make *me* into the daughter who met his high expectations and acquiesced to his decrees."

"Roarke disowned your sister?" Quinn questioned.

She bobbed her head and finally released her stranglehold on his shirt. "Yes, he denounced her right to inherit half the Sullivan fortune. He cut her off without a cent when she eloped. Papa tried to make an example of her to teach me a lesson and ensure that history didn't repeat itself."

Quinn grinned. "Guess he picked the wrong woman to bend to his will, didn't he?"

Piper nodded. "And despite what you probably think, the money I've saved up from teaching at Miss Johnson's Finishing School in Houston, while having her nag me to death for the past five years, is meant to provide me with a new start as a teacher at the garrison. Half of the funds will go to Penelope. The same goes for the pouch of jewelry that belonged to our mother and to us. Share and share alike is what I have in mind."

Quinn stared at her in amazement. This heiress, who obviously had a fortune at her disposal—if she had chosen to obey her father's wishes—had raced off alone in a coach, headed for the wilds of southwest Texas. "You are out of your mind, Piper. You had everything most people want."

She scoffed at that. "I had nothing but a gold-plated prison and a warden who tried to turn me into the image of my departed mother. To Papa, she was the ideal lady and he hasn't remarried because he couldn't find any woman who could replace her.

"After years of being told *what* to say, *how* to say it and *when* to say it, I longed to be myself and have a life of my own." She stared intently at him. "*That* is my motivation. That and the long-awaited reunion with my sister whom I haven't seen in two years. I have corresponded with her each week. I have had to be clever and discreet because Papa and Miss Johnson have tried to intercept Penny's replies. Papa wants no association between us because he has written her off and he doesn't want her to have the slightest influence on me."

Quinn watched her sink down cross-legged in front of him. She was still intense, her fists knotted on her knees, her back rigid.

She stared challengingly at him. "By confiding in you I have given you power over my destiny. My father can make you a very wealthy man if you contact him and accept the reward that he is undoubtedly offering. By now he has been informed that I left Houston. I predict that he has organized a posse or hired detectives to track me down."

Quinn predicted that she was right on that count. Now he understood why she had assumed a different identity and tried to alienate herself from other passengers. If anyone suspected who she really was she might have been turned over to her father to collect a generous reward.

She stared defiantly at him. "So, do it, Callahan," she dared him. "Telegraph my father the first chance you get. You can have the financial backing to open any business that meets your whim. People will kowtow to you, despite your upbringing because you will have the kind of money and power other people crave. This is your chance to see how the other half lives. After you locate the den of thieves and contact your Ranger battalion, then contact my father.

"But until then, I'm going to study you like a textbook, emulate your impressive skills and become just like you. Or die trying. No more tears. No more self-pity," she vowed resolutely. "You're going to look at me and see the reflection of yourself, so help me you will!"

He almost believed that because she looked so intent and driven to prove something to him. He could imagine her standing up to her father the same way, refusing to bend to his will, defying his decrees to be the woman he groomed in the image of his departed wife.

"I won't even curse you for handing me over to my father so he can make my wedding arrangements. By then it won't matter because you will have been my tutor and mentor during this journey. I will run as fast and far as I can again. *You* will still have the generous reward and eventually *I* will have the freedom I cherish."

When she sank back and heaved a deep breath his attention dropped to the swells of her breasts—again. Quinn was sorry to say that no matter how hard he tried to overlook her feminine assets he kept getting distracted, wanting things he shouldn't have.

Piper was at the top of the list of forbidden whims.

"Now then," she said, "if you want to know what I think or feel—which I doubt you do—on any other topic, just come right out and ask. I will tell you straight away. The same way *you* do with me. From now on, Callahan, when you're talking to me it will be like talking to yourself. No diplomacy, no tact, just forthright conversation."

Quinn had to battle to prevent another smile from pursing his lips. God, she was glorious. All spit and fire and challenge. "There's just one more thing I want to know."

Piper peered up at him, watching him bite back a grin and wondering what she might possibly have said to earn that glimmer of amusement. "What do you want to know?"

She held her ground, as she had taught herself to do while posing as an old crone, when he leaned in to crowd her space. The closer his head came to hers, the more difficult it was to breathe. She couldn't see past this infuriating yet intriguing man. She couldn't inhale air without drowning in his masculine scent. She couldn't concentrate on anything except the shape of his sensuous lips and the gleam in those whiskey-colored eyes that were fanned with long sooty lashes.

"I want to know what you taste like, dragon lady," he murmured as a teasing grin finally surfaced to encompass his ruggedly handsome face. "Are you fire or honey…or both?"

Chapter Seven

To Piper's stunned amazement Quinn angled his dark head and pressed his lips to hers. The kiss was nothing like she expected from a rough-edged, hard-bitten man like him. It was a baffling contradiction that crumbled her defenses in one second flat.

Piper had no clue what paradise tasted like, but if she were guessing, *this* was it. Warm. Inviting. Promising. All those marvelous sensations that made you feel good from inside and out and gave you an indescribable sense of peace and well-being. As if you had suddenly stepped over some mystical threshold and had *arrived*.

Quinn tasted like sweet, forbidden fruit. He sampled her with the same curiosity that she sampled him. They experimented with each other as their lips skimmed and darted away with the ever-changing angle of their heads—as if to savor one another from several different directions.

She leaned involuntarily into him because she felt the

need to be closer. Her palm splayed over the muscled wall of his chest, feeling his accelerated pulse matching her fast-tempoed heartbeat. She didn't even consider recoiling when he copied her gesture by laying his hand over her heart, making intimate contact with the rise of her breast.

Unprecedented sensations flooded through her body and burned deep into her core. Was this lust? Desire? Whatever it was, it seemed to have taken on a life of its own, feeding on the unexpected pleasure and the expanding heat of his kiss.

Piper opened her lips to him because it felt like the natural thing to do. When she felt the stab of his tongue searching for hers, she heard herself moan, then emulated his technique to explore the hidden recesses of his mouth.

While she was marveling at the unanticipated tenderness she had discovered in this hard-nosed man—and wanting more—he withdrew to run his fingers through her unbound hair. Disappointed that he had deprived her of her first real experience with seductive pleasure she stared up at him, *willing* him to kiss her again…and again.

"Your hair feels like silk." His voice rumbled like a purring cat. Which was only fair because her body was rumbling with astonishing sensations. "I figured as much."

"Why did you kiss me like that?" she asked directly.

"Why did you let me? I gave you plenty of time to pull away if you had wanted to."

She dodged the question, as he had dodged hers. Well, so much for forthright honesty, she mused. Some things were difficult to be honest about, for fear of being teased or rejected. But she made a pact with herself to become more courageous and less self-conscious in the future.

"I expected hard and bruising and uninvolved," she confided. "Did you kiss me because you *pitied* me after I told you my life story?"

The fact that the kiss he had bestowed on her *had* been gentle and left him feeling thoroughly involved disturbed him greatly. He really hadn't wanted their kiss to be personal, just inquisitive. But at first touch something had shifted inside him. She affected him way down deep inside, beneath those callous layers that had protected him from scorn, condemnation, and feelings of unworthiness.

She made him feel vulnerable; and that made him uncomfortable. Oh certainly, Piper was no match for him in any physical arena because he had been around the block of hard knocks a hundred times. He knew how to fight, how to survive and how to convince civilized society that its low opinion of him made no difference.

But *she* got to him. She, with her vow to become like him, to match him step for step until he looked at her and saw the spitting image of the Quinn Callahan that he projected to the world.

Well, despite *her* vow, he was not going to allow her to become like him, he promised himself.

She represented the wide-eyed innocence he had lost at age twelve. *She* was the purity that all the cleansing rituals the Kiowa and Comanche had conducted to transform him into a full-fledged Indian had not accomplished. *She* represented the hope and new beginnings that had died with each disappointing phase of life that he had undergone.

Yes, there were things he could teach Piper to survive in his world, but he wasn't going to permit *her* to forget how to hope and dream of a better future and to pursue life on her own terms. That's what she said she wanted, so that's what he would give her, in exchange for the sweetest kiss that he had ever known.

As soon as he located the den of thieves, he would take her to her sister at Fort Davis. She would have the independence she craved. As for her father, he would never learn Piper's whereabouts from Quinn. No matter how sizeable the reward or the temptation to make his life easier he would not betray her for personal gain.

"Quinn? Why are you looking at me like that?" she wanted to know.

Her question jostled him back to the present. He put on his poker face. "Like what?"

She rolled her eyes at him. "If I knew, I wouldn't have to ask, now would I?"

The sassy comment drew another grin from him. She was an expert at drawing all sorts of reactions from him, even when he usually tried not to let an ounce of emotion slip past his guard.

"I'm wondering how you're going to react when we bed down for the night on a single pallet. Worried, Sullivan?"

She flashed him a challenging stare. "I can handle it as well as you can. From now on, nothing gets to me, remember?"

He couldn't guarantee that it wouldn't get to *him* now that he had kissed her—and liked it way too much. He longed for a deep, thorough taste of her that went on and on. He predicted that he would be fighting these cravings and engaging in a battle royal, attempting to keep his hands to himself when she lay down beside him.

Because that's exactly what he wanted next—the *feel* of her silky skin beneath his fingertips. He wanted something more than the light brush of his hand over the swell of her breasts while he was kissing her. He wanted complete intimacy, wanted to savor the heady pleasure of being so deep inside her that it was impossible to tell where her body ended and his began.

The tantalizing prospect was enough to turn him hard and aching in a heartbeat. *Damn it, Callahan. Don't torment yourself by thinking about that!*

He watched Piper rise gracefully to her feet. She scooped up dirt to douse the campfire. After she rinsed her hands in the pool, she plunked down on the pallet. The tempting sight, and the erotic possibilities of joining her in bed, hit him with the force of a locomotive.

Considering how luscious this woman looked while fully clothed he could only begin to imagine how she would look, feel and taste if she were completely naked—beside him, beneath him and above him.

Quinn squeezed his eyes shut and gritted his teeth against the provocative images spinning around in his head. *Real smart, Callahan. Make it hard on yourself in spades, why don't you?*

"Damn, Agatha, where are you when I really need you?" Quinn grumbled sourly.

"Pardon? What did you say?"

"Nothing," he muttered as he watched her stretch

out on the bedroll. Another blow of pure lust hammered at him and he scowled sourly.

When she noticed his expression she said, "You need to stop grumbling and growling and be nicer to me."

"Oh? Why's that?" he asked tersely.

"Because you have an irascible disposition and I'm probably the only friend you have."

Quinn felt a chuckle bubbling up from his chest. "You've got that right."

When she patted the empty space beside him and grinned impishly at him, the control and self-discipline that he had spent thirty-three years nurturing and cultivating threatened to abandon him. Thankfully, inspiration struck when he saw the mutt lounging beside the pool.

"Come on, Lucky," he called to the dog.

A protective barrier is what Quinn needed and the dog could provide it. With the taste of Piper still on his lips, the scent of her clinging to his skin and the feel of her breasts branded on his hand, he definitely needed a buffer between them tonight.

Otherwise, she was going to lose her innocence to a man who had no right to take what could never truly belong to him.

Quinn sprawled on the bedroll, closed his eyes and focused his iron-willed self-discipline on getting some much-needed shut-eye. Even with the dog snuggled up between them he had to battle nearly overwhelming temptation—repeatedly.

"Quinn, are you asleep?" she asked a half hour later.

"Yes, so don't bother me," he grumbled.

"I just wanted you to know that I liked the taste of you."

He inwardly groaned, wondering if he could handle her new policy of outright honesty.

It took a long time for Quinn to fall asleep that night because his secret fantasies were buzzing around his head like bees swarming a hive.

Commander Scott Butler and his five volunteers held up their torches and peered grimly over the ledge where the stage wreck had occurred. He and the other Rangers had arrived at the stage station a few miles east, only to be informed by the driver and guard that thieves had attacked. According to the two men, the bandits had sent the coach, with its passengers closeted inside, racing along the sharp bend of the mountain road.

"There's debris scattered everywhere," Vance Cooper groaned. "The driver's description of the male passenger fits Callahan. Damn it, I can't imagine how he could have survived this crash."

Butler couldn't imagine, either. "The sheer drop off this cliff would be enough to kill anyone. If Cal managed to land in the swift-moving stream there's no telling where he ended up…even if he was conscious and knew what had happened."

"Not to mention the fact that this area is crawling with lobos and mountain cats."

"Look over here, Commander." Tom Pendleton directed attention to the object he noticed while scanning the area with his field glasses. "There's something snagged on that scrub bush. It looks like a black veiled hat." He glanced over at Butler. "Maybe it belonged to the old woman that was also on the stage."

"Or maybe a woman in disguise. Maybe Piper Sullivan managed to elude her abductor and used the disguise to keep her identity a secret."

"Looks like she was doomed one way or the other," Sam Garret said dismally. "She was the only female passenger reported to have been seen at the relay stations on the stage route this week."

Butler heaved an audible sigh. "I sure as hell am glad I don't have to be the one bearing the bad news to Roarke Sullivan." He glanced at Sam. "Ride back to the station with the preliminary report that Miss Sullivan might have perished in the crash. The driver on the eastbound stage can send the telegram to Galveston."

Sam wheeled around to fetch his horse.

"We'll find a path down to the stream to investigate. Then we'll meet you at the stage station at Perdition Pass."

Sam nodded, then reined his horse around to gallop away.

The remaining Rangers mounted up to locate a trail that would take them to the bottom of the gorge.

"Damn, Commander, there's times when I really don't wanna know what happened," Vance Cooper grumbled. "This is one of those times, especially if what's left of Cal is down there somewhere."

"Nobody promised this job would be easy," Butler said as he trotted west. "It doesn't get much worse than giving last rites to one of our own."

That said, the Rangers veered off the road to pick their way downhill. They found no conclusive evidence that the two passengers had perished.

No evidence that they hadn't, either.

The men clung to that small ray of hope that Cal and the woman might have survived the disaster. But from the looks of the shattered debris on the rocky slope and stream bank, Butler decided that walking away from certain death would have been nothing short of a miracle.

Piper awakened the next morning, not surprised to note that Quinn had left her alone again. She told herself not to feel abandoned and not to panic because this was a test of her fortitude and she intended to pass with flying colors. This was the first day of her self-reliance and independence. She was going to learn to depend on no one. Just like Quinn.

She smiled faintly when she realized that he had been considerate enough to leave one of his sidearms for her protection.

A wild Texas rose lay beside the pistol.

Startled, and inordinately pleased by his thoughtful gesture, she plucked up the flower, then winced when a thorn poked into her finger. Piper chortled when it dawned on her that Quinn had left behind the perfect symbol of himself. Gentle in some ways, but protected by prickly armor.

She also suspected that Quinn thought the flower was an accurate representation of *her.*

Although Piper had bathed the previous evening while Quinn was scouting the area, she decided to take advantage of the refreshing pool this morning, too. Privacy and bathing were about the only luxuries to be found out here in the untamed wilderness, she mused.

"And where have you been?" she asked Lucky when he trotted back to camp to lap up a drink of water.

Piper smiled when the pup looked up at the sound of her voice and wagged his tail. It was encouraging to know that someone around here appreciated her company.

When Piper doffed her clothes and sank into the pool Lucky took a flying leap and joined her. Chuckling, she watched the dog paddle in circles before he scrabbled up the rock ledge to shake himself off.

A few minutes later Piper emerged from the spring to dress in her breeches and blouse. While she was rolling up the pallet and gathering her belongings to secure to the back of her horse she heard the tumble of pebbles, then tensed at the sound of Lucky's warning growl.

She glanced over her shoulder, expecting to see Quinn rounding the outcropping of rock. She gasped in alarm when two renegade Indians stopped short and stared at her in surprise. Panic-stricken, Piper dashed over to retrieve the pistol she had left near the spring. Her breath came out in a pained whoosh when one of the men launched himself at her and sent her skidding across the pebbled path. Stones gouged her knees, hips, chin and elbows as the man scrambled over her in an attempt to grab the gun before she got her hands on it.

Lucky bounded atop the warrior and clamped onto his shirt, but he was knocked away. While the renegade was distracted Piper rammed her elbow into his nose, then surged forward in an attempt to take possession of the pistol. But to her frustration the second warrior darted over to stamp down on her wrist, then snatched the weapon out of her reach.

Although she bit, clawed and squirmed to escape, the warrior that loomed over her jerked her upright. He clamped his arm diagonally across her chest and laid a vicious-looking dagger against her throat.

Piper was forced to admit defeat.

Well, so much for the first day of her self-reliance and independence, she thought in exasperation. But no matter what her fate—or the lack thereof—she was not going to burst into tears, whimper and beg for mercy. As Quinn had told her, he couldn't name a single incident in his life where crying had solved a damn thing.

Her captor rattled off a comment to his companion in Indian dialect. The next thing Piper knew her arms were tied behind her with a leather strap and she was hoisted onto the back of her horse.

When the renegades stared speculatively at Lucky, Piper stiffened in outrage. "If you are wondering if that pup might look good roasting over a campfire, the answer is *no*," she said curtly. "I didn't save him to become your lunch!"

The warriors gaped at her, apparently surprised by her flare of temper and brisk tone of voice.

Obviously one good thing had come from standing up to her domineering father, Piper thought. She had learned not to subject herself to someone else's will without spouting protests.

Piper spewed her frustration at both warriors as they led her up the steep incline to fetch their horses. Now would be the perfect time for Quinn to show up, she mused. Then, on second thought, maybe not. She didn't want to see him hurt or killed because of her inability to defend herself. She was not his responsibility and these were the consequences she had to face because of her choice to strike off on her own.

Without Piper around to slow Quinn down, he could complete his mission and follow the gang of outlaws to their stronghold. She was on her own now. Whatever happened to her might become a traumatic ordeal, similar perhaps to what Quinn had endured as a Kiowa and Comanche captive.

The prospect of being mauled and abused made her cringe, but she refused to give up hope just yet. If the warriors let their guards down for a moment, she vowed to take advantage and attempt escape.

While the warriors led her due west, through the deep ravines dotted with junipers and boulders, Piper renewed her vow to take command of her own life. Or die trying. She had the unshakable feeling the pact she had made with herself was about to be put to another difficult test.

A sense of unease overcame Quinn as he made his way back to Sunset Springs. Over the past decade he had acquired the ability to sense trouble before it pounced. Now his instincts were on full alert and the hair on the back of his neck prickled in warning. He dismounted and left his horse tethered to a scrub bush. Cautiously, he made his way over the slabs of rock so he could peer down at the secluded spring in the V-shaped ravine.

Sure enough, Piper, Lucky and the horse were nowhere to be seen. All that had been left behind was the withered rose Quinn had impulsively placed beside

Piper on their pallet because its wild yet delicate beauty reminded him so much of her.

Quinn swore inventively as he bounded from one boulder to another like a mountain goat. He searched the campsite for telltale footprints and then let loose with a string of epithets when he spotted two sets of moccasin prints in the dirt.

Unless he missed his guess Piper had been captured by renegades. He felt guilty as hell because he knew her abduction was *his* fault. He had left her to her own devices again this morning. He hadn't deviated from his course of action by taking her to Fort Davis after the stage holdup, as he should have. He had been hell-bent on tracking the desperadoes to their isolated hideout.

At the very least he should have jostled Piper awake this morning and insisted that she ride with him. Instead, he had given her the chance to rest when time permitted.

He had compromised his plans to accommodate Piper this morning and look where it got both of them. Damn it to hell! Now the desperadoes were on the move northward and he had to trek west to rescue Piper before she was sold off to Comancheros or became some warrior's lusty amusement.

The prospect of Piper becoming a sexual conquest incensed him and filled him with a sense of urgency that bordered on panic. He took off at a dead run to vault onto his horse. Gouging the animal in the flanks, he clattered down the trail at a reckless pace, hoping to make up for lost time.

Two hours later, Quinn scrabbled up a rocky ridge to

pan the winding valley below. He spotted the threesome that had halted five hundred yards ahead of him. One of the warriors—a Comanche, he guessed by the long length of the fringe that adorned his buckskin breeches and shirtsleeves—had stopped to relieve himself. Since Quinn usually had rapport with the renegades he encountered from time to time, he decided to use the direct approach with Piper's abductors.

Using the familiar coyote howl to draw attention to himself, Quinn held his coiled whip over his head and waited for the renegades to whirl toward him.

He nudged his steed down the narrow path, bold as you please. He had learned long ago that Indians respected and valued courage, even in their enemies. They only relied on stealth and cunning when they were greatly outnumbered—which they had been when white invaders encroached on their hunting ground and offered worthless treaties designed to swindle Indian tribes out of their property.

Halting just out of rifle range, he called out in the Comanche dialect, "That is my woman you are making off with and I want her back."

The renegades made no move to blow him out of the saddle so he walked his horse forward. He inwardly grimaced when he noticed Piper's scraped chin and knees and saw the grime that covered the front of her blouse. Her silver-blond hair was in disarray, indicating that she had put up a fight before her capture.

Admiration swept through him when he remembered her declaration that she was going to become self-reliant. Of course, she had flunked her first test, but from all indication she had put up a fuss before she was abducted.

Quinn was so relieved to know that Piper was in one piece that he wanted to hug her close and reassure himself that she really was safe from harm. However, he had been trained not to display emotion or expose the slightest weakness. But, that didn't mean a jumble of feelings weren't bubbling just beneath the surface.

"I thought that was you, Gray Owl," one of the warriors called out as Quinn approached. "Still fighting Mexicans and white outlaws with the Rangers?"

"You *know* these renegades?" Piper asked, glancing back and forth between him and her captors.

"We're acquainted, although we have never been formally introduced," Quinn said in English before he slid his right leg over his mount and hopped to the ground. He reached down to pet the mutt that had bounded up to greet him. His gaze swung back to Red Hawk, the warrior who was on horseback. "You're a long way from the reservation. You know the army frowns on hunting expeditions this deep in Texas."

The Comanche snorted derisively. "I never met a white man whose opinion mattered much to me. Except for yours, maybe." He smiled faintly at Quinn. "But you are Kiowa and Comanche at heart. That is where it counts, my brother." He slid agilely from his paint pony, then ambled over to untie Piper's hands. "I have seen you in action against Mexican banditos. You still have the good sense to fight like one of us."

That was a fact. When it came to warfare no culture could compete with the hand-to-hand combat and guerilla skills of Indians. From childhood, Indian children were taught games that simulated the techniques necessary in battle. Quinn had mastered those skills and applied them constantly in his profession.

When Red Hawk released Piper, Quinn walked over to inspect her for injury. "You okay?" he asked softly.

"Fine, except for a few more bruises and scrapes." She stared disconcertedly at Red Hawk. "But I would dearly like to rub this man's nose in the dirt to repay him in kind for scuffing me up."

Quinn chuckled. "Spiteful little witch, aren't you?"

"I am now. I have also learned that being a woman in this part of the country affords no special privileges."

"No, it doesn't." Quinn stared somberly at her. "The next lesson you need to learn is that everyone is a potential enemy, especially in this neck of the woods. If you treat them as such then you're never surprised by an attack."

"I'll be sure to remember that." She extended her hand to Red Hawk, somewhat begrudgingly. "My name is Piper."

The tall, muscular-looking warrior cocked his raven-black head and stared at her hand, as if he wasn't sure what to do with it. Eventually he accepted it, then tried to repeat her name in awkward English.

"This is Red Hawk," Quinn said. "His clan was herded to Indian Territory two years ago." He clasped his hands around Piper's waist and assisted her from her horse. A wry smile pursed his lips as he gestured toward the warrior. "I presume Red Hawk didn't approve of the accommodations on the reservation, so he left. Not that I blame him."

He directed Piper's attention to the other Comanche who approached. "This is Spotted Deer. His father was a powerful Comanche chief who died in combat against Mexican raiders that plundered their winter encampment."

Piper nodded curtly. "He and I are more familiarly acquainted than I prefer. He tackled me, then crawled all over me while we were scrambling to get possession of your pistol."

"Who won?" Quinn asked, surveying her stained clothing.

"*Red Hawk* did. They ganged up on me. Otherwise, I might have gotten off a shot."

Quinn bit back an amused snicker. Damn if he didn't admire Piper's determination to hold her own against lopsided odds. The woman had plenty of fire and spirit. That almost made up for her lack of hand-to-hand combat skills.

"Didn't know you had a woman," Spotted Deer commented as he appraised Piper. "When did this happen?"

"A few days ago," Quinn replied as he slid his arm possessively around Piper's shoulder to verify his claim. "I don't plan on sharing her with anyone, even if the Comanche custom is to offer his woman to his brothers as a show of friendship and respect."

"Not sure I would have wanted her anyway." Red Hawk extended his hand to display the claw marks on his wrist. "She fights dirty. I do not think she will make you a dutiful wife."

"I don't think so, either. Much too feisty," Quinn agreed, grinning. "But she is pleasing to look at."

Red Hawk nodded in masculine approval. "She is

that, Gray Owl. But if you tried to bed her when she is not agreeable to it I think she might claw out your eyes."

"Would you *please* speak English," Piper insisted.

"They don't speak English. A little Spanish, yes," Quinn reported before he turned his attention to Red Hawk. "The Rangers sent me to track down a gang of outlaws that have been holding up stages, banks and depredating ranches. Have you seen them in this area?"

Red Hawk nodded grimly. "More than twenty well-armed riders have camped in *El Muerto Cañon*. They built corrals and adobe shacks. The fortress will make an attack very difficult."

"What is he saying?" Piper questioned curiously.

"They have seen the banditos," he translated. "They're holed up in Dead Man's Canyon. About five miles north-west, on the far side of Hell's Ridge. The haunt was once a sacred burial ground for the Kiowa and Comanche."

Piper suspected the warriors were not pleased to have the desperadoes tramping around on that particular site. "Would these men be willing to help us scout the hideout?"

"*Us?*" Quinn stared bemusedly at her. "I figured after this morning's incident that you would prefer I take you to Fort Davis first."

"We had a deal. I agreed to go with you to track the bandits near here and you agreed to guide me to the garrison before you contacted your battalion." She elevated her chin stubbornly. "A deal is a deal, Callahan, and we're wasting daylight."

He stared pointedly at her skinned chin and grimy clothes. "You have suffered enough already. I think I should take you to the fort first."

Piper shook her head, causing a few more recalcitrant tendrils to coil around her face. "If we are only five miles from the canyon, the sensible thing to do is check it out. I have cost you valuable time and inconvenience already. A day or two won't make that much difference to me because I didn't tell my sister exactly when to expect me."

Piper listened to Quinn make his request for assistance in the Comanche dialect. She sighed in relief when both warriors nodded agreeably. She regretted that she wasn't much help to Quinn in his reconnaissance mission, but his acquaintances could provide the needed expertise. Now that she knew neither of the Comanches who had sneaked away from the reservation were a personal threat she certainly didn't mind their company.

A tingle of pleasure shot through her when Quinn scooped her up and set her on her horse. She smiled down at him when he murmured, "I was worried about you, wildcat. I'm glad to see that you're all right."

"I was glad to see you, period," she confided. "But I thought you might decide to look the other way and go on about your assignment without bothering to track me down." Her gaze narrowed on him. "Be honest with me, Callahan. You *did* consider it, didn't you?"

"I didn't consider it for even a second," he replied, then smiled wryly. "Like you said, we made a deal and I had every intention of upholding my end of the bargain."

Piper was so pleased by his comment that she was tempted to lean down and hug the stuffing out of him. Perhaps he didn't consider her such a nuisance, after all. Plus, if he was willing to take her with him it would provide her with the opportunity to watch, listen and learn to become as self-sufficient as Quinn and these two warriors. Piper was willing and eager to develop the self-confidence needed to make a new life on the outpost of civilization.

She *was* going to become independent, she promised herself. With a few more lessons she wouldn't have to rely on any man. That thought inspired her to pick up the pace as the procession headed east.

Chapter Eight

The procession ascended the steep grade, winding through rocky gorges and juniper-choked ravines to reach the lofty peak that Quinn referred to as Hell's Ridge. Piper made an effort to emulate the way the men moved in synchronized rhythm with their horses to keep their balance. If nothing else, she was learning to adjust to unfamiliar surroundings and she was living the kind of adventure she had yearned for and had been deprived of in polite society.

For once she wasn't subjected to her father's demanding expectations.

In addition, Piper had the chance to spend time with the first man she actually found herself physically attracted to, a man she had managed to get attached to in a short span of time. When she compared Quinn Callahan to John Foster, there was simply no contest.

Quinn was a man's man, a warrior's warrior. He was the epitome of strength, courage and well-honed skills.

Her would-be fiancé was none of those things and Piper had nothing but lukewarm reactions to him. Her would-be fiancé was simply the extension of his father's will. John Foster was content to take over the business without spreading his wings and asking himself if there was another life that better suited his own wants, needs and desires.

Piper's gaze swung sideways to survey Quinn in profile. If she were forced to choose a man to spend her life with Quinn Callahan would be her pick. He excited her, challenged her and didn't condemn her because she was teeming with spirit. For sure and certain, there would be nothing dull or mundane about a match with this rugged Texas Ranger.

Piper blinked, wondering where that preposterous thought had come from. The very last thing a man like Quinn wanted was a wife. He never stayed in the same place long enough for grass to grow beneath his feet.

"Why are you staring at me like that?"

She was jolted back to the present by Quinn's abrupt question. For a moment she considered telling a fib, but then she recalled her vow of honesty with Quinn. A wry smile quirked her lips, wondering how he would react when she voiced her private thoughts. Well, there was only one way to find out, wasn't there?

"I was contemplating what it would be like to be married to you instead of the dandy Papa selected for me." She shrugged nonchalantly. "This is all hypothetical, of course. Just a way of passing the time."

He blinked, startled. "Yeah? And what did you decide? Hypothetically, of course."

Piper grinned when she noticed the sparkle of curiosity in his amber eyes. "You won hands down."

His eyebrows shot up and his jaw dropped. "I did?"

"Absolutely. Compared to John Foster you have barrel loads of personality and admirable traits. If there is one thing I can say about our association, Callahan, it is that it has been an eventful adventure."

"And *dangerous*," he emphasized, staring at her so oddly that she wondered what was running through that quick mind of his. "Ours would likely be a short-lived marriage. If we didn't kill each other first, the decreased life expectancy in this part of the country probably would."

"Nonetheless, I have done more living this past week and have gained more practical experience in the past few days than I accumulated in all the years that I resided in Houston and Galveston," she maintained. "I predict that I can cram more living into a month, while following you around, than I could in a year at home."

"So marry me," he suggested flippantly. "That would ensure that your father couldn't hand you over to this Foster character he picked out for you."

Piper stared goggle-eyed at him. It was a convenient solution to her problem, come to think of it. But what would Quinn get out of the arrangement? Other than legal license to her body for his sexual pleasure.

And hers perhaps...? A slow burn worked its way through Piper's body as she followed the trail that led to a spire of jagged rocks. For the first time in her life she wanted to know what it was like to experience passion. She'd had only a small taste of it recently—with

Quinn. The truth was that she had wanted more. But how much more?

"Snap out of it, Sullivan," Quinn demanded when she continued to stare speculatively at him. "You're staring again. A friend of mine told me that was rude."

"If we did marry," she ventured, "what would you expect to gain from the arrangement?"

"Hypothetically speaking?" he teased, his bronzed face crinkling with amusement.

"Of course," she said, enormously affected by one of his rare smiles.

"Unlimited sex comes quickly to mind," he said, waggling his eyebrows suggestively.

Piper felt her face burst into flames and she suspected that Quinn was purposely goading her. Well, two could play that game, she decided. "That goes without saying. I would be all for that, of course. I am very much interested in new experiences, after all."

It was his turn to gape at her. She also noticed that he was squirming uncomfortably on his horse. Piper was amazed that she could discuss such a private matter with a man. It certainly wasn't acceptable in polite society. But then, she had recently discovered that she felt at ease discussing almost everything with Quinn. He had become her confidant and friend, and the possibility of being his lover appealed to her far more than it probably should have.

"I thought perhaps the opportunity to share my inheritance might be the determining factor in your offer of marriage," she added belatedly.

He gave her a smoldering glance that sent another

wave of fire coursing through her body. "When I look at you, I guarantee that I don't see dollar signs, Piper," he said huskily. "Besides, I have no doubt that your father would disinherit you faster than he disowned Penelope after taking one disapproving look at me."

Piper surveyed him for a long, pensive moment, seeing a tough, courageous warrior who answered to no man. "Then my father would be a fool for rejecting you. Furthermore, he can keep his money because, from my experience, it comes with stifling restrictions and too many strings attached."

Leaving Quinn to stare bewilderedly at her, Piper nudged her horse to precede him up the trail that had again narrowed to such extremes that riding single file was imperative.

Roarke Sullivan leaned back in his chair at his desk when the city marshal entered the office. Drake's mouth was set in such a grim line that Roarke's senses went on full alert. Whatever news Drake had received obviously wasn't good.

"What's happened?" Roarke demanded immediately. "Have you received word about my daughter?"

Drake halted in front of the desk and Roarke reflexively surged to his feet. It was his policy never to allow anyone to tower over him, as if he were at a disadvantage.

"I received a telegram from Commander Scott Butler," the marshal murmured, refusing to meet Roarke's direct stare.

"And?" Roarke prodded impatiently.

"There was only one woman reported to be riding the

westbound stage from Fort Stockton to Fort Davis this past week. She was an old widow, swathed in black from head to toe. She was wearing a veiled hat that concealed her face."

Hope rose inside Roarke. "That has to be Piper. She might not have the good sense to go racing off unchaperoned, but she is certainly clever enough to disguise herself for protection and try to conceal her identity. So, has she arrived at the garrison to be with her sister?"

William Drake shook his head, then handed over the telegram. "The stage was robbed and the coach crashed on a cliff in the mountains."

Roarke howled in dismay as he read the missive.

"I'm terribly sorry, Mr. Sullivan. If you read the entire message you know that the rescue party of Rangers found part of the wreckage strewn on the mountainside and the rest washed away in the fast-moving stream below. The veiled hat was snagged in a scrub bush."

Roarke sat down before he fell down. Piper was presumed dead? His young daughter was gone? Her remains had washed downstream to be picked apart by the wolves, mountain lions or bobcats that prowled that godforsaken region of Texas?

Grief and regret plowed into Roarke so quickly that it stole his breath and drained the color from his ruddy cheeks. "Dear God in heaven!" he wheezed as he half collapsed in his chair.

"The Ranger commander promised to send a detailed report of the accident after further investigation," Drake went on to say.

Roarke heaved himself back to his feet, his mind

whirling. He had arrangements to make before his trip to Fort Davis. If this bleak report proved to be accurate then he had no recourse but to contact Penelope. Despite his disappointment in her decision to marry that army captain she had foolishly fallen in love with three years earlier he was compelled to see her again.

My God, he might have lost one daughter, but he couldn't bear to lose them both!

Leaving Drake standing where he was, Roarke pelted through the door to the warehouse behind the office. He wasted no time locating his second-in-command. He was bound for Austin on the train. From there he would hop the first stage headed southwest. If Piper had miraculously survived the catastrophe he would find her—somehow.

If she hadn't survived… The image of Piper staring up at him, bursting with irrepressible spirit and determination, nearly knocked him to his knees.

It can't be, came the frantic voice of denial. He couldn't have lost her. He had doted on Piper after Penelope defied his wishes. He had put all his efforts into molding and grooming Piper to become the perfect wife for a wealthy Galveston aristocrat.

Damnation, he'd had such high hopes for his young daughter. She had angered him constantly with her resistance and her insistence on controlling her own destiny, but he had been confident that she would eventually obey his command.

Never once had Roarke considered the possibility of losing Piper forever.

If the preliminary report was true, then Roarke had

no recourse but to bring Penelope back to Galveston, because she would be his only heir. He would dissolve her ill-advised marriage to Captain Duncan if he must, but he *would* protect Penelope, as he *should* have protected Piper from harm.

On that determined thought, Roarke made the necessary arrangements with his second-in-command. Then he dashed home to pack a bag. He would try to find Piper. He would refuse to give up hope until he knew beyond all doubt that she had perished. Then he would reconcile with Penelope and bring her home where she belonged.

Roarke had lost his wife to illness years ago, and now perhaps his younger daughter. But he would *not* lose Penelope, too!

Quinn made the arduous trek to Hell's Ridge by high noon. Although Piper hadn't voiced a single word of complaint he had kept a close eye on her and noticed she had begun to look fatigued. She'd had quite a scare that morning, followed by a difficult ride over unforgiving terrain without the convenience of a saddle to anchor herself to.

Being an inexperienced rider, she'd had a couple of near misses on the treacherous trail. Quinn could see the determination etched on her enchanting face and he knew she intended to test herself to the limits and gain experience in survival—no matter what extremes she encountered.

Although Quinn had tried hard to remain focused on his mission, it had been nearly impossible after he had impulsively popped off with the suggestion that Piper marry him to counter her father's plans. What the hell had he been thinking? And for Piper to say that she preferred him to her wealthy fiancé from Galveston? What had *she* been thinking?

Quinn sighed heavily as he dismounted to lead the procession down a winding footpath to yet another rock-covered arroyo. He was pretty sure now that he couldn't deal with Piper's new policy of straightforward honesty. True, he had informed her that he disliked deceit and manipulation. Now she was out to prove that he could trust her to say exactly what she meant and tell him exactly what she felt.

That was *good*…and that was *bad*.

He didn't want to waste time speculating on what it would be like to wed this blue-eyed siren who was so distractingly attractive that he constantly battled lust at inappropriate moments. If he weren't careful he would drive himself completely loco with erotic fantasies.

He would, however, agree to marry her in name only if it would resolve her conflict with her father and provide her with protection from adventurers looking to attach themselves to an heiress. But that would be the beginning and end of a marriage to Piper Sullivan, he told himself sensibly.

Never mind that there had been times—after discovering that she wasn't the persnickety old crone, who had given him hell for the spite and sport of it—that he had only to look at her and wanted her badly. But Quinn refused to take something from Piper that should belong to a worthy, deserving man.

"You are awfully quiet, Gray Owl," Red Hawk murmured from behind him.

"I have a lot on my mind."

All these thoughts pertaining to Piper, and most especially her comment that she wouldn't be adverse to a marriage between them, were playing havoc on his emotions. Damn, she had really knocked him for a loop with that. He still hadn't gotten past it.

"Are you thinking of the bandoleros in *El Muerto Cañon?*" Red Hawk questioned.

Not even close, thought Quinn. That's where his mind should have been. But it wasn't, damn it.

"Spotted Deer and I would like to offer our services to join the fight that will rid our sacred ground of those vicious Mexicans and white men. You could inform your commander that you have recruited us for the task," he suggested hopefully.

Quinn glanced over his shoulder to see a shrewd sparkle in the Comanche's coal-black eyes. He grinned in amusement. "That would solve your problem of being absent without permission from the reservation, wouldn't it?"

"It would," Spotted Deer spoke up. "Other tribe members have volunteered to scout for the army and the Rangers. It has to be better than confinement. And why not us? We know this territory as well as you do. And like you, Gray Owl, we have no family left that requires our assistance and support."

Quinn thought it over and decided the prospect had merit. These two warriors were a great deal like him. They were men whose way of life had been taken from them. They were also without family ties. Although some clans of the Kiowa and Comanche tribes had accepted their fate and given up the fight to save their dying culture, Red Hawk and Spotted Deer were restless spirits needing a cause and purpose.

They preferred to die in combat rather than lose their pride and rot away on the reservation. To Quinn's way of thinking he was doing the warriors a favor by allowing them to join ranks. It had to be better than remaining fugitives—waiting for the army to run them to ground and execute them for causing trouble.

It wouldn't be the first time soldiers followed their take-no-prisoners policy with Indians.

"Then you are hereby deputized as Ranger scouts," Quinn declared with an expansive wave of his arm. "You have two assignments. The first is to help me identify the white and Mexican banditos for future trial and sentencing. The second is to keep my woman safe from harm."

His woman? Damnation, he needed to call her by name instead of placing a possessive label on her. Piper was not his woman and she never would be. He would not bring her down to his lowly level and force her to face the scorn and rejection he had endured most of his adult life. Despite his good intentions, she had come to mean something special to him and he didn't want to see her hurt, shamed or shunned because of her association with him.

Plus, she was a unique experience for him and he didn't want his image of her tarnished. There would be at least one sweet memory that he could look upon in the future, something aside from the danger and violence and hatred he dealt with on a weekly basis.

He and Piper had become friends and confidants because necessity demanded it. But when he completed this assignment and delivered her to her sister they would go their separate ways. That was best for her, he assured himself sensibly.

"I really would appreciate it if you wouldn't exclude me from all your conversations," Piper commented while she and Lucky brought up the rear of the procession. "What are you three discussing now?"

Quinn studied Piper's peaked complexion and decided it was definitely time to call a halt. She looked tired and her face was flushed from too much exertion. He had been pushing her too hard and he needed to be more attuned to her needs or she would collapse in exhaustion.

"Well?" she prodded in typical Piper Sullivan fashion.

He grinned at her persistence to be included in conversation. "Our two friends have volunteered to serve as guides for my Ranger battalion," he replied. "They have no desire to be confined to the reservation."

"I can identify with that." Piper pulled a face then stared sympathetically at the Comanche warriors. "Having someone dictate what you can do and where you can go is extremely exasperating."

The warriors looked to Quinn for translation. "Piper thinks you should be allowed your freedom so you can avoid confinement in Indian Territory."

The comment earned Piper two wide grins and approving nods from the Comanches.

"You've made fast friends," Quinn assured her. "I think they regret that fiasco this morning, especially since you've taken their side."

A moment later Quinn flung up his hand. "This is a good time to break for lunch. But pemmican and water is all I have to offer."

Piper's stomach growled. She had missed breakfast and hunger had left her light-headed for the past hour. "Sounds wonderful."

She frowned curiously when Red Hawk and Spotted Deer tethered their horses and disappeared into the wild tangle of underbrush on the west side of the mountain. "Where are they going?"

"To find something more appetizing for you to eat, I expect." Quinn shepherded her toward a flat-topped outcropping of stone and gestured for her to sit down. "When I agreed to deputize the Comanche warriors I insisted that part of their duties was to provide you with protection."

Piper wrinkled her nose and flung him a withering glance. "So now I'm an inconvenience to them, too? You sure know how to make a woman feel good about herself, Callahan."

Quinn curled his hand beneath her skinned chin, forcing her head up to meet his wry smile. "I don't think they mind the extra task all that much. You might be a paleface to them, but they mentioned that they found you appealing to look at."

"Oh, well, that makes me feel *so* much better," she said, and smirked. "After all, I have been no more than a trophy and window dressing to my suitors the past few years."

Her breath stalled in her chest when Quinn leaned down to brush his lips gently over hers. Pleasure overshadowed her weariness in one second flat. Amazing what the taste of this man did for her sagging spirits.

When he tried to withdraw, Piper looped her arms around his neck and brought his head back to hers. "Not so fast, Mr. Ranger. I need more than a hasty kiss to get me up and moving again."

Piper kissed him for all she was worth, marveling at how quickly she had become addicted to the taste of him. He was like a thirst-quenching drink, a long-awaited feast. She could get used to kissing him whenever she felt like it.

Would she be just as compelled by him if they shared a bed? she wondered. Would she want more intimacy with him, just as she craved more of his kisses?

The thought whirled off in the wind when he tasted her deeply. She responded instantaneously, enthusiastically. What was there about this man that stirred so many unprecedented sensations and tender emotions inside her? Why was she reaching out to him when she had spent years dodging the unwanted advances of other men? Why did he taste like heaven to her? Why did he draw her admiration and affection without even trying?

Because Quinn Callahan isn't a man with hidden agendas, came the quiet voice of insight. *He's an honest man. Rough around the edges, to be sure. Blunt to a fault, no doubt about it. But he's solid and trustworthy and competent. Something deep inside him calls to something deep inside you and makes him impossible for you to resist.*

The crunch of stone beneath moccasined feet caused Quinn to retreat. Piper turned her head to see the warriors approaching. Her eyes lit up and she smiled appreciatively when she noticed the red berries they had gathered for lunch.

When Red Hawk extended a handful to her, Piper thanked him kindly then gobbled the treat. The berries were bittersweet but juicy and she eagerly accepted a second helping.

"What are these things?" she asked, pointing to the brown buds mixed in with the berries.

"Peyote buttons. Don't eat too many of them," Quinn warned.

"Why not?" she asked between bites.

"They are an Indian remedy for pain and exhaustion that comes from a certain species of cactus. They are also used in religious rituals to provoke insightful vision quests. But some people are highly sensitive to them and they can cause hallucinations."

Piper popped a third peyote button in her mouth and chewed. "If they relieve exhaustion and sore muscles then I need a strong dose," she contended. "I don't want to slow you down." She glanced up at him. "If you want to leave me here—"

"No," he interrupted quickly. "This morning was a glaring example of what might happen. I'm not leaving you alone again. This is not negotiable."

Piper was touched by his concern, but nonetheless she said, "I never intended to become your responsibility. My fate is my own now. No matter what happens I refuse to be on your conscience. You have enough to do without complications I might cause. I told you already that I have accepted the consequences of announcing my independence from my father."

Quinn leaned right in her face and said, "Regardless, I plan to watch out for you so you need to accept that. This is not the time to argue with me, spitfire. Take advantage of your short break because the trail to *El Muerto Cañon* is going to become more difficult. In fact, we just covered the easy part of the path."

When Quinn strode off to fetch the pemmican, Piper frowned, wondering what had caused the blurry haze in her vision. She shook her head, but it didn't help. She decided Quinn might have been right about the peyote buttons. They had a strong effect on her, especially when she'd had nothing to eat but a few berries. Suddenly she felt lethargic, as if she hadn't a care in the world.

"I think I'll catch a quick nap," she mumbled as the world began to spin around her.

Piper didn't remember much after she said that. She sort of crumpled sideways and would have landed on her head if Quinn hadn't dashed over to catch her.

Swearing, Quinn gathered her limp body in his arms and listened to her mumble incomprehensibly. He called to Red Hawk to grab the bedroll for Piper to lie on. When he put her down on the pallet, she didn't move, just sprawled motionlessly.

"How many buttons did she eat?" Red Hawk asked as he stared worriedly at Piper.

"At least three that I noticed." Quinn brushed the wild tangle of moonbeam-colored hair away from her peaked face.

"Must have been too strong a dose for a paleface's

first time," Spotted Deer said as he came to stand beside them. "If the medicine causes her to see and hear things, her outbursts might give our whereabouts away. I for one do not want to make it easy for those vicious bandits to spot us."

Quinn muttered a few more epithets under his breath. He hadn't planned a lengthy rest stop, not if he was going to reach the stronghold before dark so he could take a head count and clearly identify some of the gang members. Neither was he going to leave Piper sedated, with only the pup to stand guard over her.

"We'll eat quickly and Piper can ride with me," he decided. "I can muffle any outburst the peyote might cause."

Leaving Piper to sleep off the medication for a few minutes, Quinn wolfed down pemmican, berries and gulped water from his canteen. After he mounted up, Spotted Deer lifted Piper's limp body to him. Quinn draped her over his lap. Her head lolled against his shoulder for a moment before sliding down his arm.

"Turn her to face you," Red Hawk suggested. "You can hold onto her better and still maintain control of your horse on the narrow trail."

With the Comanches' help, Quinn turned Piper so that she straddled his hips. When her head drooped, Quinn lifted her higher onto his thighs so that her chin rested securely on his shoulder. But it wasn't until Red Hawk recommended binding her wrists together behind Quinn's neck that he could effectively hold her unresponsive body upright without fretting that she might catapult sideways and take the short way down the rocky ridge.

With Lucky trailing faithfully behind them, they moved along the trail that demanded cautious footing by the horses. Quinn scowled in frustration. He would like to skin his Comanche brothers alive for bringing peyote buttons for Piper. Plus, the feel of Piper's full breasts meshed to his chest and her hips gliding suggestively against his crotch with each motion of the horse was giving him fits. He was too close to this beguiling female. Her unique scent was wrapping itself around his senses to such extremes that he couldn't think straight.

This was not the time or place to become distracted, he reminded himself. There might be posted guards defending the bandits' hideout. If Quinn was so lost in provocative daydreams about what he would like to be doing while he had Piper this close he might not be able to sense trouble until it was too late.

Difficult though it was, Quinn forced himself to concentrate on the mission at hand and ignore the enticing woman in his arms.

Chapter Nine

Thirty minutes later, Quinn finally gave up trying to ignore the arousing effect that holding Piper so close had on him. "Red Hawk, it might be best if you and Spotted Deer scouted ahead." He reached back with his left hand to retrieve his field glasses from the saddlebag. "I'm at a disadvantage here."

Red Hawk smiled knowingly as he accepted the spyglass. "But a pleasant disadvantage, I think. Not to worry, Gray Owl. We will lead the way while you proceed at a slower pace."

Forty-five minutes later, Piper stirred sluggishly and nuzzled her cheek against Quinn's neck. A bolt of red-hot lust shot straight to his loins when the V of her legs brushed against his erection. The woman was killing him and she didn't even know it.

When she moaned softly, then pressed a row of warm kisses against his throat and the underside of his chin, Quinn gritted his teeth against the tantalizing sensations flooding through him. The torment he had endured during his first two years of captivity with the Kiowa had never been as maddening as this! It was enough to make a grown man howl.

"Piper, wake up," he said.

"Mmm," she mumbled, still showering him with kisses. "I want you. Teach me how to please you."

He angled his head away to study her droopy-eyed expression and the seductive smile playing on her lips. Lust struck like a lightning bolt, sizzling to his very core. He squirmed atop his horse and muttered succinct curses.

"Damn peyote," he said, and scowled. "Piper, pay attention to me. You have to remain quiet."

"I can do that," she said in a loud whisper. "Kiss me and I'll hush up."

Quinn was reasonably certain that the peyote buttons had unleashed every inhibition Piper might have had. She arched suggestively against him, rubbing the pebbled peaks of her breasts against his chest. When she clamped her legs tightly to his hips he nearly came unglued. Hungry need swamped and buffeted him before he could call upon his reserve of self-control and he felt himself arching instinctively against her.

Yep, this brand of torture was the absolute worst he had ever withstood, he realized. Piper was burning him up from inside out and she showed no signs of letting up.

"I said, kiss me," she demanded a little too loudly.

So he did, if only to shut her up. In a heartbeat she was devouring him. Her tongue mated with his as she pressed her supple body ever closer. She gyrated her hips against his and Quinn muffled a tormented moan.

What she was doing to him was guaranteed to drive a man insane. Quinn broke out in a sweat and his over-loaded senses whirled like a pinwheel. Between her provocative gestures and the rhythmic motion of the horse stepping down the steep slope, the lower portions of their bodies kept moving together then apart. He was so hard and needy that breathing suddenly became a vol-untary task.

He finally had to admit defeat because he couldn't muster the willpower to resist Piper's peyote-induced seduction. He kissed her as if there were no tomor-row. As if there weren't a stronghold of bandits on the far side of the ridge. As if he had every right to take what Piper offered him and enjoy every delicious mo-ment of it.

He halted the horse and his arms contracted tightly around her. He crushed her against him so tightly that there wasn't room for a gnat to breathe. They fit together like two pieces of a puzzle and his body surged urgently against hers. He resented the layers of clothing that sep-arated them. He wanted to possess her completely, to meld his flesh to hers until they were one living, breath-ing essence lost to the frantic urgency of desire.

"More," she breathed against his lips. Her bound arms pulled his head back to hers. "I need more of you."

His lips slanted over hers, devouring her. He was driven by the kind of insatiable impatience he barely recognized in himself. His left hand slid between them to cup and knead her breasts. His right hand dipped be-neath the waistband of her breeches to clamp his fingers into the satiny curve of her hip and guide her against his throbbing arousal. Pleasure coursed heavily through him and he swallowed a groan of unholy torment.

Quinn had never wanted anything as badly as he wanted to unleash this raging passion inside him. His male body was straining eagerly toward hers and he felt his tenuous grasp on control slip another dangerous notch.

The world suddenly shrank to a space no larger than they occupied. For this moment out of time nothing mattered except holding her, touching her familiarly and savoring those dewy lips that begged for his kisses. Dozens of heady sensations bombarded him as he caressed her and she responded wildly.

Not so long ago—only a few hours, in fact—Quinn had sworn to restrict himself to an occasional kiss. Now he wondered if he could summon enough self-restraint to retreat before things got completely out of hand. To his dismay, he discovered he couldn't stop himself from crossing the line and exploring her satiny flesh with intimate caresses.

He marveled at the feel of his questing fingertips skimming inside her blouse to map the soft, feminine contours of her body. Needing more, he loosened the buttons of her blouse, then glided his hand beneath her lacy chemise to make contact with the hard crests of her breasts. And then he dared to taste her there, suckling her, exploring the texture of her skin while his thundering pulse roared in his ears and uncontrollable need blurred his vision.

She whispered his name with a ragged moan and Quinn swore he had never heard a voice so inviting and compelling.

"Please... I need you... I need to touch you...."

Her bound hands pressed against the back of his neck while she fought the restraints. Quinn lifted her arms over his head, then felt her fingertips spearing beneath his shirt to explore the width of his chest. When she arched up and kissed him with the kind of wild desperation that he had never experienced the world all but crumbled around him.

That was when he knew this was the woman he had waited for all his life and never expected to find. She preyed on emotions buried deep inside him, provoked sensations so intense and profound that they made his head spin.

Despite how fiercely and instinctively he was drawn to her this could only be a temporary fascination, he reminded himself realistically. They had nothing in common except this forbidden attraction that made him wish for things that could never be.

She will never be yours, in body or spirit. You are worlds apart. It is only blind lust that makes you wish for what you can't have. Stop this madness before you complicate your life and ruin hers more than you have already.

Quinn jerked himself upright, turned Piper around on his lap and hooked his arm around her waist to steady her. "Fasten your blouse," he demanded more gruffly than he intended. Unfortunately tormented frustration was eating him alive. "No more of this nonsense, Piper. I mean it, damn it—"

His voice dried up when she slumped abruptly against him. Her tousled blond head dangled over his arm and her thick lashes fluttered against her pale cheeks. Cursing a blue streak Quinn fastened her blouse, then took up the reins.

Maybe it was a good thing she had conked out again, he decided. At least he was granted time to regroup and cool down. Damn, what he wouldn't give for a quick plunge into an icy spring pool!

Holding on to Piper so she wouldn't pitch off the horse, Quinn quickened the pace. Five minutes later Piper jerked upright and tried to let out a wild shriek. He clamped his hand over her mouth to muffle the sound. When she tried to twist away from him, he tightened his grip before she unseated them both. He wrestled with her for several minutes before she finally quieted down again.

Curse it, the peyote was causing weird hallucinations. He made a mental note never to let her touch the stuff again. *Neither* of them could handle it when she was under the influence.

Thankfully, Piper didn't rouse for another half hour and Quinn was able to make better time. When she did wake up, she seemed to be in reasonable command of her senses once again. Quinn was mightily relieved when she pushed herself upright on the horse and glanced questioningly at him.

"Where are we? The last thing I remember was blacking out."

Quinn wished that was the last thing *he* remembered. Instead, he was battling erotic memories and feeling immensely guilty for taking advantage of Piper when she wasn't fully aware of what was transpiring between them.

"We're approaching the stronghold," he reported. "Red Hawk and Spotted Owl are scouting the trail."

Piper swallowed with effort. Then she glanced curiously at her bound hands. "Why am I tied up again?"

"Because I had trouble keeping you on a horse. I had to loop your hands around my neck so you wouldn't fall off. There isn't a soft place to land on these rugged crests and I didn't want you hurt." He reached behind him to grab the canteen. "You probably need a drink. Peyote usually leaves you with dry mouth."

Piper eagerly gulped water, and then she heaved an audible sigh. "Remind me never to partake of peyote buttons again. I had the strangest dreams you can imagine."

"Oh?"

Piper shifted uneasily as wild sensations and brightly colored images flashed through her mind. She decided that her evocative speculations about sharing Quinn's passion must have gotten tangled up in her dreams while she was sedated. Even now, her body thrummed with pleasure.

If her dreams were this arousing she could only imagine what the reality of unleashed desire might be like.

Someday, before Quinn dropped her off at the garrison and rode away, she would like to find out for certain. It might be the first and last time in her life that she experienced passion, because having known Quinn, she wasn't sure she wanted to satisfy her growing curiosity with any man but him.

Piper came to attention when she saw Red Hawk and Spotted Deer, leading her horse behind them, appear from a winding ravine. Although her senses were still groggy she noticed that both warriors were grinning at her for reasons she couldn't account for.

When Red Hawk spoke to her she waited for Quinn to translate. "They want to know if you feel rested," he repeated. "They also apologize for giving you those buttons."

"Tell them I'm feeling much better and that I intend to avoid peyote unless I'm suffering extreme pain." She frowned disconcertedly. "The dreams caused by that Indian remedy were *unsettling* to say the least."

An hour later Piper was on her hands and knees, following the Comanches who led the way across the rocky cliff that overlooked the outlaws' hideout. In the distance she could see two dozen men, whiskey bottles in hand, lounging outside their adobe headquarters. A makeshift corral, filled with stolen cattle, was butted up against the perpendicular canyon wall to the east. Another pen, erected two hundred yards to the north, held a herd of horses. Also stolen, she suspected.

It looked as if the bandits were celebrating another successful robbery. Piper squinted into the setting sun to survey the gang members who were both Mexican and white. She recognized three of the men from the stage holdup.

When she glanced over at Quinn, she noticed that he was flat on his belly, staring through the field glasses. "There's only one way into this canyon," he murmured as he carefully surveyed the encampment. "Posted lookouts are at the south entrance. It would be impossible to send a strike force of Rangers into the mouth of the canyon without risking numerous casualties."

"Then how are you going to capture them?" Piper asked worriedly.

The prospect of Quinn being wounded during the skirmish did not set well with her. She suddenly found herself wishing he had a safer profession. Like an accountant at her father's shipping office.

Piper silently chuckled at the absurdity. Quinn would go stark raving mad if he were confined to the cramped spaces of an office because the wilderness had been his domain most of his life. He was accustomed to mobility, dangerous adventure and constant challenges. Plus, he would have to alter his manner of dress to fit into society and she suspected he would find that as unpleasant as having a hangman's noose wrapped around his throat.

Her gaze settled on him again, marveling at his ability to focus on his task of reconnoitering the bandits' nearly invincible fortress. She swore not a single detail of the area or the roaming gang members escaped his notice. He was making mental notes again, just as he had done immediately before and during the stage robbery. No doubt, the knowledge that his colleagues' lives would be in jeopardy prompted Quinn to be thorough and conscientious.

She turned her attention to Red Hawk and Spotted Deer, noting they wore the same look of profound concentration as they looked at the canyon that was once a sacred burial ground. They had a vested interest in routing these bandoleros, and they were paying strict attention to detail as well.

Piper decided this was the perfect opportunity to practice her skills of observation.

She had recently discovered that paying close attention to your surroundings was crucial, especially in this barely civilized part of Texas. If she was going to be able to fend for herself at the fort, she would need this skill.

Piper was thoroughly convinced that what she couldn't learn from these three experienced men she probably didn't need to know when it came to survival. She was training with the best.

Only when darkness blanketed the valley and the echoes of rowdy laughter and drunken voices filled the air did Quinn give the signal to retreat. He grabbed Piper's hand and led her into the rock-filled ravine, then towed her up the steep grade to reach their waiting horses.

Lucky barked and whined to show his displeasure at being tied up and left behind. When Piper walked over to release the mutt, Quinn shook his head.

"We need to keep Lucky on the leash until we're a few miles from the stronghold. The last thing we need is for the bandits to realize they were tracked to the canyon. We'll make camp in a couple of hours, if you're up to the ride."

Even if Piper had been dead on her feet and half-starved, she wouldn't have objected. She wasn't about to be the cause of another delay. In addition, Quinn had become very businesslike since she had awakened to find herself riding double with him. She wanted to attribute the emotional distance she felt between them to his single-minded focus on his assignment, but she sensed that something else was bothering him.

Had she done something to annoy him? Perhaps he

was aggravated that he had to tote her with him on his horse while she was lost in those strange dreams. Whatever the reason for his detachment, Piper felt awkward and uncomfortable around him for the first time in days. She sorely missed the easy camaraderie that had developed between them.

Later, when they made camp, the Comanche warriors went in search of something besides pemmican for their supper. Piper watched Quinn pace from one side of their encampment to the other and she wondered if he resented the fact that he had to remain behind to keep an eye on her.

The thought depressed her. She had finally met a man who interested her and aroused her and he considered her an inconvenience, no matter how hard she tried to match his pace. Piper knew all too well that she wasn't right for Quinn, knew she couldn't fit into his tumbleweed lifestyle, even if she spent months perfecting her skills. But that didn't diminish her fascination with him.

If only they had met under different circumstances. But then again, it probably wouldn't have mattered. Quinn Callahan wasn't about to change for her and she wouldn't truly fit into his world. This ill-fated attraction was going nowhere, she told herself sensibly. It was high time she accepted the fact that her infatuation with Quinn was simply a brief chapter in her life.

She had come west to claim her independence and prove her self-reliance, she reminded herself. So why didn't that seem as important as it had two weeks earlier when she had planned her trip to Fort Davis?

Because she had met an unconventional man and her attraction to him had sidetracked her and altered her priorities.

"Here, drink." Quinn thrust the canteen at her.

Piper took a sip, then peered into his ruggedly handsome face that was a study of angles and shadows in the campfire light. "Are you angry at me?" she asked.

Yes, he was, Quinn thought. Well, to be fair, he was angry with *himself.* He was frustrated that he cared so much about Piper. He also felt guilty as hell because he wanted to avenge Taylor Briggs's death and his friend had been the farthest thing from his mind this afternoon. He was angry that he was putting Piper through this strenuous ordeal and that he had touched her so familiarly when he never should have touched her at all, especially when she didn't recall the incident.

And worse, he still wanted her like hell blazing, and *not* touching her right now was driving him crazy!

"What makes you say that?" he asked, keeping his voice carefully neutral and his gaze on anything but her.

She frowned at him in exasperation. "Your attitude has been standoffish since this afternoon. I have gotten to know your mannerisms and facial expressions pretty well since we have spent so much time together. Something is wrong and I want to know what it is."

Quinn shifted uneasily from one foot to the other and stared at the air over her head. "Everything is fine."

"No, it isn't." She flashed him an impudent grin. "You need to know that I have a habit of badgering a person until I find out what I want to know. Save yourself some time and just tell me. If I'm causing too many delays and too much inconvenience then just say so. I'll try harder to match your pace."

"I do not want to have this conversation right now," Quinn grumbled before he went back to his restless pacing.

"Too bad. We *are* having it."

When she bounded to her feet to stand toe-to-toe with him Quinn felt himself instinctively reaching for her. He had to fight like the very devil to keep his hands fisted at his sides.

"I expect the same honesty from you that you demand from me. What have I done to upset you?"

"Nothing. Everything is fine," he repeated through clenched teeth.

She crossed her arms over her chest and raised her chin challengingly. "I don't believe you. What's wrong?"

Quinn raked his fingers through his tousled hair, muttered under his breath at her refusal to back off, then said, "Okay, Piper, you asked for it. I feel damn guilty because this afternoon you were all over me while we were riding double and I was all over you. Those weren't dreams you were having. That was *reality.*"

There. He had said it out loud. Now *she* could deal with it.

Her silver-blue eyes widened and her mouth dropped open.

"You wanted to know," he defended himself tersely. "It happened. And now it's not enough because I want more from you. But that is a very bad idea, because you can do a hell of a lot better than a man like me and I know it."

Her mouth dropped open another notch and her eyes popped.

"Satisfied yet? You wanted to know so I'm *telling* you that if you expect to keep your innocence intact that you need to keep a wide berth and stop asking what I'm thinking and feeling because you are probably offended by what you're hearing. Now I'm going to shut up and you should do the same."

He veered around her, then plunked down beneath the overhanging ledge where he had built the campfire to prevent easy detection.

To his dismay, Piper strode up in front of him again. Damnation, didn't this woman know when to back off? But then, when had she ever? She just kept on coming at him, defying the danger and threat he represented, ignoring his warnings.

"I tried to seduce you while I was under the influence of peyote?" she asked as she stared intently at him.

"Didn't try—you succeeded," he said, and scowled. The campfire spotlighted her curvaceous physique and enhanced the delicate features of her face. Another jolt of awareness zapped him. "Go away, Piper. I'm tired and cranky and lust is making me edgy. I intend to deliver you to the fort in the same condition I found you, so keep your distance."

She shook her head and sighed audibly. "If you could see yourself through my eyes, you wouldn't make the ridiculous remark that I can do better than a man like you. There are none better."

"Right," he snorted. "I'm a regular Prince Charming with all the proper manners and social graces." He gestured toward his shaggy mane of hair, his stubbled jaw and the odd combination of clothing that reflected his unusual upbringing. "Do I look like any gentleman you've ever met?"

"No, but in my eyes you *are* a Prince Charming."

"Then you need to have your vision checked, sweet-heart," he drawled sarcastically. "All you will ever get from me is a tumble in the hay and no promises of ever after."

When she grimaced at his blunt remark he realized the only way to discourage her from making the biggest mistake of her life with him was to drive her away. "Is that what you want? A quick tumble on the ground, just to find out what lust feels like? You won't have to ask me twice, but you need to remember that I'm not accustomed to bedding a real lady and there will be no strings attached."

"You asked me to marry you, remember?"

Damn it, he should have expected that she would throw that in his face right now. The woman was too quick-minded. Plus, matching wits with her was a bad idea when he was in a mood. And he *was* in a bitch of a mood right now.

"Don't push me, Sullivan," he said warningly.

He reared back when she dropped down on her knees in front of him, then got right in his face—a technique he noted that she had borrowed from him.

"Maybe I do want one night with you, just to find out what desire is all about," she dared to say. "Maybe I do want to take you up on your offer to provide the protection of your name so my father has no legal control over me. I can handle a tumble on the ground—as you so delicately put it," she said caustically. "After all, I have met every other challenge you have tossed at me, haven't I?"

Yes, she had, which made her all the more irresistible to him. He had never met a woman like Piper. She was lovely beyond compare, spirited beyond belief and determined to the extreme. He liked her way too much and that worried him.

"Well, haven't I?" she persisted as only Piper could. "So, maybe the truth is that *you* can't handle my fascination and attraction for you. Just why is that?" She didn't give him time to reply, just hurried on. "I think it's because you have been made to feel unworthy and unwanted when you were ostracized by your own culture. Well, here's a piece of news for you, Callahan, *I* want you, whether you think anyone else does or not!"

The bold comment simultaneously pleased and tormented him. But Quinn quickly reminded himself that Piper was young and reckless and too daring for her own good. She might be singing a different tune if he took her to bed and she discovered that sharing his passion didn't meet her idealistic expectations.

"Furthermore, you don't have to fret about promises or commitment if they don't interest you. I would marry you this very minute. I would hold no future expectations. I know you don't want me around permanently to cramp your style or get in the way of your obligations as a Ranger."

She stared at him. "*I* get the legal license as proof of

our marriage and *you* get all the freedom you want. It's a situation that's good for both of us."

Quinn gaped at her and tried to breathe, but he couldn't seem to drag air into his deflated lungs. She was offering him what every man wanted? No charge? No commitment? No consequences?

When he finally recovered his powers of speech he frowned disapprovingly at her. "Your father would pitch a fit if he could hear you. Your sister, too, I suspect."

She flung her arms in expansive gestures. "Do you see either of them here right now? Even if they were here, this is still *my* life and *my* decision. And why, I would dearly like to know, do men seem to think women and children should be seen and their opinions *un*heard? I object to that philosophical nonsense!"

No surprise there, he mused, biting back a grin.

"Why shouldn't women want the same things men do? Answer me that, Mr. Rough, Tough Texas Ranger. And while you're at it, please explain why men *think* they know what is best for women. I am curious to know why men think we should want to exist contentedly within the confining boundaries and restrictions you have set for us. I am here to tell you that is the very last thing *I* want!"

When her voice rose sharply and her chest swelled with indignation, Quinn chuckled out loud. Lord, she was glorious when she was in a fit of temper.

She shook her finger in his smiling face and said, "Do not try to speak for me or think for me, Callahan. I happen to know my own mind, thank you very much!"

His attention dropped to her breasts when she sucked

in a deep breath. He was still hopelessly distracted when she snapped, "Do you know what your problem is?"

"Other than you?" he asked as he lifted his gaze to meet her flashing blue eyes. "No, but I'm betting you're going to tell me."

"Darn right I am. You have more honor and integrity than you give yourself credit for and it is getting in the way of what I want from you."

"Are you about done ranting?" he asked, trying to keep a straight face and failing miserably.

"Pretty close. There's just one more thing."

"What's that, wildcat?"

She flung her arms around his neck and toppled him to his back. The kiss she delivered packed as much heat as two blazing Colt .45s. Then, a mind-boggling moment later, she scrambled off him and bolted to her feet.

"When you think you can handle what I have to offer, let me know, Callahan. But rest assured that you aren't dealing with a submissive female who stands around, meekly waiting at a man's beck and call. You will be doomed to disappointment because I pride myself in being assertive. *Not* holding back feels a natural part of who I am and I have *you* to thank for teaching me to come right out and say what I mean!"

"Don't put all the blame on *me*," he grumbled as she turned around and stamped off. "While you were posing as Agatha Stewart you didn't mince words. I should know because I was on the receiving end of that sharp tongue more times than I care to count!"

She glared over her shoulder at him and, not to be outdone, he glared right back.

"I'm going down to the spring to bathe so don't bother to check on me. If I meet with trouble I intend to handle it without any help from you."

When she disappeared from sight Quinn propped himself against the stone wall and sighed heavily. Knowing that Piper was recklessly willing to offer him what he wanted from her was not making it easier for him to resist her.

Damn it, she could have ranted all night without saying exactly what he wanted to hear.

There was probably a lot of irony in that, he decided. Too bad that he was so frustrated at the moment that he couldn't figure it out.

Chapter Ten

Quinn was mightily relieved a half hour later when the two warriors returned to camp with a skinned rabbit and rock squirrel for supper. Piper had returned from bathing and had been giving him the cold shoulder. The silence in camp had been deafening. He definitely needed a break from Piper.

Leaving Piper to herself, Quinn struck up a conversation in Indian dialect while supper roasted. He inquired about conditions at the reservation in Indian Territory and asked after several acquaintances he had made while living with the Kiowa and Comanche.

Anything to distract himself from the disturbing confrontation with Piper. He was flattered, in an exasperated kind of way. And tormented beyond measure because he wanted her so badly that the prospect of having her colored every thought.

But his conscience was beating him black and blue for even imagining what it might be like between them.

"You would not like the reservation," Spotted Deer commented bitterly. "Our people are watched over like misbehaving children. We have been ordered not to practice our former way of life and have been made to adopt the paleface ways."

"The army delivers rancid beef that makes our people ill and the traders at the fort steal from our portions of food to sell to whites for their own profit. The children have been sent to schools in the East to be indoctrinated to the white ways as well," Red Hawk added resentfully. "It is not a life we would wish on anyone."

Although many of Quinn's memories of life in Indian camps were bitter and tragic, he had eventually adapted and had come to think of himself as more Indian than white. The prospect of being contained like prisoners on infertile lands the government considered useless to white expansion angered him.

Quinn knew he walked a fine line between two contrasting worlds and consequently held mixed opinions and philosophies. He resented what the Indians had taken from him. Yet, ironically, he was grateful to them for teaching him to become a competent, self-reliant man. Conversely, he disliked the way whites treated him because of circumstances beyond his control. In addition, he despised his own kind for their cruel treatment of his adopted people.

There was so much conflict of emotion pulling him in so many different directions at once that there were times when he wasn't sure who or what he was. And worse, the overwhelming temptation to take Piper up on her reckless offer of passion was yet another internal battle that was wearing him out.

Feeling the need for privacy, Quinn left Piper and the warriors to eat their meal without him. Giving the excuse of scouting the area in case of trouble, he ambled away from camp.

Quinn was sorry to say that most of his thoughts kept centering on his conversation with Piper. Need and desire kept getting in the way of his common sense. That woman stuck in his mind like a cactus needle and Quinn couldn't shake her loose, no matter how hard he tried.

He stared skyward, requesting divine guidance. "What am I going to do about that woman?"

When he was met with nothing but silence, he sighed heavily. "Why is it that I always have to figure things out by myself?"

Piper's attempt to keep her mind on learning the Comanche translation for squirrel, rabbit, campfire—to name only a few of the words the warriors were trying to teach her—failed dismally. Her mind and her gaze kept drifting to the path Quinn had taken when he disappeared from sight.

True, she had come on way too strong earlier that evening. But his detachment had cut to the quick and she had wanted to know what was bothering him. She wanted things to be right between them again.

Now the situation was worse than before.

The impossible man! She was ready to live each day as it came and refused to let anyone plan her future. And Quinn, damn his fierce sense of honor, was almost as bad as Roarke about decreeing what he had concluded was best for her.

Piper shook her head in dismay. Why couldn't men understand that trying to overprotect and dominate women was offensive? At least it was to her.

When Quinn returned to camp, looking refreshed after bathing and shaving at the small spring she had made use of earlier, Piper found herself ignored.

Which did nothing for her disposition.

Quinn spoke quietly to the warriors who nodded at her, then walked off into the darkness.

Puzzled, Piper stared after them. "My, you *do* have a knack of offending a person and provoking them to get up and leave, don't you?"

"I asked them to grant us privacy for the night," Quinn said as he came to stand over her.

She rose to her feet. "I expected you to bed down as far away from me as you could get after you turned tail and ran off earlier."

His gaze narrowed on her, not that she was the least bit intimidated. No matter how aggravated she made him, she had discovered that he would never raise his hand to her. His voice? Yes, on occasion. But she had the same habit so who was she to complain about that?

"You are trying to provoke me again," he grumbled.

"Agatha would be so pleased."

Quinn pivoted on his heels to stride over to the pallet. "I've thought it over and I've decided you're right."

"About what?" She walked over to sink down cross-legged in front of him.

"You want a marriage license for protection and convenience and you want instruction on passion, so I'm going to make you a deal."

Her surprised gaze swept up to meet his carefully blank stare. Was he teasing her? Most likely. But she couldn't resist saying, "I'm humbled by your self-sacrifice on my behalf. You will, of course, be monetarily compensated."

"You are annoying me again," he said, his deep voice rumbling with warning.

"And if you become much more romantic in presenting your proposal I will surely swoon at your feet—"

Her taunting voice trailed off when he cupped her face in both hands and stared intently at her. "I am giving you one last chance to change your mind, Piper. If you wake up tomorrow full of regret and realize you have made a hasty decision that you would like to retract then it will be too late."

The gentle touch of his hands stirred an undeniable longing inside her. It was proof enough that her body called out to his. She *did* want him. She wanted the intimacy she had rejected until she met a man who thoroughly intrigued and fascinated her.

He was the one. She wasn't sure how she knew that, but she did.

One night with Quinn was a memory she knew she would cherish in the years to come. She would have one bright, shining moment of pleasure to savor. Surely it would be worth the hurt of watching him ride out of her life.

And he would; she had no illusions about that.

"When we reach Catoosa Gulch we will make this

marriage legal in the white man's culture and you will have your signed document. But in the ways of the Kiowa and Comanche, a woman has only to give her assent and join a warrior in his tipi to make the marriage binding." His thumbs brushed over her lips and he smiled wryly. "The wilderness is my tipi, Piper. You are already here. Are you absolutely certain this is what you want?"

"Yes," she murmured as she pressed her lips to his.

Her frustration melted away as his sinewy arms enfolded her. Hungry need surged through her as she savored the addictive taste of him and reveled in the feel of his muscular body melded familiarly to hers. His hands glided over her hips and she shimmered with radiating pleasure that burned to her very core. He nipped at her bottom lip, tugging at it the same way that erotic sensations tugged at her feminine body.

When she moaned his name he responded with a rumbling growl. And then the palm of his hand settled between her legs and red-hot desire coiled deep inside her. Piper forgot to breathe—couldn't remember why she needed to—when his questing hand glided beneath the waistband of her breeches to brush intimately against her. He caressed her with thumb and forefinger, penetrating her heated flesh until she gasped and shivered and pressed eagerly against his hand.

Piper felt herself falling deeper into the sensual web of breathless need as he stroked her gently. His tongue plunged into her mouth, mimicking the rhythmic motion of his fingertip. Sensation after inexpressible sensation converged on her, burning her up from inside out.

Quinn explored the hidden secrets of her body and marveled at the pleasure he derived from touching her so intimately. When she melted around his fingertip he swore the earth had shifted beneath him. Pleasure rippled through him and his body clenched with throbbing need. He longed to bury himself in her velvety heat and burn alive in the hottest sweetest fire he had ever known.

"I want you," he whispered as he tugged impatiently at her breeches. "I want to be inside you. Now. This very minute."

"That's where I need you," she said with a ragged breath. "Now. This very minute."

She reached for the placket of his buckskin breeches, wanting to touch him as familiarly as he had touched her, wanting to return the incredible pleasure that rippled through her.

Suddenly she heard the clatter of hooves on the ledge above them. Voices echoed in the still of the night, jostling Piper from her pleasure-induced daze. Before she could react to the possible threat of danger Quinn was already on his feet. He jerked her up beside him and snatched up their bedroll. He bustled Piper beneath the outcropping of rock then smothered the small campfire.

Piper was still trying to regain her senses when Quinn pressed a pistol into her hand. "Stay here and pay attention."

"But—"

He touched his forefinger to her lips to shush her. "This is when you obey my orders without question."

Grabbing his bullwhip, Quinn scurried around the corner. When the pup, that had been napping by the fire before they abruptly disturbed him, tried to trot after Quinn, Piper cuddled him close. She sat frozen to the spot when she heard the unidentified riders moving closer. Everything inside her rebelled against allowing Quinn to confront the intruders alone, but she did as she was told.

Staying put didn't stop her from fearing for Quinn's safety. Once again, she chastised herself for being incompetent. This might be the one time Quinn needed someone to watch his back and she didn't possess the skills to assist him.

That realization tormented her to no end while she waited helplessly for Quinn's return. And he had better come back in one piece or she would never forgive herself.

Quinn crouched beside an oversize slab of rock to appraise the five riders that filed along the trail that lay ten feet below him. Mexican banditos. He had a pretty good idea where they were headed. There was nothing he would like better than to take the men captive and interrogate them. He wanted to be well informed before his Ranger battalion laid siege to the remote stronghold.

Pensively, he contemplated the best method of attack—and wished there had been time to alert the two Comanches for backup. Well, it wasn't the first time he had worked alone, he thought as he waited until the last rider passed directly beneath him.

Like a pouncing cougar, Quinn sprang from the ledge to catch the rider unaware. The butt of his pistol connected with the bandito's skull and put him out like a doused lantern. When the man slumped forward on the skittish horse, Quinn bounded into the saddle to grab the reins. He hauled his unconscious captive up in front of him like a shield.

When the nearest rider swiveled in the saddle to determine the cause of the muffled sounds, Quinn lashed out with his bullwhip. It curled around the second rider's neck like a striking snake. One quick jerk sent the man cartwheeling off his horse to collide with the perpendicular wall of stone.

Quinn was ready and waiting when the other three men tried to wheel their horses around, only to become log-jammed by the walls of the narrow ravine. Their mounts collided as they grabbed for their pistols. Quinn's whip cracked and hissed repeatedly as he sent the weapons leaping from the bandoleros' hands.

Shouts and curses of pain erupted while Quinn thrust out his whip to jerk one man after another from the saddle.

"Very impressive," Red Hawk called from somewhere overhead.

"Thanks for nothing," Quinn snorted while he held the four conscious outlaws at gunpoint.

Spotted Deer grinned. "If you had needed our help we would have joined in."

Quinn heard the cascade of sand and pebbles that indicated the Comanches were sidestepping down the slope above him.

"Besides," Red Hawk said, smiling wryly, "we had farther to come since you sent us away from camp."

"We have money to trade for our freedom," the pot-bellied Mexican negotiated in Spanish.

"Robbed another stage, did you?" Quinn pushed the unconscious outlaw into Red Hawk's arms, then dismounted.

"No," the rail-thin bandit hurriedly denied. "It's our hard-earned wages."

"Doubt it," Quinn smirked as he went over to remove the lasso attached to one of the men's saddles.

With the Comanches' assistance he secured the bandits' hands in rope, then herded them to camp. The warriors trailed behind him with the confiscated horses.

A pleased smile pursed Quinn's lips when he rounded the corner to find Piper exactly where he had left her. She released Lucky and the mutt trotted over to thump his tail against Quinn's leg in greeting.

"A gaggle of Knights, I presume," Piper said as she inspected the men who were strung together like a chain gang. She glanced approvingly at Quinn and the warriors. "The three of you work well together."

"We *could* have if those two sleepyheads had arrived sooner. They left me to do all the work," Quinn replied.

Piper's wide-eyed gaze lifted to him, amazed by his nonchalant acceptance of his impressive abilities. She would have been thrilled if she possessed a third of his skills.

When Quinn gestured for the bandits to sit down, they reluctantly obliged. After he had secured the ends of the rope to a juniper, one of the men glanced back and forth between him and the two warriors. "What are you gonna do with us?" he asked in stilted English.

Piper wasn't surprised that Quinn ignored the question. She had discovered early on that Quinn only offered information sparingly. Apparently, he planned to let the desperadoes stew in their own juice for the night.

To her amusement she watched Quinn shake out the bedroll then encircled it with the pistols, rifles and knives that he had confiscated from his captives. After she and Quinn bedded down side by side, the Comanches retrieved their gear and returned to camp to guard the prisoners.

Well, so much for the complete intimate knowledge she had hoped to gain of Quinn tonight, she thought, disheartened.

"Maybe this was a sign that it wasn't meant to be," Quinn murmured as he stretched out next to her, placing himself directly between her and the string of bandits.

She levered herself up on her elbow to peer down at him. "Or perhaps it was just a sign that this was the wrong time and place." She smiled impishly. "I'm still holding you to our agreement, so don't think you can weasel out of it."

The smoldering look he flashed her served to soothe her disappointment. Then his expression sobered. "This is when you sleep with one eye open," he insisted. "Never take for granted that just because men are tied up that they can't find some way to get loose. So don't get *too* comfortable."

She cast the banditos a wary glance as she settled beside him on the pallet.

"And Piper?"

Her gaze swung back to him. "Yes?"

"Thanks for staying where I left you. I needed to know you were safe so I could focus on my duties."

She pulled a face at him. "I can help you the most by doing nothing at all? You might as well come right out and say I have no use whatsoever."

"You have your *use*. We just got interrupted."

Her head snapped up, and she was tempted to whack him soundly on the head for insulting her. When she noticed the teasing grin that quirked his lips she settled her ruffled feathers.

"A shame that," she replied saucily. "Because I had planned for *you* to be well used and completely worn out by this time of night."

When his jaw fell open and he gaped at her, she turned her back on him. She was pleased with herself for giving him food for thought while they both slept with one eye open, deprived of their chance to take up where they had left off an hour earlier.

The next morning Piper awakened to the sound of voices and the smell of coffee brewing on the campfire. Apparently Quinn had rummaged through the bandits' saddlebags to make use of their supplies. She presumed the warriors had been hunting again because there were two rabbits roasting over the fire.

Her mouth watered in hungry anticipation.

Rolling to her feet, Piper ambled over to survey the other items Quinn had confiscated from the saddlebags. Her gaze widened in alarm when she recognized a jewel-studded ring and gold watch that were among the stolen loot.

"What's wrong?" Quinn questioned warily.

"These belong to my father," she murmured as she stared at a large wad of bank notes that lay beside the watch. "He must have figured out where I was going and decided to come after me himself."

The prospect of her father meeting with calamity because he was chasing after her was unsettling. Piper wanted her freedom but certainly not at her father's expense. Conversely, the thought of reaching her destination, only to have Roarke waiting to cart her back to Galveston sent her spirits plummeting.

Confound it, if not for the holdup and delays she might have reunited with her sister before Roarke arrived. The last thing Piper wanted was for Penelope to have to deal with their father's unexpected arrival alone.

A sense of urgency had Piper pacing around camp, busying herself with rolling up the pallet and tucking away supplies. Quinn must have sensed her apprehension for he was on his feet, keeping pace beside her.

"I questioned the bandits about the stage robbery. It didn't take place on the same stretch of road where we were held up," he assured her. "The three passengers were unharmed, but they were left to walk the last several miles to the next stage stop."

Piper's shoulders sagged in relief. Her father had been robbed, but he was unhurt. Now all she had to do was deal with his temper. No doubt, the inconveniences he had endured during the trip would do nothing to sweeten his disposition.

"We'll head for Catoosa Gulch after breakfast," Quinn informed her. "As soon as I jail these outlaws and notify my commander I'll take you to the fort." He grasped her arm to halt her nervous pacing. "I will also be there to ensure Roarke doesn't force you onto an east-bound stage with him."

Piper smiled appreciatively at his insistent tone. "Thank you. I'm not looking forward to that confrontation, but I will handle Papa myself. There is no need for you to escort me to my sister if I can catch a stage headed south."

"We made a deal," Quinn reminded her. "One of several bargains we made. There is also the matter of the license. If nothing else, you will have that…if you still want it."

"I wanted more," she told him honestly, then glanced at the string of Mexican prisoners whose unexpected arrival last night had interrupted them at an inopportune moment. "But we don't always get our way, do we?"

"No, sometimes we get what's best."

Quinn gestured for Piper to make use of one of the saddled horses rather than riding bareback. He could tell by her hurried motions that she was anxious to get moving. Her plans were falling apart around her and she dreaded the confrontation with her father.

It amazed Quinn that he was more concerned about resolving Piper's problems than assembling a strike force to attack the stronghold so he could avenge Taylor Briggs's death. Damn it, he had lost his single-minded focus this past week. It was impossible to concentrate on his mission when Piper preoccupied his thoughts.

Wheeling around, Quinn strode over to dole out food

to his captives. He noticed that Piper had separated herself from the men and chose to take her meal alone. No doubt, she was mentally rehearsing what she intended to say to Roarke.

He should have made a beeline to the garrison, Quinn scolded himself. If he had, Piper and Penelope could have presented a united force when Roarke showed up.

Although Quinn had heard that old cliché about how things usually worked out for the best he had never really believed it. He had been there on too many occasions to observe how things worked out for the absolute *worst*. But despite Piper's determination to face her father alone, Quinn intended to be there to provide reinforcement.

He had come to care more for Piper than he should have and he couldn't ride away until he knew her life was back on course. He vowed to make damn sure that she acquired the freedom and independence that meant so much to her.

If *he* had any say in the matter, Piper was going to get her heart's desire. She sure as hell deserved it after all that he had unintentionally put her through the past several days.

Roarke Sullivan was not in the best of moods while he hiked downhill to the crude station that stood right smack dab in the middle of nowhere. He had been cramped up on a train, and then a stagecoach for three days. Then he had been robbed at gunpoint and forced to walk half the night. He had to rely on the kindness of the proprietor to provide a meager meal because his money had been stolen, along with his valuable ring and his watch.

Begging for charity did not set any better with Roarke than being robbed.

The meal he choked down was the worst food he had ever tasted. The thought of Piper being subjected to these despicable accommodations incensed Roarke. Worse, the prospect of never seeing Piper again haunted his every waking hour.

When Roarke finished his tasteless meal he was offered a straw mat on the floor to catch a nap while he and the other two male passengers waited for the next stage. While he lay there staring up at the cobwebs on the ceiling, he wondered if he would reach a community that had a bank or telegraph office. He needed to replenish his funds to complete this disastrous journey.

A trip to hell and back, he thought as he rolled to his side and closed his eyes. He was never venturing this far west until the railroad was up and running, he promised himself. And how in God's name had Penelope adjusted and survived in this vast wasteland that was rife with bandits, scorpions, rattlers and who knew what other vicious varmints?

For sure and certain, Penelope was coming back to Galveston to resume her rightful place as heir to the Sullivan fortune. As far as Roarke was concerned, her noaccount husband could sit out here by himself and rot. The man should be shot for forcing his blue-blooded wife to endure such a dismal existence.

Captain Matthew Duncan better believe that Roarke was going to have a few things to say about dragging Penelope out to hell's fringe and forcing her to live like a commoner!

Chapter Eleven

Piper was enormously relieved when the procession veered down from the treacherous stone ledges and V-shaped ravines to follow a broad valley that led southwest. When Quinn noticed riders approaching from the west he grabbed one of the Mexican's wide-brimmed sombreros and crammed it on Piper's head. She stared curiously at him when he draped one of the men's grimy serapes over her shoulders.

"No sense putting you at risk," he explained. "The disguise isn't as effective as the snippy old widow Agatha's, but this will keep you from drawing unwanted attention. Just keep your head down."

Piper ducked her head and pulled the foul-smelling serape around her. She made a mental note to rent a hotel room in the community where Quinn said they would stop. The hat and garment reeked of whiskey and sweat and she couldn't wait to cast them aside, draw in a fresh breath of air and enjoy a long-awaited bath.

Her attention shifted to the six rugged-looking riders that trotted toward them. She watched interestedly when a smile kicked up the corners of Quinn's mouth and he raised his hand in greeting.

"Well, if you aren't a sight for sore eyes," the man with the salt-and pepper-colored hair said as he halted beside Quinn. His sharp-eyed gaze settled on the Mexican captives. "Looks like you've been busy. We've been searching the area for the past few days and we seem to have been a few steps behind the road agents." His disapproving stare landed squarely on the Comanche warriors. "Why aren't these renegades bound up?"

When Quinn gestured for the riders to follow him out of earshot, then motioned for Piper to join them, she trotted forward. She was inordinately pleased that Quinn was considerate enough to include her in the conversation. She wanted to reach out and hug him, but she ducked her head and hunched her shoulders forward instead.

"I deputized these warriors," Quinn announced. "They are former acquaintances. They also know this country as well as I do. I request that you pull a few strings, Commander Butler, and take advantage of the expertise they can offer during the strike against the bandits' hideout."

Piper blinked, suddenly aware that this ragtag group of men was a battalion of Rangers. They wore no distinguished uniforms to set them apart from brigands. They looked as hard-bitten and well armed as Quinn. She assumed they made it a practice to conceal their badges until proper identification was necessary.

"What tribe do they hail from?" Butler questioned as he carefully studied the warriors' buckskin garments. "Look like Comanches to me."

"They are." Quinn smiled wryly as he glanced back at Red Hawk and Spotted Deer. "They pointed me in the direction of the Knights' stronghold in Dead Man's Canyon. They also helped me scout the hideout in preparation for our attack."

Commander Butler eyed the warriors speculatively. "Are you sure they are reliable?"

Quinn nodded. "I will take full responsibility for them. Their English is practically nonexistent, but you can communicate with them in Spanish."

After the company of frontier fighters nodded agreeably, Butler shrugged. "If you can vouch for them, then they are hired as scouts."

"Thank you, sir." Quinn frowned curiously at the assembled battalion. "I thought you were waiting for my missive before you rode out here. What changed your plans?"

Butler pulled off his dusty hat and slapped it against his thigh. "We were sent out to locate a kidnap victim. So far we haven't had any luck tracking her down. Which doesn't bode well for the poor woman, I'm afraid." He arched a questioning brow. "Ever heard of the Sullivans from Galveston?"

Piper jerked up her head, her confused gaze darting to Quinn who wore a carefully neutral expression. *Kidnap victim?* Where had that ridiculous rumor come from?

"I've heard the name," Quinn replied blandly.

"According to the girl's father, she was abducted and

was presumed to have been on a stage bound for Fort Davis. Can't fathom how Mr. Sullivan knew that, but he sent us to rescue the girl."

Quinn smiled faintly. *He* could fathom how that might have happened. No doubt, Roarke had twisted the story a bit to make sure that he acquired the assistance of the Rangers.

The man didn't waste time with underlings, Quinn mused. Roarke had gone straight to the top to enlist the services of the state's most reputable fighting force. Then he must have decided to head west to be on hand when Piper was located—*if* she were located.

"Unfortunately," Lieutenant Vance Cooper spoke up, "we have reason to believe that she might have disguised herself to elude her captor. We found evidence of a woman passenger on the doomed stage that wrecked on a cliff." He grinned in relief. "We figured you might be on the same stage and we were damned worried about you, Cal. Guess you've got as many lives as a cat or you wouldn't be here right now."

"I *was* on that stage," Quinn confirmed. "Close call."

Butler's thick brows rose sharply. "Was there a female passenger with you? Did she mention that she escaped from her captor? Do you know if she's still alive?"

Quinn reached over to pluck the sombrero off Piper's head, allowing her curly blond hair to cascade around her shoulders. All six men's eyes popped in surprise as they stared at her. "Does Piper fit the description you were given?"

Butler nodded as he stared at Piper in astonishment.

"You have been in the wilds with Cal this entire time, Miss Sullivan?"

"Yes, sir," Piper replied, then smiled wryly. "It has been an eventful week."

"But how did you elude your kidnapper?" Butler questioned, bemused.

When she squirmed uneasily beneath the commander's probing stare Quinn spoke on her behalf—and then realized he was probably stepping on her independent toes. "There seems to have been a misunderstanding. Miss Sullivan left on her own accord. Her father must not have been fully aware of the circumstances surrounding her disappearance."

"That is Callahan's subtle way of saying that my father obviously resorted to any method necessary to see that you tracked me down," Piper interjected. "I also know that he was on the stage that was robbed by these Mexican bandoleros. I identified his ring and watch among the stolen items Quinn confiscated from them. I can't say how much money he was carrying, but I'm sure part of the cash Quinn recovered belongs to him."

She frowned worriedly. "Did you send word to my father that I might have died in the stage wreck?"

Commander Butler shifted uneasily in the saddle. "Yes, ma'am, I did. I'm sorry. But we couldn't fathom how anyone could have survived that disastrous wreck." He glanced curiously at Quinn. "Just how *did* you get out of that stage alive?"

"Long story," Quinn said. "I'll explain it later."

The commander opened his mouth, then clamped it

shut. Clearly he was curious about the details of the holdup, but Quinn had more pressing matters to discuss.

"Our foremost concern is jailing these outlaws and formulating a plan of attack," Quinn insisted. "The bandits will become suspicious when their Mexican cohorts don't return to the hideout promptly."

When the Rangers reined back in the direction they had come Quinn requested that the Comanches bring the prisoners forward. The procession picked up the pace and trotted west.

"We have received some disturbing information since we last contacted you, Cal," the commander reported grimly. "We have been informed of a plot to lure in Rangers for extermination."

Quinn jerked up his head and frowned. "What sort of conspiracy are we facing?"

"The Knights of the Golden Circle are trying to rid themselves of as many Rangers as possible for capturing and killing their cohorts and kinfolk," Butler elaborated. "We think the reason for this rash of robberies in the area is twofold. Not only are these bandits padding their pockets with stolen money and the profits from horses and cattle, but also they are trying to gain our attention. They are trying to provoke us into coming after them."

"You will understand why they want us to come to them when you get a look at their stronghold in Dead Man's Canyon," Quinn muttered. "With its steep cliffs, the box canyon they've got set up makes one hell of a fortress. There is one obvious way in and we will be sitting ducks if we strike as a united force."

He hitched his thumb over his shoulder. "That's another reason why the Comanches will be beneficial to our siege. They can lead a flank of men along the little-known trails on the ridges. Our only hope of success is to surprise the outlaws that are tramping all over sacred Comanche burial ground."

Butler glanced back at the warriors. "That should guarantee that they don't try to double-cross us."

"Double-crosses are not the Comanche way," Quinn said in defense of his adopted clan. "It has always been the white man who goes back on his word repeatedly." Long-held bitterness crept into his voice. "You get the truth from the Comanche, whether you want to hear it or not."

The Rangers chuckled in amusement and six pairs of eyes settled speculatively on Quinn.

"So that's where that trait of yours comes from," Cooper mused aloud. "Always wondered about that."

Quinn knew he had nothing on Piper these days when it came to outright honesty. She had begun to speak her mind, even when there were times when he wished she would keep some of those unsettling thoughts to herself. He did not, however, voice that comment to his companions. But he and Piper did exchange significant glances. He swore she knew what he was thinking when she smiled impishly at him.

"I've been a Comanche longer than I have been white. But the point is that these warriors are trustworthy, experienced in battle and they won't betray our cause. I'll stake my reputation on that."

"Then we won't be wary about relying on them to

guard our backs, if necessary," Cooper declared, then
frowned curiously. "How many Rangers do you think
it will take to seal off the canyon and make a strike on
the bandits?"

"How many men can we spare for this siege?"
Quinn asked.

"We have a battalion at Van Horn that consists of
eight seasoned fighters. It would take at least a day to
contact our reinforcements."

"If we have explosives and considerable firepower at
our disposal, then we should be able to launch an attack," Quinn speculated. "We spotted two dozen outlaws milling around the hideout. These five Mexicans
will be out of commission, but that doesn't mean there
aren't other road agents targeting banks and nearby ranches that have yet to report in."

"Oh, good. Outnumbered again," Butler said, and
snorted. "Can't imagine what it would be like to engage
in a battle where we weren't on the short end of lopsided odds."

Piper was greatly relieved when the men picked up
the pace. She wasn't sure where her father was, but if
she could reach the garrison before he surprised Penelope she would be grateful. She could only hope that discovering that she was alive would make Roarke easier
to deal with. But she had the unmistakable feeling that
her near-brush with catastrophe would have the opposite effect on him.

Quinn dropped back beside her as the procession
moved west. "Discovering that you're alive and well
should soften up your father," Quinn said, smiling en-

couragingly at her. "Roarke might be so relieved that he'll be more receptive to your announcement of independence and agree to anything."

Piper snorted in contradiction. "If you knew my father you would realize that he will likely blame *me* for putting him through undue stress. He will be outraged that I put myself in danger." She frowned contemplatively. "I'm beginning to wonder if the purpose of his journey southwest, upon hearing that I might have perished, is to drag my sister back to become the surviving heir. The fur will fly if Papa demands that Penny pack up and leave her husband."

Quinn studied her speculatively. "Perhaps your sister is tired of doing without luxuries and yearns for a more active social life," he ventured.

Piper tilted her chin and said, "Penny is devoted to Matthew. It is a Sullivan family trait. We do not bail out when things become difficult. If that were the case, I would still be bawling my head off back in one of those nameless canyons and demanding that you take me to Galveston."

Quinn shrugged a broad shoulder. "It wouldn't be the first time a woman with stars in her eyes came west to join her husband at an isolated fort, then had a change of heart. I've seen it happen repeatedly."

"We Sullivans are not fainthearted," Piper said defensively. "When you meet Penny you will realize how badly you have misjudged her."

"If you don't mind, I'll reserve judgment until then," he said skeptically.

"Fine, then prepare to be mistaken. If I, being a Sullivan, announced that I would follow you to the ends of the earth because I loved you, then I would honor the commitment. Penny has done the same thing."

Quinn stared pointedly at her. "I would never ask a woman to make such a sacrifice and endure unnecessary hardship."

"That's probably because you have never fallen in love," she countered. "You would have no problem imagining your life without a woman in it. But Matt rescued Penny from a robbery attempt three years ago. At first meeting she swore she had met her soul mate. After that, she and Matt were inseparable, despite Papa's objections. They defied him because they are deeply committed to each other and that makes all the difference."

Quinn decided that debating the issue with Piper was a waste of time. She stood firm in her idealistic beliefs, but he was a realist and he had seen marriages fail among military officers whose duty it was to defend the frontier. Many of the army wives chose to live in the East and lead separate lives.

"I still wouldn't ask a woman to make that kind of sacrifice," Quinn said, determined to get in the last word—for once.

She smiled tauntingly at him. "*You* won't have to because *our* arrangement doesn't require that. *I* know what you think of me, Callahan. The last thing you want is to have me tagging along behind you indefinitely."

She didn't have a clue what he secretly wanted, he reflected as he watched her nudge her mount to trot up beside Commander Butler. As for love, Quinn wasn't sure there was such a thing. There was wary respect, sexual attraction, vengeance and several other emotions that influenced a man's actions. Quinn had no experience whatsoever with love and he wondered if his upbringing had made it impossible for him to feel anything remotely close to that sentiment.

Furthermore, emotional attachments were painful when they ended abruptly. Quinn had suffered loss more often in his life than he cared to count.

He was *not* going to make the foolish mistake of falling in love with Piper and that was that.

He did admire and respect her, though. And true, he was unwillingly attracted to her. Also true, being with her brought unexpected happiness and unfamiliar pleasure. That is, when she wasn't making him loco by debating with him or defying him.

Quinn had never allowed himself to form a strong emotional bond with anyone the past two decades. Aside from Taylor Briggs, of course. He had suffered grief and anger when Taylor died. Quinn had vowed not to make the mistake again because every close association in his life had ended badly. He had endured more than his fair share of emotional upheaval. He was not going to let Piper so close that leaving her behind colored every one of his thoughts and left him pining for things that could never be.

No, he told himself. He was sticking to his original plan. He would marry Piper for her convenience, if that protected her from her domineering father. But he wasn't going to get so attached to her that losing her would devastate him and leave him vulnerable and restless.

The more he thought about it the more convinced he

became that it was a good thing the Mexican bandits had shown up when they did last night. He was probably better off not knowing what he was missing with Piper. It would only make it more difficult when they parted company.

Piper noticed that Quinn had become more standoffish after reuniting with his squadron of Rangers. She also noticed that the lawmen had a great deal of respect for his ideas and opinions. Among his peers he was a valued member of a clan of fighters who had dedicated their lives to protecting helpless citizens from danger. She could understand why Quinn had made a place for himself with the renowned Rangers. It was a life that would never include her, even if she were foolish enough to fall in love with him.

As if you haven't fallen a little bit in love with him already, said that annoying voice inside her head.

Well, it didn't matter how she felt, Piper told herself as she followed the Rangers into a settlement of adobe and timber buildings that was nestled beside a bubbling spring. Her foremost concern was obtaining a marriage license. The next thing on her agenda was to make the two-hour ride to Fort Davis so she could alert Penny to their father's imminent arrival.

When Piper noticed Red Hawk and Spotted Deer's wary regard for the Mexican and white settlers in Catoosa Gulch she took it upon herself to provide suitable shirts and breeches for the Comanches so they could fit in, now that they had been deputized. The men had supplied her meals, guided and protected her from harm and now she had the chance to repay them—even if the gesture might put a dent in her limited funds.

Piper had discovered that she could subsist with the barest necessities after her trek through the wilderness. She could manage until she received pay from teaching school at the garrison.

While the Rangers incarcerated the Mexican bandits at the shabby adobe jail and began their interrogation, Piper made a beeline for the dry goods store. She returned several minutes later with four plaid shirts, four pair of breeches and two hats. When she offered the gifts to the Comanches they stared at her, dumbfounded.

"In appreciation for your protection and preparation for your new profession," she declared, although the men couldn't understand a word she said. "I didn't want you to stand out in a crowd. Hopefully these garments will help you fit in easily."

She started when a deep voice rumbled behind her. She pivoted to find Commander Butler smiling at her. He translated in Spanish and the warriors reached out to pump both of her hands simultaneously.

When they strode off to change clothes in the alley behind the store Scott Butler grinned at her. "That was mighty nice of you, Miss Sullivan."

"Please call me Piper," she requested. "The warriors were exceptionally helpful to me and I wanted to show my gratitude."

Butler shifted awkwardly from one scuffed boot to the other. "I wanted to apologize again for any duress I might have caused your family. When we checked the stage station to discover that only one female passenger had taken this route west, then investigated the wrecked coach that was scattered down the mountainside we assumed the worst." He studied her pensively. "I assume you were traveling in disguise for your protection."

Piper nodded and grinned. "The tactic worked superbly until that fiasco with the holdup and runaway coach."

"I would dearly like to know why you struck off on your own, considering your background," he remarked.

"As Quinn said, it's a long story. The boiled-down version is that my father refused to let me visit my sister at the garrison so I made the traveling arrangements myself. I had planned to telegraph him shortly before I reached my destination."

"What's important is that you were in capable hands when disaster struck. Cal might be a bit unconventional in his manner, but he is one of our best men. I suspect that you owe him your life."

Piper chuckled. "Believe me, commander, I am vividly aware that Callahan spared my life several times this week. I have also learned a tremendous amount about survival, thanks to him. It has been an adventurous and educational experience, to say the least."

"I reckon so. Fortunately you lived to tell about it." He waited a beat then said, "I also hear tell that you and Cal plan to wed."

Piper blinked, surprised that Quinn had imparted that information to Butler. "Uh…yes, we do."

He cast her a fatherly smile. "This is none of my business, of course. I am the first to admit that Cal is a rare individual, but he isn't exactly the kind of man a woman of your social status takes as a husband." She watched him choose his words carefully as he continued. "If he behaved in a way that um… Well, if he—"

Piper flung up her hand to forestall him. "I appreciate your concern," she said, "but I found no fault with Quinn's behavior." Except that he dragged his feet about introducing her to passion, she amended silently. "Ours is a marriage of convenience, one *he* suggested as a solution to my father's constant interference in my life. But rest assured that I don't intend to complicate Quinn's life or interfere with his duties."

"I am married myself," Butler confided as he took her arm to escort her across the street to the town's one and only hotel. "Unfortunately, my wife objected to my continued absence. It might not be my place to offer advice, and I know I have no right to meddle, but I feel compelled to warn you those high expectations can lead to disappointment. I would spare you and Cal the frustration my wife and I dealt with."

Piper smiled warmly at the crusty veteran Ranger. "Believe me, I have no expectations whatsoever. Quinn has my gratitude, respect and admiration. But I am fully aware that he is committed to his duties and takes them very seriously."

Butler patted her arm. "Glad to hear that you both have your eyes wide open going in. Quinn explained that he wants to escort you to the garrison before we surround the mountain hideout. I'm sending a courier west to the Ranger encampment near Van Horn. Our reinforcements should be here tomorrow.

"In the meantime, if there is anything I can do to assist you, all you have to do is ask. As I said, I regret any distress my preliminary report might have caused your family." He bowed slightly. "I will be at your service if there is anything you need, Piper."

She pushed up on tiptoe to give him a peck on the cheek, then grinned impishly. "Between you and me, I think your wife made a serious error in judgment. I don't believe she is aware of the good deal she had going."

Butler tossed back his head and laughed. "You, my dear, are a delight. Now I understand why you captured Cal's attention and prompted him to offer his services." His hazel eyes sparkled with amusement. "I think you have been a positive influence on him, too. There's something different about him these days. I think you might have something to do with that."

When the commander strode back to the jail, Piper stared after him. Her attention shifted to the two men who exited the alley, garbed in their new attire. A pleased smile pursed her lips when Red Hawk and Spotted Deer lifted their right hands, palms forward, to acknowledge their appreciation.

Piper watched the men turn their attention to the commander then quicken their steps to overtake him. Wheeling around, she strode into the hotel—if one could call it that. The two-story structure of stone and timber offered crude accommodations. Piper wondered if she could make arrangements for a bath in preparation for her hasty wedding ceremony. From the looks of the place, it wasn't promising.

Her footsteps stalled and wary consternation puckered her brow when she surveyed the stubble-faced clerk—or proprietor, whichever he was—who leaned negligently on the counter. Her suspicions doubled when she saw the bandana tied on the left side of his neck. If she wasn't mistaken, the kerchief matched the ones worn by the gang of outlaws.

The man's facial features reminded her of a turtle, with his close-set eyes, beak nose and nonexistent chin. He also seemed familiar to her, but Piper couldn't make a connection, especially when the greasy-haired man leered disrespectfully at her. Of one thing she was certain though, this man was somehow connected with the network of thieves.

"Don't get many lookers like you in these parts, sweetheart," he declared as he raked her up and down— twice. "The name's Roy Morrell. Would you be wantin' somethin' besides a room for the night?"

If the gap-toothed grin he flashed her was supposed to be seductive it fell well short of its mark. A wave of repulsion rolled over Piper and it was all she could do not to shudder in disgust. "My *fiancé* will be joining me shortly," she informed him.

"Hey! Get outta here, mutt!" he growled suddenly.

Piper glanced over her shoulder to see Lucky perched on the threshold. The dog barked and growled at the clerk. Piper decided the mutt was a good judge of character. She didn't like this scoundrel any better than Lucky did.

The man slapped a key on the counter. "Room seven. Top of the stairs, darlin'. Second door on the left."

"I would also like a bath," she requested.

Another devilish grin exposed his missing teeth. "Whatever you want, honey. I'll be more than happy to scrub your back for you."

"That will hardly be necessary, because I can manage that by myself. I will return in a few minutes, *after* the tub has been filled and you have left the room." She spun on her heels and strode off. No way was she going to enter her room and risk being trapped alone with this lecherous cretin.

Once outside, Piper drew in a restorative breath, then took off toward the jail. When she heard a loud yelp, she hesitated before knocking on the door. Unless she was mistaken, one of the Rangers was applying some form of persuasive tactics to convince the bandits to supply needed information. When she rapped on the portal, it was a long moment before Commander Butler allowed her entrance.

"A problem?" he questioned, then cast a glance toward the cells in the adjoining room.

"I would like a quick word with Quinn."

Butler smiled evasively. "I'm afraid he's busy at the moment. He just found out that these five bandoleros are the gang's over-the-border connection for selling stolen livestock."

Just as Piper predicted, it was Quinn who was in charge of gleaning information. "The hotel proprietor, Roy Morrell, is wearing a bandana that's tied in the same fashion as the Mexican bandits and road agents we encountered," she reported.

Butler's thick brows nearly rocketed off his broad forehead. "An informant?"

"Perhaps. I'm not an expert in these matters, but I spent enough time with Quinn to learn to be observant. I wouldn't be surprised if the proprietor plans to send a message to the stronghold, informing the outlaws of the Mexicans' capture. Considering the close proximity to their headquarters, and the fact that the Mexicans are an important link in the operation, it occurs to me that you might be able to lure the Knights to you, if the outlaws decide a jailbreak is in order."

An approving smile quirked Butler's lips. "You have a quick mind, Piper. If you have a hankering to work undercover for us, let me know. You would be an asset to our organization. Brains and beauty. That combination has been the downfall of men for centuries."

Piper beamed proudly. "A Ranger spy? The prospect is tempting. I will certainly keep that in mind since I plan to locate in this area."

Another howl erupted from the back room. Piper cocked a brow. "Quinn seems to be very thorough. Considering his background, I suspect he's good at finding out what he wants to know from reluctant outlaws."

Butler grinned, then scratched his head. "The best, as a matter of fact. He usually gets the results we want."

"Tell Quinn I will be in room seven when he's finished here," Piper requested as she spun toward the door. "Our arrangements shouldn't take long."

On her way down the street Piper stiffened her resolve. She had automatically come running to find Quinn when she sensed trouble at the hotel. Well, no more of that, she thought determinedly as she retrieved her satchel from her horse. If that scraggly ruffian tried to assault her under the pretense of filling the tub, then *she* would handle the situation.

Quinn wasn't going to be around in the future and she had to learn to deal with trouble, she reminded herself.

Piper noted Roy Morrell wasn't stationed at the counter when she ascended the steps. Her senses went on full alert as she opened the door to her room. Sure enough, the turtle-faced man was pouring a bucket of hot water into the tub.

She positioned herself beside the commode—close to makeshift missiles that she could launch to discourage any attack. She hoped the greasy-haired hombre had the good sense not to bother her because she had no intention of being manhandled without putting up a fight.

Apparently Roy hadn't been blessed with an abundance of good sense. He ambled over to close the door. When he turned toward her, a lusty grin split his stubbled face. When the man took two threatening steps toward her Piper snatched up the pitcher. She stepped behind the chair that sat beside the bed and raised her improvised weapon threateningly.

"Keep your distance," she demanded.

He sniggered at her attempt to protect herself. "You think I'm afraid of a little piece of fluff like you? Not a chance. I also think this supposed fiancé you mentioned doesn't exist." He moved in closer. "We're going to get to know each other better—"

When he lunged abruptly, Piper swung the pitcher, knocking him on the head. He staggered back, then snarled mutinously at her.

"You'll pay dearly for that."

Piper hurled her satchel at him, but he kept on coming so she snatched up the chair and slammed it into his shoulder.

He erupted in another vicious snarl as they wrestled for control of the chair. When he ripped it from her grasp, Piper decided it was time to run. Screeching at the top of her lungs, she sprang toward the door, but the ruffian launched himself at her. Piper crashed into the wall, but recovered quickly enough to thrust her leg out behind her, catching him in the groin.

He sneered as he grabbed the shoulder seam of her blouse and whirled her to face his malicious glare. When he grabbed the front of her blouse the fabric ripped and her temper exploded. She uplifted her leg to catch him squarely in the crotch, then clawed his face until he recoiled backward.

Piper plunged toward the door and exploded into the hall. Her breath came out in a whoosh when she collided with Quinn's muscled chest. When his arm came protectively around her she slumped shamelessly against him, momentarily forgetting her vow to rely on no one but herself for her protection.

"I heard there might be a problem," he murmured as he steadied her on her wobbly legs. "Is there one?"

"Unfortunately, yes," she said on a seesaw breath.

"Then let's fix it," he growled as he barreled through the door.

Chapter Twelve

Quinn burst into the room to find the scraggly hombre who sported a familiar red bandana blotting the scratches on his cheeks. Fury boiled through Quinn at the thought of this two-bit ruffian putting his filthy hands on Piper.

"You messed with the wrong man's woman," Quinn growled ominously. "It's high time you found out what it feels like to be mauled."

Pulling back an arm, he punched the man in the nose. The blow packed enough wallop to send the proprietor crashing against the wall. That should have been enough to appease Quinn, but it wasn't even close. Not only did he plan to thoroughly avenge the assault on Piper, but he also intended to ensure this despicable excuse of a man went running to the brigand in Dead Man's Canyon in search of reinforcements.

When the bastard bounded to his feet, bowed his neck and tried to plow into Quinn's midsection, he agilely leaped sideways and scissor-kicked with his legs.

The hombre tripped and sprawled facedown on the floor. Quinn shoved his foot into the small of the man's back, then reached into his holster for his badge.

He dropped the tarnished star beneath the man's bloody nose. "You have a choice," Quinn snarled as he loomed over the man. "Get to your feet and I'll put you down again. Or you can crawl out of here on your hands and knees like the swine you are."

The would-be assailant muttered a foul oath.

"If you ever look at my fiancée the wrong way or lay another hand on her again, I will personally see to it that you are fitted for a pine box. Guaran-damn-teed. Do we understand each other?"

The man nodded his greasy head, then skedaddled off on all fours. He didn't glance up when he passed Piper who clutched modestly at her torn blouse. Damn good thing he didn't because Quinn was just looking for the excuse to beat that disgusting bastard to a pulp.

His outrage turned to amusement when Piper kicked her assailant in the seat of his homespun breeches on his way by. When he glared at her over his shoulder she gave him another boot in the rump for good measure.

Her retaliation seemed to have soothed her indignation. She hauled in a fortifying breath and gathered her composure as she turned to face Quinn.

"I'm sorry you had to intervene on my behalf again," she said as she closed the door with one hand and held her blouse together with the other.

Quinn arched a muddled brow. "Why's that?"

"Because I want to learn to deal with situations myself." She frowned disconcertedly as she set the upended chair on its legs. "Apparently I'm going to have to get a bigger stick or carry a firearm if I expect to be taken seriously. Whatever it takes, I intend to protect myself from the lusty heathens of this world."

Quinn bent at the waist to retrieve his badge. "I've been lax about teaching you to handle a pistol. We'll work on that during our jaunt to Fort Davis."

"Thank you, but it won't be necessary. I'll ask my brother-in-law for instructions." She glanced over her shoulder at him. "If you don't mind, I would like to have some privacy while I wash off the stench of close contact with that offensive swine. I will be ready to meet the justice of the peace in a half hour. I know you have obligations with the Rangers and you are pressed for time."

"Piper?"

She raised a perfectly arched brow. "Now what?"

"Are you sure this is what you want?" he had to ask again.

"It is precisely what I want," she said without the slightest hesitation. "I have decided not to marry for love or money, but for protection and convenience. If you are having second thoughts then kindly point me in the direction of one of your unmarried associates. Perhaps he wouldn't mind doing me this favor."

Much as he hated to admit it, the prospect of Piper married to anyone but him was unacceptable. "No, I'm prepared to seal this deal," he replied as he wheeled toward the door. "I'll stand watch in the hall so you won't be interrupted."

"Thank you," she said stiffly.

When Quinn exited Piper peeled off her clothes. She sighed appreciatively as she sank into the warm water. Since this morning she had set aside all her foolish romantic fantasies and had begun to look upon her hasty marriage as a necessary solution to her problem with her father. Knowing he was in southwest Texas and she would inevitably confront him, Piper intended to be well armed.

The marriage document would accomplish that purpose. Furthermore, she had decided to forego a wedding night with Quinn. All she really needed was the license, after all.

The problem was that she had gotten caught up in the heat of the moment and had become thoroughly mesmerized by him. She didn't need a memory to cherish in the future, she convinced herself. She did not need to experience passion for the sake of passion, either. She would do herself a tremendous favor if she considered this wedding nothing more than a simple business arrangement.

For sure and certain Quinn had no sentimental attachment to her and she would only get her heart broken if she yearned for more than he was prepared to give.

Piper sank beneath the water to wash her hair, then shook her head in self-disgust. Yesterday she had all but demanded that Quinn make love to her. Today she had turned a complete about-face.

For a woman who claimed to know her own mind she certainly had become wishy-washy, hadn't she?

Why was that? she asked herself pensively. Because she was falling in love with a man who didn't want or need her in his life and she was trying to protect her heart? Because she was afraid that ending up in his bed would verify that her feelings for him went far beyond desire? She was pretty sure that if she offered Quinn her body that her foolish heart would go right along with it.

Well, so much for trying to adopt men's policy of passion for the sake of passion. She sighed heavily. This was a fine time to discover that she was a sentimental romantic and that deep down inside she really wished Quinn *would* fall madly in love with her.

But that was not going to happen. If she had the good sense God gave a goose she wouldn't let herself forget that.

After rinsing her hair, Piper scrubbed herself squeaky clean, then grabbed the towel to dry off. She was going into this wedding ceremony with a clear head, she decided. All that mattered was obtaining that official piece of paper that had her name scribbled beside Quinn's.

And honestly, she was better off *not* knowing what it was like to share Quinn's bed.

Reaffirming her vow that she didn't need a man to complicate her life, Piper dressed in the frilly blue satin gown she had packed in her satchel. Quinn kept telling her to be very sure about what she wanted. Now she was. She had no illusions. No silly fantasies. And by damn, she was going to be as detached and distant as Quinn, she promised herself.

Piper twisted her damp hair into a fashionable bun, then pinned the curly mass atop her head. After a quick glance at her reflection in the mirror, she strode determinedly across the room. *Mrs. Piper Callahan. In name only,* she repeated silently as she grabbed hold of the door latch. What was in a name anyway? It didn't change who she was or what she wanted from life. She was sticking to her original objective of reuniting with Penny and becoming a teacher.

And all men everywhere could go hang! They were a constant source of frustration and she didn't need any of them. This was her life and she was living it by her own rules for once. She was going to become one of the new breed of women and no one was going to stop her from enjoying her freedom and independence, she decided resolutely.

Quinn nearly swallowed his tongue when Piper swept into the hall, garbed in the fanciest dress he had ever seen. The diving neckline, stitched with delicate ribbon and lace, accentuated the rise of her creamy breasts. The trim-fitting gown emphasized the small indentation of her waist and glided provocatively over the shapely curve of her hips.

Sweet mercy, she looked as if she had stepped from a book of fairy tales and Quinn couldn't drag his eyes off her. She took his breath away when she was all spruced up like the fashionable lady she was.

The differences between them couldn't have been more obvious, Quinn mused. She looked like a fairy princess.

He looked half-civilized—which he was.

"Give me a minute," he requested as he scooped up his saddlebags and darted into the room.

Quinn jerked off his clothes, then fastened himself into the gambler's garb—minus the gaudy red vest. Clean-shaven though he was, his hair dangled around his shoulders in disarray. He untied the beaded head-band, pulled his thick hair back, braided it then secured it in place. He tucked the braid beneath the collar of his white shirt.

A little better, he decided as he appraised his reflection. His clothes didn't begin to compare to Piper's expensive gown, but this was the best he could do on short notice. He frowned when he realized this was the first time he had made a conscious attempt to give a better impression of himself.

His frown deepened when he admitted that he wasn't doing it for himself. He was doing it for Piper's sake. Because *her* opinion of him mattered.

Which said a little too much about how important she had become to him.

Deciding not to dwell on that uneasy thought, Quinn stepped back into the hall.

Piper surveyed his appearance, then smiled wryly. "You didn't have to change clothes on my account. I thought you looked perfectly fine, just the way you were."

Her comment pleased him. But since he had stumbled over that unnerving epiphany a moment earlier he wasn't as surprised by the feelings of pride that assailed him. Bottom line, Quinn thought. Everything Piper said and did was beginning to influence him and he needed to guard against that.

"Thank you. You look breathtaking. All decked out in your finery. But you didn't have to change on my account, either." He extended his arm politely. "Shall we?"

Arm in arm, they descended the steps and Quinn felt as if he were escorting royalty. He blinked, startled, when he saw his battalion—minus Tom Pendleton who had ridden to Van Horn to gather reinforcements—waiting by the abandoned counter.

"The clerk lit out of here like a house afire," Vance Cooper remarked as his gaze flooded over Piper in masculine approval. "He looked a mite roughed up. That your doing, Cal?"

"Piper had to fend off his attack," Quinn explained.

"And you provided the muscle to emphasize her distaste," Butler speculated as his eyes roamed appreciatively over Piper. "I figure we have spare time while that informant runs off to tell his cohorts that we're in town and the Mexicans are in jail. We thought we might attend your wedding."

"Should be something to see," Remington Simms, the dark-haired Ranger said, grinning. "Congrats, by the way, Cal. Don't know what the lady sees in you, but I guess we all have our special brand of charm."

Quinn ignored the teasing grins that flew his direction. He knew damn well what his associates were thinking. Mismatch if ever there was one.

When he glanced down at Piper's shiny blond head, undeniable emotion hit him like a bullet in the chest. His wife-to-be? This beguiling heiress, who probably had a pedigree as long as his arm, was going to take his name? He still couldn't believe they were going through with this, couldn't believe she *wanted* to be hitched to the likes of him.

He should have kept his big mouth shut and dreamed up another solution to her problem with her father. For instance, he could have threatened the man within an inch of his life if he tried to interfere in Piper's plans.

Quinn could have done that easily enough. He was the Rangers' answer to persuading reluctant outlaws to offer needed information, after all. He was pretty sure he could have brought Roarke Sullivan around to Piper's way of thinking. So *why* had he offered marriage?

He was still mulling over that bothersome question when the procession stepped into the justice of the peace's office. Quinn came down with the worst case of the jitters he had ever experienced, thinking that his motives weren't as honorable as he wanted to believe. He shot Piper another uneasy glance, noting that she had that determined look he had come to recognize at a glance. Well, if she had the gumption to marry him then he would see this through.

He wished he could figure out why he had suggested this marriage in the first place. Could it have been because of vanity? Good God, was he like every other man who secretly wished to claim her as his own—just because of her striking beauty and enormous wealth? Damn it, that put him in the same category with the long list of suitors she had rejected. Quinn cringed at the thought of being included in that list.

And what if she met some young officer at the fort and fell in love? Then what was she supposed to do about the husband she had married for convenience? The solution to one problem could cause more problems, Quinn mused as he watched the official fumble around in his desk to locate the necessary document. What if Piper decided to divorce him in six months?

How would he feel about cutting her loose to marry another man? Or worse, what if she considered divorce an unacceptable solution and decided to have an affair with someone else?

"Where are those confounded licenses?" the official muttered, jolting Quinn back to the present. "Ah, yes, here we go."

The bald-headed justice of the peace laid the license on his desk, then glanced up. "Do you have a ring?"

Quinn dug into his pocket to retrieve the silver band he had purchased at the general store. It was cheap and unpretentious, but it was the best he had to offer on the spur of the moment.

It was an appropriate symbol of himself, he thought as he tucked the ring on his pinky finger for safekeeping.

His mind reeled as the official conducted the brief ceremony. Quinn choked out his I-dos and Piper did the same. And suddenly, they were man and wife.

When the official told him to kiss his bride, Quinn half turned to her, troubled by his ulterior motivations and feeling as awkward as all get-out about kissing her in front of his grinning colleagues. But when he stared into those silver-blue eyes and focused on those lush lips, he forgot there was anyone else in the office.

His mouth slanted over hers and his pulse kicked up. When he raised his head the taste of her was on his lips and desire sizzled in his loins. He was still staring into those hypnotic eyes when the Rangers closed in around him to pat him on the shoulder and whisper that they were envious of the fact that he had taken such a lovely bride. Disgruntled, he watched the five men place smacking pecks on Piper's cheek to offer their congratulations and good wishes.

Quinn slipped his arm possessively around her waist and shepherded her toward the door before his so-called friends helped themselves to a second round of kisses.

"Not so fast," the official called after him. "Sign your John Henry or this won't be legal."

Piper pivoted around to sign on the dotted line, then handed the pen to Quinn. With a quick slash of ink he made their marriage legal. Amused, he watched Piper roll up the document, then cram it into the sleeve of her gown.

She had what she wanted.

Why didn't *he* feel completely satisfied with this arrangement?

When they exited the Rangers announced they were going to the saloon to drink a toast to the newlyweds.

Piper glanced up at him. "I have reconsidered and decided you are right."

He frowned, bemused. "I'm right about what?"

"There is no need to make more of this marriage than what it is intended to be. If you want to join your friends, then feel free to go. I will have no difficulty occupying myself."

He should have been relieved that she had come to her senses and decided that consummating the marriage was a bad idea. Instead he felt hugely disappointed, even if it had been *his* suggestion. Nodding curtly, he turned to leave.

"Unless you can think of some reason why—"

"There's no reason to complicate matters," he interrupted abruptly, then mentally kicked himself when her shoulders stiffened and she glanced the other way.

"Right," she murmured. "Well then, I presume we will be leaving for the fort at dawn. I will see you then."

"Piper?"

When she turned back to him he noticed that her smile was strained and her chin had tilted to a defiant angle. "Good day, Callahan. Thank you for your cooperation. I appreciate the gesture."

And then she swept regally across the street, and Quinn wanted to shake her for being as detached as he tried to be. He expelled a frustrated sigh, recalling that when Piper was forthright and honest with her feelings he squirmed in his skin. When she closed up tighter than a clam he felt…well, he wasn't sure how he felt. Deprived, perhaps. A mite shut out, ignored and dissatisfied.

Hell! He had been married all of ten minutes and already he didn't know how to deal with his wife.

Scowling, Quinn traipsed down the street, then halted when he saw Red Hawk and Spotted Deer.

"So you made this marriage legal in your culture as well?" Red Hawk asked.

Quinn nodded.

Spotted Deer watched Piper disappear into the hotel, then turned his attention back to Quinn. "What strange custom doesn't allow a man to accompany his wife to his bed?" He shook his head in confusion. "I will never understand the ways of the palefaces, even if I now dress like one while riding with the Rangers."

"I will never understand *women*. One in particular," Quinn muttered in English.

The Comanches stared curiously at him.

"Never mind. I'll fetch you a drink to celebrate. Might even have a drink—or three—myself."

Then he walked into the saloon, wondering why Piper had become distant and standoffish today. Had he done something to upset her? Had he made her feel excluded during the trek to Catoosa Gulch? Or had she simply come to her senses and realized the worst thing she could do was to become physically involved with a man so far below her social status?

Quinn had felt rejected, discarded and unwanted plenty of times in his life. But every insecurity and inadequacy he had ever encountered converged on him abruptly.

Well, so what if Piper had changed her mind about bedding him. She wasn't the only female in town who could accommodate him. He could find companionship if he wanted it. And from someone who knew how the game was supposed to be played, he reminded himself.

On that sour thought he walked into the saloon to join his compatriots.

Piper paced from wall to wall, telling herself that she had made the right decision by retracting her request to experiment with passion. Too bad restless need had her fidgeting and wishing for something to occupy her mind.

Blast it, Quinn could have said something if he wanted to consummate their marriage. She had given him the opening and he had rejected it immediately. And why would he turn down such an offer? It didn't make sense.

Men! she thought in frustration. She would never figure out what made their minds work. Piper threw up her hands, muttered under her breath, and then shed her gown. She hurled the expensive garment against the wall in a fit of temper then scolded herself for behaving childishly.

When the license rolled from her dress sleeve she scooped it up. She had what she needed—the document that placed her beyond Roarke's control. It was better this way, she tried to convince herself for the umpteenth time. She had come to realize that she wanted all or nothing from Quinn. If she couldn't have his love then she wouldn't accept his lust, because she would ultimately wind up getting hurt.

"You are going to drive yourself crazy with thoughts like that," she admonished herself. "I doubt Quinn has been shown enough affection in his life to know what love is. Determined as you are, you can't *force* him to feel something for you that he doesn't feel. And you can't fault *him* because friendship is all he can offer you, either."

And curse those bandits for their untimely interruption last night, she fumed as she went back to circumnavigating the perimeter of her room. She could have satisfied her feminine curiosity and she wouldn't be wondering what she had missed and second-guessing herself right now.

She had no right whatsoever to be annoyed with Quinn, she reminded herself again. He had done nothing but save her life about half a dozen times, teach her to survive in the wilds and then marry her for *her* convenience.

He had done everything that a woman could ask of a man—except love her back.

"Stop wanting what you can't have," she scowled at herself.

Piper flounced on the bed and watched the lantern light flicker over the cracked plaster on the ceiling. Instead of wallowing in misery she should be anticipating her reunion with her sister and mentally preparing herself for her encounter with her father. A shame that Quinn's image kept bounding across the center stage of her mind to distract her.

The long and short of it was that, despite her sensible decision to marry him so she could gain control of her own destiny, she wanted *Quinn,* desired *him.* But the depressing truth was that he didn't need her. Her only lure and appeal was that she was *female.*

And if he sought out another women on their wedding night she was going to strangle him!

Quinn did not make a habit of overindulging in whiskey because he preferred to keep his senses sharp and his wits about him. But he was sorry to say that he showed no restraint whatsoever while drinking with his friends.

He was shamelessly drunk when he finally wobbled from the saloon. His bleary gaze went immediately to the hotel where a dim light burned in room seven.

"The hell with her," he mumbled as he staggered down the street.

It was *her* fault that he couldn't see straight right now. *Her* fault that the prospect of seeking out another female felt like betrayal and held no appeal for him.

This is what happened when a man stopped being realistic and started entertaining impossible whims, he decided.

And why *had* she changed her mind this evening? Quinn frowned. Or at least he thought he did. His facial muscles were so numb that he couldn't be sure. Well, he was gonna march right up there and ask her why she had decided not to consummate their marriage. She could tell him the truth flat-out like she used to do before he did whatever the hell he had done that caused her to retreat emotionally from him.

"Yeah, that's wha' I'll do. Jus' ask her," he mumbled. "Ooooff—" Quinn staggered back when he collided with a solid form in the darkness.

"Where are you going, Gray Owl?" Red Hawk asked.

"To see my wife."

Spotted Owl turned him around then gestured east. "This direction. But I think you have had too much firewater."

Quinn shrugged off their concern and lurched from their grasp. Straightening his twisted jacket, he weaved unsteadily down the street. "I'm takin' Pipe' to the fort, t'morrow. Report to Butler."

That said, he started off. When he entered the hotel he grabbed a quick breath then tackled the mountain of steps that stood between him and his maddening bride.

Piper shot straight up in bed when she heard the clatter and thud in the distance. Like a shot, she bounded from bed to grab the chair as her impromptu weapon.

Cautiously, she stepped into the hall. Another grunt and thud caught her attention so she went to investigate.

To her stunned amazement she saw Quinn sprawled at the bottom of the stairs. "What the blazes happened?"

"Missed a step," he mumbled as he rolled onto his back then peered up at her.

The slur in his voice indicated his condition. She frowned disapprovingly. "You are drunk."

"I know." He stirred like an overturned beetle, then came to his knees to clutch at the banister. When he tried to stand up he swayed and nearly fell off his feet.

"Oh, for heaven's sake." Ignoring the fact that she was clad in nothing but the chemise that barely covered her thighs, she bounded down the steps to offer support.

With his arm draped over her shoulder and one hand secured to the railing she assisted him up the steps. Huffing for breath, Piper steered him into the room, then went back to retrieve the chair she had left in the hall.

"Your garb's a mite skimpy. Walk out like that in public and you'll land flat on your back. Guaran-damn-teed."

"I hadn't planned on leaving the privacy of my bed until someone tumbled down the steps." She crossed her arms over her chest and stared at him. "Why are you here, Quinn?"

He drew himself up, then sucked in a deep breath that made his chest swell like an inflated toad's. Piper bit back a grin. The man looked adorably rumpled and not at all his usual well-disciplined, restrained self.

"Wanted to ask you a question."

"Fine. Fire away."

"What'd I do to make you change your mind?" He

shrugged off his coat and tossed it at the chair—and missed it by a mile. "Las' night you wanted me. Today you don't. Honest t' God, Pipe'. I dunno know how to deal with you and it's drivin' me nuts."

He plopped down on the edge of the bed to battle his way out of his shirt. When he launched it across the room it landed in the basin on the commode. "And you know what else?"

"I give up. What else?" she asked, muffling an amused snicker.

"I was gonna trot down the street to find a willin' female, just to show you."

She arched her brow and jealousy shot through her like venom. "To show me what? That this marriage isn't worth the paper it's written on and that I mean nothing to you?"

"To show you that I didn't care if you brushed me off. O'course, we both know it's better this way. I didn't deserve you in the first place. Sure as hell don't deserve to be married to a blue-blooded heiress."

There he went again, selling himself short. Piper refused to listen to that nonsense. She stamped up in front of him to wag her finger in his bronzed face. "You listen to me, Callahan. You don't get to criticize yourself. That's what *I'm* here for. What you *do* deserve is the *hangover* you'll likely wake up with tomorrow. And that is *all*. The fact is that *you* happen to be the nicest man I know. I will not tolerate these self-deprecating comments from you, so please hush up."

She yanked off his boots then tossed them aside. He braced himself on his arms and peered at her with those hypnotic golden eyes that were fanned with long, tangled lashes. The woebegone expression on his face made her chest cave in. If he didn't stop burrowing into her heart she *was* going to fall head over heels for him. Completely overwhelmed by a myriad of tender feelings for him.

And then where would she be? So deep in longing and misery that she would never find her way out.

"I couldn't bear the thought of touching another woman when you're the only one I want," he murmured.

His admission hit Piper right where she lived. She would have thrown herself into his arms if he hadn't looked so unstable and disoriented. Plus, she couldn't be certain that it wasn't whiskey-induced lust talking.

Maybe she had unintentionally set herself up as a challenge to him after she had denied him his husbandly rights. That, after practically begging him to make love to her the previous night. And still nothing had happened between them.

Just as nothing was going to happen tonight. Quinn was so soused that he probably wouldn't even *remember* if she seduced him now.

Just as she hadn't remembered what happened between them while she had been under the influence of peyote.

Exasperated, Piper grabbed his legs and swung him onto the bed. She wheeled around to douse the lantern she had forgotten to attend before she had fallen asleep. Padding barefoot to the bed, she noticed Quinn had already conked out. She shoved his shoulder, encouraging him to roll over so she could lie down beside him.

"Honest to goodness, you and I simply have one devil of a time getting our timing right, don't we?" she asked her oblivious husband. "Between unexpected interruptions and on-again-off-again fits and spurts of desire, we might never share one night together." She sighed heavily as she stared down at him. "Maybe you're right. Maybe this *thing* between us—whatever the devil it is—simply isn't meant to be."

Now here was a wedding night that will go down in the annals of marital history as disaster, she thought in exasperation.

When Quinn sighed heavily in his sleep, Piper instinctively cuddled up to him. She looped her arm around his waist and pressed her cheek to the muscled contours of his back. She knew she was missing out on her last chance at passion with him. It was that disgruntled thought that followed her to sleep.

Chapter Thirteen

Sometime during the night Quinn rolled sideways and felt a soft, fragrant presence beside him. Although his senses were still a bit groggy he knew instinctively that he was in bed with Piper. He couldn't recall how he had gotten here and the distasteful prospect that he had forced himself on her while intoxicated made him feel like a jackass.

Sweet mercy, had he hurt her?

The thought made him grimace. He shifted again, and then realized he was still wearing his breeches. Surely that was a good sign. Hesitantly he reached over to brush his hand over Piper's hip and made stimulating contact with her silky flesh. He swallowed hard as he skimmed his hand higher to find the soft fabric of her chemise gathered around her waist.

Damn it to hell, if he had taken her innocence with no regard for her pleasure he was going to climb right out of this bed and shoot himself.

"Piper?" he whispered as he pressed a kiss to her cheek.

She moaned softly, then squirmed closer. Her breasts brushed against his chest and her knee insinuated itself between his thighs. Desire rocketed through him and intense need left him hard and aching. Drawn to her, he tilted her face to his kiss, striving for tender patience as he savored the delicious taste of her.

"Mmm," she murmured drowsily. Her arm glided over his shoulder to caress him. "Do that again."

And so he did. He lost himself in the seductive scent and feel of her. His hands drifted down her hip to trace her inner thigh, then ascended to encircle her breasts. She arched toward him, filling his hand with her satiny flesh. He angled his head to flick his tongue over her pebbled nipples and felt her tremble against him. Her soft sigh left him yearning to draw more of those satisfied sounds from her.

Shifting beside her, he explored the length of her legs, the shapely curve of her hip and concave belly. He tossed aside the sheet to study her in the moonlight that sprayed through the window—and lost his breath when he stared at feminine perfection. Her pale skin glowed pearly white in the light and his admiring gaze swept over her again and again.

Awed by the sight of her lush body, he bent his head to spread a trail of featherlight kisses from the crests of her full breasts to her belly button.

Caught between dreams and wakefulness she arched toward him and his name tumbled from her lips. Quinn knew beyond all doubt that he wouldn't be satisfied until he had learned her luscious body by touch and taste, until he had given her pleasure to counter whatever pain and disappointment he might have caused her earlier.

Nudging her thighs apart with his elbows, he eased between her legs. When he brushed his fingertips over her secret flesh he found her hot and wet and so tempting that he shuddered with a need so intense that it shocked him. As much as he wanted to sink into her sultry fire and surround himself in the sweet essence of her body, he refused to rush this moment. He stroked her gently, felt her burning his fingertips like sensual lightning and savored her uninhibited response to his touch.

When he flicked at her with his tongue and offered her the most intimate of kisses she hissed out her breath and quivered around him. Her hand clamped on to his shoulder, as if anchoring herself against the rush of pleasure that crested upon her.

Quinn smiled against her flesh when her nails dug deeply into his skin, testifying that she was teetering on the edge of wild abandon. That's exactly how he wanted this maddening female who turned him wrong side out, upside down and backward. He wanted her *wild* and *abandoned* and so hungry for him that nothing else mattered. He wanted the memory of his touch to be burned forever on her body, claiming her as his own.

And that, he realized suddenly, was the reason he had been so troubled and tormented on the way to the wedding ceremony. Marrying her was his excuse, but the real reason was that deep down, he did want her all to himself, despite what was best for both of them.

He felt the ripples of pleasure assail her body as he

dipped his fingertip inside her and stroked her gently. He heard her breath catch when he glided two fingers deep inside her, stretching her tight passage to accept him.

He reached down to free himself from his breeches, then kicked them away. When he stared down at Piper her eyes were wide open and she was peering up at him with an expression of urgent need. He bent his head, letting her taste the flavor of her passion on his lips as he moved carefully against her.

Ardent desire hammered at him, but he forced himself to slow down, allowing her time to adjust to his masculine invasion. He felt her body stiffen momentarily, felt her hands lock behind his neck as her breath came out on a wobbly sigh.

When he sank into her satiny warmth and felt the fragile barrier give way he squeezed his eyes shut, relieved that *this* was their first encounter and that he hadn't come to her in a drunken daze.

At least he had done something right. For once.

"I thought I would never have you," she whispered against the side of his neck. "You were well worth the wait…is there more?"

Quinn grinned at her naivete. "Wait and see."

He withdrew slightly, drawing her mumbled protest. Then he drove into her and she purred her pleasure. He hooked his elbows under her knees and pressed closer still before he pulled away once again.

Her eyes widened as he buried himself to the hilt and then eased away. "Tormentor of women," she accused, then smiled impishly and said, "More."

He chuckled, amazed that he felt like laughing and

screaming simultaneously. He should have known that bedding his spirited wife would be as unique and unforgettable as she was. Whatever Quinn had felt after other liaisons didn't compare to the feelings and emotions that bombarded him when he was with Piper.

It would have been easier if this was purely physical, he knew. But there was nothing simple or uncomplicated between them. Sparks always flew between them, especially now.

When she urged him deeper Quinn braced his hands beside her shoulders and moved above her, inside her. Need expanded and devoured as he drove against her, faster and faster when she demanded even more from him. He felt like a blazing meteor hurtling toward its own fiery destruction, felt his pulse pounding in his ears as overwhelming desire avalanched upon him.

When Piper's body contracted around him and her breath hissed from between her clamped teeth he felt immeasurable pleasure burgeoning, exploding, and catapulting him into oblivion. He shuddered helplessly and collapsed against her.

When he realized that he was squashing her he braced himself up on his elbows, preparing to move away.

"Not yet," she insisted as she clamped her arms around his waist. "I swear I'll feel empty without you."

The fact that he was thinking the same thing unsettled him. Quinn was very much afraid he would never experience this much intense emotion and pleasure again in his life. He had discovered it only when he and Piper were one living, breathing entity.

That was such a dangerous thought that Quinn quickly discarded it and tried to pull away.

"You're doing it again," she said quietly.

"Doing what?"

"Shutting me out. Tell me what you're thinking."

He wasn't sure he wanted her to know that she had gotten to him as no one ever had, didn't want her to know that he was dreaming of impossibilities in a future they would never share together. This had to be just about passion, no matter what else he thought he was feeling at the moment. He had to remember that. For *her* sake as well as his.

"I'm thinking that I need to ask you a favor, considering that you owe me a few times over for saving your life."

She smiled, her eyes sparkling in the dim moonlight. "Since you put me in such an agreeable mood, ask away."

He traced the curve of her Cupid's bow lips with his forefinger. "Passion could be the illusion that makes you agreeable at the moment. But whatever you do, Piper, don't fancy yourself in love with me. That's the last thing either of us need."

Her smile vanished. "Why would that be so bad?"

"Because as good as it is between us, we have no future," he told her solemnly. "No matter which way we turn it, we both know I'm the last man you need and that I have nothing to offer you."

When he withdrew, making the distance between them seem like miles, Piper turned her back to him. He was still doing it, damn him. He was trying to dictate what was best for her.

God save her from men who kept trying to save her from herself!

"Someday you are going to wish I loved you if only so you could say that someone had," she told him. She fought back the tears that sprang to her eyes—and hated the display of weakness. "Then it will be too late."

"Piper, the last thing I want to do is to hurt you," he whispered as he stroked her arm, trying to soothe her.

She silently cursed him, thinking he was hurting her *now* and wanting to clobber him for taking something so incredibly remarkable and satisfying and ruining it by telling her what she should or shouldn't do.

Piper squeezed her eyes shut and held on to the sweet, delicious memories of their passion. He couldn't steal them from her, ever. For one marvelous, mind-boggling moment out of time in a place where outside influences couldn't interfere Quinn Callahan had belonged to her completely.

That would have been enough to satisfy her, if she had wanted passion only for passion's sake. But she wanted his heart and soul, as well as his body.

Dream on, silly fool, she chided herself before she drifted off to sleep. *You will never have his heart. That is the one irrefutable fact that you can't change.*

The next morning Piper eased off the bed and dressed in her riding breeches. A smile pursed her lips as she glanced back at Quinn who was sprawled facedown in bed. The night they had spent together had been everything she had anticipated and more.

Except for the fact that he was never going to return these tender feelings she held for him.

She could have loved him forever if he had let her.

Her thoughts trailed off when he shifted and the sheet glided to his hips. Piper stared at the puckered red scars that crisscrossed his back. Again, fury at his unfair mistreatment hurtled through her and she silently cursed the bastard who had taken a whip to Quinn.

She eased down on her knees to lightly trace the scars, wishing she could magically erase the hardships and pain he had suffered in his lifetime. When she thought of how many times he'd had to harden his heart to endure rejection, scorn and mistreatment she realized why it was difficult for Quinn to reach out to anyone. Even her. Life had taught him to be overly cautious and to harbor no dreams and expectations.

Withdrawing, Piper crammed her clothes into her satchel then tiptoed toward the door. She planned to be ready and waiting to ride to the fort when Quinn ventured downstairs.

She had just finished strapping her belongings behind the saddle of her horse when she heard the jangle of harnesses and clatter of a wagon approaching. Her eyes widened in disbelief when she saw the blond-haired woman perched on the seat beside a uniformed officer.

"Penelope?" she shrieked excitedly. She dashed into the street, startling the guards that surrounded the army supply wagon.

And found herself staring at the spitting end of several army-issued pistols.

Penelope bolted to her feet and motioned for the

guards to holster their weapons. "Piper, you're finally here! Dear God, I was so worried when I heard that two passengers were believed dead after a coach crash on the stage route."

When Penelope alighted from the wagon Piper dashed around the team of horses to give her a fierce hug. Dozens of pleasurable childhood memories enveloped her while she clung to Penny for a long, gratifying moment.

Penny reared back to look at Piper. "You look absolutely wonderful, except for that tan on your face." Her blue eyes sparkled with familiar mischief. "Papa would pitch a fit. After all, proper ladies are supposed to have milky white complexions, you know."

Piper snickered as she studied her sister's tanned cheeks, sun-bleached blond hair and trim, statuesque physique. "We are a discredit to our elevated status in society. 'We are *the* Sullivans of Galveston and we have our reputations to maintain,'" she declared, quoting the comment she had heard their father make endless times. "Speaking of which, Papa is on his way here. I thought perhaps he had beaten me to the fort after the wreck waylaid me and I had to take a time-consuming detour with my guide. I expect Papa to show up any time."

"Papa is coming?" Penny's eyes rounded. "To drag you back, no doubt. This should be interesting."

Piper pulled a face. "Doesn't sound like that much fun to me." She glanced at the armed guards then frowned curiously. "What are you doing here with this entourage?"

Penny gestured for the driver to toss down her carpetbag. "A friend of mine lives on a ranch between here and the garrison. I spent the night with her, then caught the freight wagon into town while Matthew is checking out the rumor that Apaches are roaming the area. I was hoping that I might come across you here so we could ride back to the fort together."

She directed Piper's attention to the armed guards. "Matthew insisted that a patrol accompany me during my ride home." She wrinkled her nose disconcertedly. "He has become overly protective of late because we are expecting a child in seven months."

Piper chuckled delightedly as she hugged Penny again. "I'm going to be an aunt? Splendid!"

Grabbing Piper's hand, Penny pulled her toward the general store. "I need to pick up a few supplies before we head back to the garrison. We can be on our way in just a few minutes."

Piper glanced back toward the hotel, wondering if Quinn would make an appearance before she left town. Maybe it would be best if he didn't, she mused. Considering the *favor* that he asked of her last night, perhaps she should leave him to his duties without awkward goodbyes. Escorting her to the fort would only cause another delay and she had caused him enough of them already.

When she noticed the Rangers lingering around the jail she wrung her hand from her sister's grasp. "I'll be along in a minute. I need to say goodbye to the Rangers."

Penny glanced at the hard-bitten group of men, nodded, then headed into the store.

"My sister, Penelope, arrived unexpectedly," Piper explained as she halted in front of the men.

Commander Butler chuckled as he watched Penny disappear from sight. "So we noticed. Two peas in a pod, I'd say. We were standing here, trying to decide which one of you is the most attractive. Then we gave up and called it a draw."

Piper smiled impishly. "Unfortunately for both of us we have similar dispositions. Our father swore we were the curses of his life."

"With two fetching daughters to watch over and protect, I'm not surprised. It would be a daunting responsibility."

Piper frowned pensively, wondering if Butler had hit upon a fact that she had overlooked. Perhaps their father had gone overboard on being domineering and protective because he felt he had been left to single-handedly raise and groom his daughters to take their place in society. Reason or not, it had been difficult to deal with Roarke's exasperating decrees and his habit of trying to map out his daughters' lives.

"Since Quinn hasn't come downstairs yet, tell him there is no need to escort me to the fort," Piper requested, tossing aside her thoughts. "Four armed soldiers will accompany us."

Butler studied her speculatively for a moment. "Are you sure that is what you want?"

"I'm sure," Piper confirmed before she held out her hand. "It was an honor and privilege to meet all of you."

That said, she spun on her heels and strode into the store to join Penny. Within a few minutes the freight wagon headed off to restock supplies in San Antonio and Piper and Penny left town, accompanied by Lucky, surrounded by an armed patrol.

"I want to hear all about your journey west. Your courage impresses me, Pi."

Piper gaped at her sister. "*My* courage?"

"Heavens, yes. You struck out on your own without a chaperone to face unforeseen difficulties in this wild country. Most women wouldn't attempt the feat."

"You were the one with gumption," Piper contended. "You stood up to Papa and held firm when he rejected *you* and loudly objected to your decision to marry Matt."

"But I had Matt for moral support and protection, not to mention the patrol of soldiers that accompanied us west," Penny countered. "What I did was nothing in comparison. But then, *you* always were a bit more precocious and daring than I was. So...tell me about your adventures and how you survived the wreck."

While they followed the route into another mountain range of jutting stone peaks and deep canyons Piper offered her sister a detailed account of the trip, while disguised as an old crone.

Penny snickered in amusement. "I wish I could have seen your impersonation of Miss Johnson. She is a sourpuss of the worst sort." She shook her head in dismay. "I cannot tell you how many times I wanted to whack that pucker-face old bat for sniping at me to stand up straight and harping at me to watch my disrespectful tone of voice."

"The plan worked perfectly to ensure men kept their

distance. Obviously the male of the species doesn't appreciate Miss Johnson's sharp tongue and snippy remarks any better than we do."

Piper went on to describe the stage wreck and her arduous journey to Dead Man's Canyon to reconnoiter the outlaws' stronghold with Quinn. However, she didn't mention her hasty marriage. Piper decided to save that until Roarke showed up to drag her home—which was *not* going to happen, she promised herself resolutely. She had come too far and endured too much not to see her dream of independence come true.

And where was Roarke? she wondered as she glanced back in the direction they had come. Wherever he was, Piper doubted that he had given up, turned around and gone home. She also wondered if Roarke would reverse his decision to disown Penny when he learned that he would soon be a grandfather.

Discovering that Penny was expecting and that Piper was married should set Roarke back on his heels, she predicted. Plus, with Penny's husband on hand, and surrounded by a garrison of soldiers, Piper was fairly confident she wouldn't be hauled away against her will.

For once Roarke would be out of his element and unable to wield the power of his influential position in Galveston. Piper smiled wryly at the thought.

Her thoughts wandered back to Quinn while Penny chattered about the new accommodations that had been constructed at the fort and then described the rancher's wife she had befriended. Hearing that Penny was satisfied with her life on the frontier filled Piper with a sense of envy. Penny had Matt's complete devotion and affection. Piper had no one who cared deeply about her. A shame that Quinn wasn't capable of that kind of commitment. Piper would have gladly compromised her independence in order to share his life.

But he didn't want her. He might as well have come right out and said so last night.

She glanced at her sister who looked happy, healthy and well-adjusted. She and Quinn might have had the same thing if he could have returned her affection. But he couldn't. Or wouldn't. It didn't really matter which, she supposed.

The humiliating truth was that he simply didn't want her.

Well, she hoped Quinn was happy that she had ridden out of his life. As for Piper, she missed him already and she had only been gone an hour. She tried to convince herself that a promising new life awaited her, but she wanted more.

Who would have thought that her cherished freedom would become a distant second to what she suddenly wanted in life?

"Good God…" Quinn groaned when he awakened to hear tom-toms thumping against his skull. He swore that a miniature war party was practicing its usual ritual before charging into battle.

His mouth felt like cotton. Even his eyelids ached. Much as he hated to do it, he pried open one bloodshot eye then slammed it shut when piercing sunlight tried to bore holes in his eyeballs.

This, he reminded himself, was why he didn't drink to excess.

His stomach pitched and rolled as he crawled off the edge of the bed. With extreme effort, he raised his head and opened both eyes. The room spun furiously and he breathed deeply until his groggy senses cleared up. Somewhat at least.

A few minutes later he rose to his feet and scrubbed his hands over his face. He glanced around the empty room, noting that Piper and her satchel were gone. No doubt she had gone over to the café to grab a bite to eat before they headed to the fort.

Sluggishly, Quinn walked over to soak his head in the basin of water Piper had refilled after her unpleasant encounter with the ruffian. Feeling a mite refreshed, Quinn gathered up his clothes and grimaced at the thought of jostling around on the back of a horse with a queasy stomach.

Well, one good thing might come of this, he mused as he fastened his moccasins and leggings in place. If they should happen onto Roarke Sullivan, Quinn would be in the perfect mood for a fight, because right now it wouldn't take much to aggravate him.

Scooping up his gear, Quinn headed downstairs. When he stepped outside he inhaled a deep, cleansing breath. Then Quinn made a beeline for the café to gulp down a much-needed cup of coffee.

He nodded a greeting to the Rangers who were lounging at a table, and then he frowned curiously when he didn't see Piper with them. He wondered if the Comanche warriors were dogging her steps to keep a close eye on her as he had asked. He certainly hoped so. Quinn had certainly fallen down on the job after last night's losing battle with whiskey.

Commander Butler smiled wryly as Quinn took a seat at the table. "You look like hell."

"Glad to hear I don't look better than I feel." Quinn mumbled a quiet, "Gracias," when the Mexican waitress set a cup of steaming coffee in front of him. He glanced at Butler. "Are the reinforcements here yet?"

"We're expecting them anytime," he replied. "I sent Cooper to alert the townsfolk that trouble might be brewing. I'm hoping Piper's suggestion of letting those bandits come to us works. I don't relish the thought of riding through rough terrain to reach their canyon fortress. If they want their Mexican cohorts freed from jail then they can ride into town and try to take them from us."

Quinn sipped his coffee, then turned his attention to the plate of food the waitress delivered. He was halfway through his meal when Tom Pendleton strode inside, followed by eight Rangers that patrolled the area west of Van Horn. While Butler briefed the men on the situation, Quinn heaved himself to his feet.

"Where are you going?"

"To find Piper. The sooner I deliver her to the fort the sooner I can get back here."

"She left already."

"What?" Quinn hooted then grabbed his sensitive head.

"Her sister came up with the supply wagon and then they headed toward the fort with an armed patrol." Butler grinned. "It was quite a reunion. Piper and Penelope nearly hugged the stuffing out of each other in the middle of the street. Oh, and Piper said to tell you goodbye."

Butler stared intently at Quinn, as if gauging his reaction. "She seemed to think you would be relieved that you had fulfilled your obligations to her."

The news left Quinn with an odd, empty feeling in the pit of his belly. She was gone from his life? Just like that? She planned to take on her father alone?

Of course she did. Knowing her, she had decided that dealing with Roarke was just another obstacle she had to overcome, another test she had to pass to gain her long-awaited freedom.

Maybe this was for the best, he mused. He and Piper had parted company without any awkward goodbyes. Now he could focus on his vow to see the bandits brought to justice. Taylor Briggs might have paid the ultimate sacrifice, but those bastards were not going to get away with murder, not if Quinn and the other Rangers had a say in the matter.

When the commander requested that Quinn add his two cents' worth to preparations for the upcoming confrontation Quinn tried to concentrate on his duties. But an uneasy feeling kept hounding him. True, things felt unsettled between him and Piper, but something else niggled him.

Finally he shrugged off the unexplainable sensation and chalked it up to the unfamiliar emotions Piper stirred in him. Then he got down to the serious business of planning an attack on the desperadoes who had been creating havoc in southwest Texas.

Chapter Fourteen

Roy Morrell touched his swollen lip, then cursed the spitfire who had defied his amorous advances and clobbered him with the porcelain pitcher and the chair. He spat another curse at that vicious Ranger who had come to the woman's defense. Both of them were going to pay dearly for the assault, he vowed spitefully.

He had ridden half the night to call in reinforcements from the stronghold that he and his brother had established the previous year in Dead Man's Canyon. He and his brother, Sam, had amassed a small fortune and their organized ring of thieves had raked in profits galore. But those pesky Rangers constantly caused interference by capturing or killing their gang members.

Now, the Mexicans that were a crucial part of the operation were locked in jail. Two of the Morrell cousins were serving time in the penitentiary at Huntsville. And some of them were dead, their youngest brother Charley included.

"Those sonsabitches will rue the day," Roy muttered to Sam.

From their vantage point on the hill overlooking Catoosa Gulch, Roy peered through the spyglass. He carefully appraised the group of Rangers that exited the café. Then he glanced south to survey the small army patrol that followed the road to the fort. A devilish grin spread across Roy's lips, and then he winced at the pain caused by the mind-boggling blows he had sustained the previous afternoon.

"Ah, good fortune is with us," Roy declared when he noticed the two blond-haired women riding with the soldiers.

"Good fortune?" Sam Morrell snorted derisively. "Not when those devil Rangers have decided to sit back and make us come to them. Curse those stupid Mexicans for getting themselves jailed! We could have used their firepower to battle the Rangers. Now there they sit."

He scowled in disgust. "Our connections across the border won't do us any good if we can't sell the stolen beef in Mexico. We damn sure can't drive the cattle north to the railheads without inviting more trouble from those roaming bands of Rangers."

Roy sniggered as he handed the spyglass to his brother. "Our ace in the hole. One of the women with the patrol is that bastard Ranger's woman. The other one is a soldier's wife. I've seen her before. We'll have all the bargaining power we need if we take the women captive."

A wide grin spread across Sam's stubbled face as he peered at the procession in the distance. Then he glanced at the well-armed men who awaited his orders. "There are plenty of box canyons in these mountains to serve as a deathtrap for the Rangers. Phantom Springs comes quickly to mind."

Roy nodded in fiendish delight. "Perfect for our ambush. Even better that half the cavalry at the fort is out chasing a supposed band of Apaches that raided two ranches to the west."

"Hell of an idea you came up with to impersonate renegade Indians and have some of our men loot the ranches. The Apaches are taking the blame for those robberies."

Roy smiled, well pleased with himself. "We'll keep the army confused while we take our revenge on those cussed Rangers."

"It shouldn't be too hard since we outnumber the Rangers more than two to one. Plus, the army troops won't even know about the kidnappings until it's too late because they are tracking the imaginary Apaches."

Sam handed the spyglass to Roy, then motioned for his cohorts to follow the ridge that overlooked the road. "We'll come at the military patrol from three directions at once," he ordered. "They will have nowhere to run except straight up the stone cliff beside them."

"I get first turn with that wildcat that tried to claw out my eyes," Roy insisted as the bandits rode south.

Sam raised a thick brow and smirked. "Think you can handle her? Looks like *she* left her mark on *you* before the Ranger roughed you up."

"I'll handle her all right," Roy growled. "When I'm through with her I'll pass her around among our men.

That devil Ranger that dresses like a savage won't want her when we've finished with her. Not that he'll have the chance because he's the first man I want to see dead."

Piper marveled at the perpendicular walls of the western cliff that looked to be layered in limestone, sandstone and granite. The steep rise of the mountains beside the trail was every bit as rugged and impressive as the range to the northeast where she and Quinn…

Don't think about him, she lectured herself. He preferred to be a closed chapter in her life and there was nothing she could do about that.

"Why so glum, Pi?" Penny questioned perceptively. "Having second thoughts about living in the middle of nowhere?"

Piper gave herself a mental shake and flashed a smile. "No. I'm exactly where I want to be," she said, although her first choice would have been to be with Quinn.

"Then what's bothering you? And don't tell me *nothing.* We might have been separated for two years, but I *know* you."

Piper had intended to delay her announcement about the marriage, but she suddenly felt the need to confide in her sister. For a time Quinn had been her confidante, but the closeness they had shared was over and done and she had to accept that.

"There was this man," she began.

"Ah, isn't that the story of a woman's life." Penny snickered as she swept out her arm in an expansive gesture. "Just look where my handsome prince brought me. My castle is the mountain range and my knights are soldiers." She shrugged lackadaisically. "Ah, well, my fairy tale might be a bit off the mark, but I'm not disappointed."

Piper grinned. "This region seems to agree with you."

"It does," Penny said, then frowned curiously at Piper. "Did this man you mentioned jilt you? Is that why you decided to head west?"

"No. I met him on the stage and he has saved my life several times since then."

Penny raised her brows in surprise. "This Callahan character? The Ranger looking for the bandits' stronghold? *He's* the one?"

Piper fidgeted beneath her sister's probing stare. "Yes, we sort of made a bargain."

Penny's gaze narrowed warily. "*Sort of?* What does that mean *exactly?*"

Piper inhaled a deep breath then said, "He agreed to marry me for protection against Papa's inevitable attempt to drag me home."

Penny's astounded gaze dropped to the plain silver band on Piper's finger. "You married the Ranger you had only just met?" she croaked.

Given Penny's shocked reaction Piper could only imagine Roarke's response. No doubt, he would erupt like a volcano.

"It is a marriage of convenience that provides me with a legal document," she explained. "Plus, spending days on end together in the wilderness is more intense than your courtship with Matt. I observed the best and worst of Quinn's moods. I was also impressed by his skills and learned a great deal about survival from him. How long did it take *you* to gain that kind of insight about Matt?"

Penny chortled at the challenging question. "Okay, Pi, you've made your point. We did face a period of adjustment after our wedding. But *really,* a convenient marriage? I thought that was exactly what Papa had planned for you with that dandy named Foster." She shrugged nonchalantly. "Well, at least you didn't fall in love with Callahan. That would have been a disastrous complication."

When Piper stared straight ahead, refusing to meet her gaze, Penny frowned suspiciously. "Please tell me that you don't have romantic feelings—"

Piper never had the chance to reply. A volley of bullets erupted from out of nowhere and she sprawled over her horse as Quinn had taught her to do. Penny had the good sense to do the same. The soldiers encircled them as gunfire rained down from three different directions. Piper muttered in dismay when she saw the band of desperadoes, a few of whom she recognized from the stage holdup, pour down from the tumble of rocky hills.

When one of the soldiers grabbed his shoulder then toppled from his horse, Piper dismounted to grab the pistol he thrust at her.

"Head to the fort as fast as you can!" he said with a pained grimace. "We'll try to provide cover."

To Piper's way of thinking there was no holding off these banditos. The hapless patrol was woefully outnumbered and surrounded. Clutching the reins to her jittery mount, she pulled herself back into the saddle then fired the weapon wildly.

She wasn't sure who was more surprised when the discharging bullet caught one of her attackers in the thigh. But it gave Piper time to dig in her heels and thunder down the road, with Penny matching the swift pace she set.

Piper cursed in frustration when ten scraggly outlaws appeared to block her escape route. Ten loaded pistols were aimed at her chest and she had only one firearm aimed at the vicious-looking group of banditos who held her and her sister at gunpoint. She growled under her breath when she recognized the greasy-haired scoundrel who had tried to attack her at the hotel the previous afternoon.

"So we meet again, bitch," Roy Morrell snarled hatefully. "Wanna guess how our next encounter turns out?"

Despite the lopsided odds, Piper kept her weapon trained on her nemesis. She glanced at the outlaw beside him—the one she had nicknamed Silver Spurs during the stage robbery. The family resemblance between these two men was striking. Brothers, she guessed. Same greasy hair and beady black eyes. Same beaked nose and nonexistent chin.

"I've heard about you," Silver Spurs said. "Roy had nothing good to say, of course."

"We've met before," Piper surprised him by saying. "Obviously you have forgotten the old widow from the stage holdup."

Silver Spurs's bushy brows shot up. "Should've known. Same smart mouth." He glanced at his brother. "I'll be next in line after you take your turn with her, Roy."

Piper refused to react to the intimidating threat. Neither did she drop the pistol when ordered to do so. She knew she couldn't shoot her way out of here, but innate defiance wouldn't allow her to meekly submit.

"Sam, take her pistol. If she so much as blinks I'll blow her out of the saddle."

Piper waited until Sam was directly in front of her before she gouged her heels into her mount's flanks. The two horses collided. Her forward momentum caused Sam's horse to rear up. Then Piper headed directly for Roy.

Penny was right behind her, plowing into the other horses, causing them to bolt skittishly away.

Piper and Penny might have had a sporting chance, too, if one of the nearby riders hadn't lunged sideways to club her in the back of the head with the butt of his rifle. Behind her, she heard Penny's outraged shriek, but there was nothing Piper could do to help her sister. The blow to her head caused her to wilt forward in the saddle. Piper battled valiantly to remain conscious while Penny's railing voice sentenced every last desperado to the farthest reaches of hell.

Piper tried to upright herself when Sam jerked the pistol from her fingertips. But her body slumped again and she blacked out, serenaded by her sister's colorful curses.

Her last thought was that Roarke would suffer apoplexy if he could hear Penny swearing like a soldier.

After lunch, Quinn was beginning to feel human again. He had met with the reinforcements from Van Horn twice, then returned to the jail with Commander Butler on his heels.

He had heard firsthand from one of the Mexicans that

there was indeed a plot to lure the Rangers into a death-trap—to retaliate against the death of the ringleaders' younger brother. Roy Morrell was the rascal Quinn had tangled with in Piper's hotel room. According to the information Quinn gleaned, Roy and his brother, Sam, had blamed the Rangers for Charley's cold-blooded murder.

"Never heard such a twisted version of that show-down at Wolf Creek," Butler said as he came to stand on the boardwalk beside Quinn. "Hell, I was there last year. Same as you were. Horse and cattle thieves, every last one of them. We had the branded animals as evidence. If memory serves that gang of outlaws fired on us first. That young outlaw fell off his stolen horse with his pistol still smoking in his hand."

"My recollection exactly. One of the bandits winged Tom Pendleton and he has the scar to prove it. Of course, you can't expect a gang of liars, murderers and thieves to get their story straight. Haven't met one of them yet who didn't crow about a case of mistaken identity and swear on a stack of Bibles that he was completely innocent."

Butler snickered. "That is a fact, Cal. I—"

His voice trailed off when he noticed two men from the army patrol riding into town. He jerked upright, then darted toward them.

An uneasy sensation skittered down Quinn's spine as he followed in the commander's wake. "What's wrong?"

"These men escorted Piper and her sister to the fort. Damn it, where is the rest of the group!"

Quinn forgot to breathe as he surged past Butler to

reach the soldiers who had been tied to their saddles. His heart plummeted to his belly when he noticed the padded black gown Piper had worn while charading as Widow Agatha. The garment was draped over one of the horses.

Fury blazed through Quinn's veins and curses exploded from his lips. He had sworn all manner of vengeance after these bandits killed Taylor Briggs. Quinn promised even more wrath now because what he had felt for his friend didn't compare to the intensity of emotions that riddled him now.

Knowing how daring and defiant Piper could be, Quinn cringed at the prospect of her response to being captured.

He didn't even have to ask to know that Piper and Penelope had been adducted as bait for the trap. The grim expression on the soldiers' faces told the tale.

"Cap'n Duncan will have our heads," the injured corporal muttered. "His wife is with child and the cap'n didn't want her to make this trip in the first place. But she's a determined lady and wouldn't be refused her request."

If Quinn hadn't been so worried, he might have smiled at the comment. He had the unmistakable feeling that Penelope was as headstrong as Piper.

"I swore that daredevil sister of Miz Duncan's was gonna get herself killed when the bandits surrounded her," the dark-haired sergeant spoke up. "She charged directly toward the ones named Sam and Roy. She might have pulled off the unexpected attack if one of those hombres hadn't knocked her over the head with his rifle."

Quinn winced. He was almost relieved that he hadn't witnessed Piper's reckless daring. Damn it, she had taken a few lessons in survival and now she thought she was invincible.

"Where are the women now?" Butler demanded.

"The bandits said they'd be waiting at Phantom Springs with their hostages," the corporal replied.

Quinn's jaw clenched and he went perfectly still.

"You know the place, Cal?" Butler asked grimly.

"Exceptionally well," he muttered.

It was the place where he and his father had built their ranch house and watched it burn to the ground the day the Kiowas swooped down on them. It was the place where his life had changed forever and his hated enemies had become his adopted people. He had avoided that lush oasis in the valley for years. He had refused to face the long but never forgotten memories that had turned a terrified child of twelve into a bitter, mistrusting cynic.

"Perfect death trap, I presume," Butler grumbled. "Hell and damnation. Those bastards found a way to outsmart us. They hold the upper hand now and they know it."

Quinn tried to think past the upheaval boiling inside him. If Piper died on the very site that had once been his family's ranch he would swear his life had been doubly cursed.

"Cal?" Butler prompted.

Quinn shook himself loose from the paralyzing emotions that haunted him. *Think, damn it,* he ordered himself. It took a moment to get his mind back on track.

He glanced up at the two soldiers. "How long will it take to ride to the fort and retrieve every spare mount you have?"

The sergeant frowned, bemused. "You want army horses?" When Quinn nodded grimly, he said, "Almost two hours down and two back. We'll be lucky if we can have the herd here by dusk."

Quinn smiled faintly. "Perfect. Meet me at the mouth of Phantom Springs Canyon as soon as you can."

When Quinn cut the soldiers loose, they wheeled around and thundered off. He swore the next four hours were going to be the longest of his life. Every worst-case scenario of Piper's captivity kept buzzing in his head. He had seen too many unfortunate victims during his service with the Rangers. The prospect of adding Piper's name to the list of the departed made his blood run cold.

"Swear to God," Quinn muttered resolutely, "if those cutthroats leave even one mark on Piper I won't rest until all of them are standing at the door to the jail. Or at the gate to the cemetery. Whichever. I promised Taylor Briggs vengeance and the same goes double for Piper and her sister."

"Would you mind filling me in on what you have in mind?" Butler requested. "What are you going to do with a herd of army horses?"

"Old Comanche trick, and I need two Comanches to help me pull this off," Quinn said before he wheeled around and stalked away.

"I know from experience that Comanches have more than one trick," Butler called after him. "Be more specific."

Quinn didn't respond. His concern for Piper was eating him alive. The possibility that he might lose her forever was driving him half-crazy. He had every intention of giving her up for her own good, but he couldn't imagine a world without Piper in it somewhere.

Piper regained consciousness to find her hands secured to the pommel of the saddle and her feet lashed to the stirrups. Serenaded by the buzzing in her ears and the agonizing throb in the back of her skull she opened her eyes without changing position on the horse. She glanced discreetly at her sister, being careful not to alert the bandits to the fact that she was awake.

Penny's wrists and ankles were also tied to the saddle. The procession was moving along a narrow trail that led into a steep-walled canyon.

Her mutinous gaze landed on Roy's back and she cursed the bandit for allowing his revenge against her to spill over to Penny. She wasn't sure *she* was going to escape from this nightmare alive, but she would be damned if Penny had to suffer also.

Resting her cheek against the horse's neck, she surveyed the rugged terrain. Considering the armed bandits that bookended her, she didn't think she could thunder off and expect to get very far before being apprehended again. She asked herself what Quinn would do in this situation, but she didn't have a clue. Plus, analytical thought was difficult when her senses were groggy from the splitting headache and nausea.

"The whole lot of you must be suicidal," Penny declared brazenly. "Whatever beef you have with the

Rangers will only be half of your worries when my husband learns I have been taken captive."

Piper bit back a grin while she pretended to still be unconscious. Penny was in her usual form and she kowtowed to no one. She, of course, had learned the tactic after years of watching Roarke operate, just as Piper had.

"Shut your mouth," Roy snarled at Penny.

"This stunt of yours will bring the wrath of the army down on your heads," Penny prophesied, ignoring Roy's terse demand. "You won't be able to run far enough or fast enough to find refuge. My husband will do whatever it takes to hunt you down. On that you can depend."

"Just shut up!" Sam snarled. "Don't know why you should concern that blond head of yours with events you won't be around to watch unfold."

"That hardly matters," Penny said boldly. "The point is that you and your brother will hang from the tallest tree in Texas or face a firing squad. I vote for *both*."

"You have a mouth as big as your sister's," Roy muttered. "Why don't you give it a rest before we decide to rest it for you." He gestured his greasy head toward Piper. "Far as I'm concerned, you can both ride slumped over the saddle. It's a hell of a lot quieter and more pleasant for the rest of us."

Piper felt herself tense in anticipation as the procession dropped in single file to pass through a bottleneck ravine. This was her chance to escape. There was only one rider ahead of Penny, who was directly in front of Piper. Using the element of surprise, Piper might be able to jam the narrow passage long enough for her sister to plow against Roy and perhaps unseat him on her way by.

Plus, there were enough scrub bushes and junipers lining the path to provide protection while Penny scrambled uphill to take cover behind the gigantic slabs of rock and oversize boulders.

Waiting until her horse was halfway through the shadowy tunnel of stone, Piper bolted upright to claw at the reins and force her mount backward. The horse behind her slammed against a jutting rock. Whirling wildly the horse rammed into the one behind it. Hooves clattered on the path. Horses panicked when they found themselves jammed up in confined spaces. Bandits cursed as they collided with the jagged rocks in the tunnel and hurriedly tried to regain control of their frantic mounts before being unseated and trampled.

Nudging her horse forward Piper rammed into Penny's mount, sending it lunging into Roy's horse. Yelping in surprise, Roy half turned in the saddle. Piper was pleased to note that Penny uplifted her elbow and caught the stubble-face cretin in the jaw on her way by. His head snapped back against the stone wall, then he dropped to the ground and lay there motionless.

"Shoot the horses out from under them!" Sam roared.

Piper gouged her horse, sending it into a gallop. She held her position to protect Penny's back until the path widened so they could ride abreast.

"We have to split up," Piper called out. "I'll lead the bandits west while you take cover on the hillside. But whatever you do, don't risk injury."

Amid whistling bullets that scattered the pebbles beneath the horses' hooves and zinged off the perpendicular wall of rock, Piper veered off the trail and headed straight into the lush valley.

Penny scrabbled uphill and disappeared from sight, thank goodness.

Whatever else happened Piper intended to provide a time-consuming distraction for her sister. For the first time in more than a week Piper was *grateful* to be an annoying inconvenience and the cause of a delay. She knew the Rangers were out there somewhere and she refused to become the bait that endangered their lives.

Penny was right when she said these desperadoes were inviting a full-fledged war with the army, Piper thought as she raced headlong through the panoramic canyon. There would be revenge for kidnapping Penny, she assured herself. Matt wouldn't rest until he had Penny back and made certain those responsible paid in full.

Piper might become the sacrifice made to ensure justice was served, but these bandits would not escape unscathed. Quinn and Matt would see to it.

Quinn didn't love her, but he *would* avenge her. She thundered toward the stream that glowed like mercury in the sunlight. All that mattered now was leading the bandits on a wild-goose chase so Penny would survive and have the chance to raise her child.

She glanced over her shoulder as she wrested her hands free from the leather strap. The bandits were closing in on her. There was no way out of this box canyon. The outlaws would overtake her and her luck was about to run out.

Piper wished that she had found the courage to tell Quinn that she had fallen in love with him when she'd had the chance. Now it was probably too late.

Chapter Fifteen

When the overloaded coach finally reached Catoosa Gulch Roarke stepped down to work the kinks from his neck and shoulders. He elbowed his way through the congregation of men who were asking directions to the nearest saloon. He frowned disconcertedly at the backward community that offered none of the luxuries he was accustomed to. The only appealing feature was the town square where a small spring gurgled into a rock-rimmed pool then trickled southward.

Roarke breathed a relieved sigh when he noticed the café that sat across the dirt street. At least his evening meal might offer something besides the mushy beans and stale hoecakes he'd eaten at the last stop.

Thank God for small favors, he thought as he hiked across the street.

According to the driver, the stage would make a two-hour layover to repair a broken spring on the undercarriage of the coach. Just what he didn't need, another infuriating delay.

Restless and irritable, he breezed into the restaurant and parked himself in a chair. It was then that he remembered he didn't have any money to pay for his meal. The thought didn't set well with him. Roarke had begun his life back East as a poor farmer's son. He had sworn thirty years ago that he would never again be without the funds that could provide the luxuries and influence that his own father had spent his entire life trying to achieve.

Now here Roarke was, right back where he had started. And that didn't set well with him.

"You missed all the excitement, *señor,*" the young Mexican waitress remarked as she ambled over to his table.

"I've had more than enough excitement this week already," he muttered. "The stage holdup left me penniless."

The woman smiled, then appraised his clothing. "I'm sure my papa will agree to trade your fine jacket for a meal. Money is not always the medium of exchange in these parts, you know."

Scowling at the fact that he had to give the coat off his back to get a meal, Roarke shrugged out of the expensive tailor-made garment and thrust it at the waitress. "Bring me whatever this will buy," he said deflatedly.

When the waitress returned with a glass of wine Roarke decided things were looking up. He could enjoy wine rather than the rotgut whiskey the other passengers were probably gulping down at the moment.

"At least your trek to the fort should be free of trouble by the time you are back on the road," the waitress said conversationally. "There is a Ranger battalion in the area and they are hot on the heels of the bandoleros that kidnapped two white women this morning."

His arm stalled in midair, his glass a few inches from his lips. "Two women?" he chirped. Damnation, the waitress couldn't possibly be referring to his daughters, could she? That's all he needed on top of everything else! "Two *blond* women?"

The waitress nodded her dark head. "*Sí*, one is the wife of an army captain. The other is her sister. They were taken hostage this morning. The ransom demanded that the Rangers release part of the gang that was locked in jail."

Roarke's arm jerked uncontrollably, splattering wine down the front of his shirt.

The waitress spun on her heels. "I'll fetch a rag to blot your shirt, *señor.*"

Roarke's hand shook as he set down his glass. He was overjoyed to discover that Piper had somehow survived and had reunited with Penny. But stark fear and concern tormented him to no end. He didn't want to contemplate the horrors his daughters might endure at the hands of ruthless outlaws.

This was the last straw, Roarke vowed stormily. He wanted his daughters back alive—and he damn well better get them back alive or those outlaws would find their footsteps dogged by every private investigator, gunslinger, bounty hunter and law official in this state! He would make examples of every last one of those cutthroats. The bounty on their heads would be so astronomical that the thieves would turn on each other like a pack of wolves to collect the rewards.

And curse those daredevil daughters of his for thrusting themselves into harm's way by tramping around this lawless country. Neither of them should be here in the first place. They were *Sullivans* and a better life awaited them in East Texas. And by damn, Roarke was going to take them home where they belonged. This was one decree that his contrary daughters were *not* going to defy!

Now, all he had to do was pray that the Rangers could rescue Piper and Penny from disaster. Then Roarke was going to stuff them in a stagecoach and head back to Galveston, whether they opposed the idea or not!

Piper shrieked in frustration when the loop of a lariat settled around her throat. The tug of the rope burned against her neck and jerked her sideways. If her feet hadn't been tied to the stirrups she would have cartwheeled to the ground to be dragged and trampled by the circling horses.

She found herself staring at two dozen angry men. But at least all of them had taken after *her* and given up looking for Penny.

Or perhaps the threat of inviting the outrage of the army had persuaded the outlaws to settle for one hostage. Whatever the case, all the bandits were accounted for and Penny had the chance to ride to safety.

"You are trying my patience, bitch," Roy growled as he trotted up beside her. "If we didn't need a live hostage to lure in the Rangers I would shoot you where you sit."

Piper was led toward a lone cottonwood tree that stood beside the creek that bisected the lush green valley. Craggy stone ridges rose two hundred feet high on all three sides of the canyon. Momentarily distracted, she stared at the shiny slabs of stone that shimmered in the waning sunlight. It looked as if the creek was fed by an underground spring that trickled down the hillside.

Her thoughts scattered abruptly when Roy slashed the ropes that bound her feet, then jerked her off the horse. Smirking in fiendish glee he tethered her to the tree.

"When this showdown is over you will be our spoils of victory," he said menacingly. "After the men and I use you for our pleasure I will take personal satisfaction in hearing you beg me to kill you."

If he was trying to terrorize her it wasn't going to work, Piper promised herself. She raised her chin in defiance. "Don't hold your breath waiting for that to happen. I will be cursing you for the beast you are with my dying breath."

"You will be singing a different tune by morning," Sam smirked. "Torture is everything it's cracked up to be."

"I suspect *you'll* be dead by then," Piper dared to say. "The Rangers will have sent you to hell where you belong."

Snarling, Sam backhanded her across the face. Her head slammed against the tree trunk, but she refused to give him the satisfaction of crying out in pain. She enjoyed a small measure of vindication by spitting the blood from her split lip at him.

Swearing profusely, he bounded onto his horse and reined away, signaling for the brigands to follow him.

Piper watched in dismay as the bandits took strategic positions behind the boulders on all three sides of the canyon. Within a few minutes it was difficult to tell where the snipers were waiting. She couldn't imagine

how Quinn and a dozen Rangers were going to overcome these odds. The valley itself was as much a fortress as Dead Man's Canyon.

A curse tumbled from her swollen lips when she saw
five riders enter the mouth of the canyon an hour later.
She recognized the horses, sombreros and serapes and
realized that the Rangers had been forced to release the
Mexicans from jail. Muttering, she watched the Mexicans scatter to take their positions on the rugged hillsides for the impending ambush.

The odds against the Rangers had just increased,
Piper thought. She would never forgive herself if Quinn
and his battalion came to harm because of her.

Two hours later Piper heard a strange rumble in the
distance. She glanced toward the storm clouds that had
piled up on the northwestern horizon, but the ominous
sound didn't seem to be coming from that direction.

Her eyes widened in surprise when she saw a herd
of at least a hundred horses thundering into the valley
in a fog of dust. Gunfire erupted from behind the massive slabs of stones and boulders that surrounded her.

Piper smiled triumphantly when she realized Quinn
had cleverly outsmarted the desperadoes. The Rangers
hadn't come charging into the valley of death to risk
being picked off like ducks on a pond by the bushwhackers. This had to be Quinn's ingenious idea, she
guessed. He had devised a way to counter the odds.

While bullets zinged around her, ricocheting off pebbles and splattering the water in the stream, Piper stared
at the approaching herd. Her jaw dropped open when

she noticed three men hanging off the sides of their sad-
dleless horses. Their clothing matched the color of the
buckskin horses they were holding on to. Quinn and the
Comanche warriors were plastered so closely to their
galloping steeds that it was impossible for the desperadoes to get a clear shot while the rest of the herd raced
beside them, stirring up a cloud of dust.

The wild-eyed herd circled the tree and splashed
through the creek. Thoroughly impressed by the tactic,
Piper smiled when Quinn dropped to the ground beside
her, his dagger clamped in his teeth. In less than a minute he had cut her loose, while Red Hawk and Spotted
Deer kept the moving barricade churning around them.

"Who hit you?" Quinn growled when he noticed her
bloody lip. His forefinger brushed lightly against the
rope burns on her throat and he gnashed his teeth. "Who
did this to you, Piper?"

"Doesn't matter," she said as she watched the circling
horses. "How are we going to get out of here?"

"It matters to me. Who…hit…you?"

"Sam and his brother, Roy, but how—?"

Her words died abruptly when Quinn grabbed the
bullwhip that hung diagonally across his chest. With an
effortless snap of his wrist, the whip curled around one
of the horses' necks. He gave a tug and the winded steed
skidded to a halt.

"Quinn, there's something I need to tell you," Piper
hollered over the whine of bullets and thundering hooves.

"Save it until later. We're getting the hell out of here
while the getting is good."

Hooking his arm around Piper's waist, he tossed her

on the sidestepping horse. An instant later he was sitting behind her. He shoved her forward until she was draped over the mount like a saddle blanket. Her breath came out in a whoosh when he collapsed upon her and shouted something in Comanche.

Piper held on for dear life as the horse plunged back into the circling herd. With Quinn's muscular body plastered over hers, protecting her from gunfire, he gouged the steed into its fastest clip. Piper frowned in confusion when she heard unexpected explosions erupting on the hillsides.

"Commander Butler and four other Rangers posed as the released Mexican bandits," Quinn shouted over the clatter of hooves. "The unit from Van Horn provided the dynamite for the fireworks. The explosions are the signal for my battalion to advance from over the rise of the mountain to bear down on the bushwhackers. Some of the soldiers arrived back at the fort in time to bring up the herd and join forces with us so we wouldn't be outnumbered."

Piper craned her neck to see dozens of riders, armed with rifles and explosives, firing down at the bandits who suddenly found themselves trapped on the wrong side of the massive slabs of rock and boulders.

She smiled in satisfaction, then winced when the cut on her lip began to sting. "Remind me never to try to outsmart you, Callahan. If these desperadoes can't get it done, I doubt I can, either."

Quinn held on to Piper as the herd picked up speed and surged toward the mouth of the canyon, while explosions and gunfire echoed around them. Now that she was safe and sound, and huddled protectively beneath him, Quinn heaved an enormous sigh of relief.

Of course, it went without saying that he was furious with her for luring the bandits after her so her sister could escape unscathed. Piper was *not* supposed to scare him half to death by putting her life on the line like that. Plus, he would dearly like to strangle her for whatever defiant remark she had made that had resulted in Sam Morrell's vicious retaliation.

But at least she was alive and still in one piece. He was grateful for that.

Quinn jerked on the bullwhip that he had looped around the horse's neck to slow the pace as they rounded the canyon wall. There were several soldiers waiting to bring the herd to a halt. When Red Hawk and Spotted Deer dropped to the ground, Quinn pulled his mount to a stop so he could hand Piper down to them.

"What are you doing?" she asked as he drew his feet beneath him to launch himself onto the saddle horse Captain Duncan had waiting for him.

"Riding back in to settle a score," he said before he charged off in the direction he had come.

"Wait! I want to tell you—"

Quinn couldn't hear her over the rumbling explosions and spitting gunfire. Whatever she thought she needed to say would have to wait.

Hearing the clatter of hooves behind him, Quinn twisted in the saddle to see the Comanche warriors mounted on army horses. "What are you doing here? Stay with Piper."

Red Hawk shook his dark head. "She is in good

hands. This is as much our fight as it is yours. We want the men who trampled Comanche burial ground. We also want revenge against the men who staked out your wife and split her lip."

Just what was there about Piper that demanded a man's allegiance? Quinn asked himself as he approached the battlegrounds on the rocky hillside. He didn't have time to figure it out at the moment, but nonetheless he was driven to avenge her mistreatment and retaliate for Taylor Briggs's senseless death.

And by damn, when he got through with Sam and Roy Morrell they were going to be dreadfully sorry they had incited his fury.

Piper found herself reunited and immediately enveloped in her brother-in-law's fierce hug and he didn't release her for a long moment. When he did, he smiled appreciatively at her. Piper studied his dark eyes, dark hair, bronzed skin and realized she and Penny had a weakness for ruggedly handsome men.

"You spared Penny from harm," Matt Duncan murmured. "For that, you have my eternal gratitude."

"Where is she?" Piper glanced around his broad shoulders.

"I made her lie down under the nearest tree," he replied, then grimaced. "Damn near had to tie her up to keep her there. She insisted on being on hand when Callahan went in after you."

Piper stared in the direction he pointed, then trotted over to join her sister. When Penny came to her knees and braced herself against the tree trunk Piper flung up her hand. "Don't get up. You are under strict orders to rest after your ordeal."

Penny pulled a face. "I swear Matthew has become so protective that I can't even hiccup without provoking his concern. Seven more months of this and he will drive me crazy." Her gaze narrowed in concern when she noticed the dried blood caked on Piper's lip. "What did they do to you?"

Piper sank down cross-legged and smiled reassuringly. "It's nothing. It was my fault, actually. I never have learned when to keep my trap shut."

Penny grinned mischievously. "Definitely a Sullivan family trait. I can't keep my trap shut, either." Her smile faded as she clutched Piper's hand. "I can never repay you for protecting my unborn child and me. If you hadn't led those scoundrels on a merry chase through the valley I wouldn't have been able to escape over the ridge." Tears clouded her blue eyes. "Whatever you want or need, Pi, just ask and I will see it done."

Piper chuckled. What she *wanted* and *needed* was for Quinn to fall hopelessly, completely, madly in love with her. She doubted her sister could grant her fondest wish.

A week ago, gaining her independence had been foremost on her mind. Now, her freedom seemed a hollow victory because she had lost her heart.

The clatter of an approaching coach caught Piper's attention. She glanced up to see a silver-blond head appear from the window. "What miserable timing," she mumbled. "Brace yourself, Penny. Papa has arrived."

"Halt!" Roarke bellowed at the driver.

In the gathering darkness Piper and Penny stared apprehensively at each other as their father barreled down the steps even before the coach had rolled to a complete stop. His silver-blond hair glinted in the waning light and his pale blue eyes widened in concern.

"My God!" Roarke howled as he scurried over to his grimy-faced daughters. "Are you two all right?"

"We're fine," Piper insisted. "Nice to see you again, Papa."

Roarke's face puckered in irritation as he thrust back his shoulders and crossed his muscular arms in a gesture of disappointment, and then he let out a snort. "*Now* do you see why I wanted the two of you to stay home where you belong? You came to this godforsaken wilderness and look what happened. You nearly got yourselves killed—or worse!"

His broad chest swelled as he sucked in a deep breath, then ranted on. "I have been through sheer hell just getting here. Now that I'm here I damn well intend to—"

"Sir," the driver interrupted. "We're several hours behind schedule. Are you climbing aboard or not?"

Roarke wheeled around to take command of the situation. "Yes, I am and so are my daughters. You two—" He made a stabbing gesture toward two men seated beside the coach windows. "Climb atop the stage and give your seats to my daughters."

Piper and Penny found themselves hoisted to their feet and bustled toward the coach. Roarke crammed them inside, forcing the other passengers to huddle together.

"This is no place for sophisticated ladies," Roarke lectured before he motioned for the driver to head to the fort. "Stage holdups, kidnappings, renegade Indians running loose and only God knows what else. The two of you are definitely coming back to Galveston with me and I will hear no argument. Have I made myself clear?"

Piper rolled her eyes at her father's take-command attitude, then leaned toward Penny. "Are you going to tell him that we aren't leaving or shall I do the honors?"

Penny stared at Roarke who had crossed his arms over his chest, thrust out his chin and flattened his mouth into a familiar expression that invited no argument. "I suggest that we gang up on him," she recommended confidentially. "Maybe we should give him the night to rest, recuperate and calm down. He looks too unapproachable at the moment. I think we should break the news to him tomorrow."

Piper studied her stiff-necked father pensively. "I don't think it's going to matter," she murmured. "He isn't going to take the news well whether it's now or later."

"He always gets defensive and cantankerous when someone challenges his authority," Penny whispered. "Most especially when we are the ones who challenge him. I still think we should wait and give ourselves a chance to mentally rehearse what we want to say to him."

Piper acquiesced, and then suddenly realized the explosions and gunfire had ceased. She predicted the Rangers had won the skirmish and were gathering prisoners. She also predicted that she wouldn't see Quinn again. When he discovered that she had reached the garrison safely his obligation to her would be over. She expected he would ride off to take another of his endless assignments with the Rangers.

Well, what had she expected? Piper asked herself as she settled in for the coach ride to the fort. That Quinn would come to the garrison to scoop her up in his arms and declare that life without her would be no life at all? That only happened in whimsical fairy tales. As Penny said, her own fairy tale hadn't played out exactly as she had envisioned.

Piper suspected that they rarely did.

Despite the fact that Quinn had come charging into the canyon to rescue her again today he wasn't going to magically reappear so they could live happily ever after. She predicted she wouldn't even have the chance to tell him that she loved him, despite his request that she view their intimacy as merely passion for the sake of passion.

Piper smiled ruefully when the memory of Quinn clinging to the side of the horse while he raced into the canyon to rescue her came to mind. Emotions had welled up inside her until she swore she was about to burst. The moment she had seen him she had ached to tell him how she felt about him, but he had been in no mood to listen to anything she had to say.

He had been focused on getting her to safety.

"I intend for us to be packed and ready to take the first eastbound stage out of this hellhole," Roarke declared thirty minutes later. "When we get to Galveston I insist that you two take a month to rest and acclimate yourselves to civilization. Only then will you be allowed to accept social invitations." His gaze narrowed meaningfully on his daughters. "I sincerely hope you haven't forgotten how to behave like the aristocrats you are."

"Papa, I think you—" Piper's voice dried up and she

winced uncomfortably when Penny gouged her in the ribs and threw her a look meant to silence.

Resigned to being lectured and ordered about for the rest of the evening, Piper sank against the seat and kept her mouth shut. Considering the mood she was in, objecting strenuously to Roarke's plans probably wasn't a good idea. The weary travelers probably wouldn't enjoy witnessing a Sullivan family squabble this evening.

Quinn eased a hip onto a chair-size boulder in the valley that had once been his home. He watched lightning flicker in the darkness, but the brewing storm had nothing on the emotions roiling inside him. Since his capture two decades earlier he had forcefully blocked out thoughts of the ranch that he and his father had moved west to establish after his mother's death. He and his father had found peace here, even though they had foolishly laid claim to land that was inhabited by Indians.

Thunder rumbled in the distance, vibrating through him like the upheaval of emotions he had experienced that day when the war party of Kiowas had descended from the ridges to reclaim their land from invading whites. Then Quinn's life had changed abruptly again. He'd barely had time to deal with the loss of his mother and his unborn brother before he reeled from witnessing the death of his father. He had also undergone the difficult transition from white to Indian culture, carrying a bitterness within him that refused to die.

For as long as Quinn could remember he had been thrust from one perplexing phase of life to another, swearing he had been cursed for reasons he didn't understand. There were always difficult challenges to face, a riptide of emotions he had to bury deep inside in order to cope with unfamiliar situations.

He had given up trying to dream of a better life. He had simply learned to exist and do what he did best— fight to survive.

Quinn stared in the direction of the distant fort that was nestled at the mouth of another rock-strewn canyon. The sky flared with streaks of sizzling lightning, followed by resounding crashes of thunder. A whimsical smile pursed his lips, as the world around him grew dark and silent for a few moments. He wished he were cuddled up in Piper's arms right about now. Being with her, teaching her the skills she needed for survival and matching wits with her had made him happier than he had been in twenty years.

True, there had been times when that sassy female had frustrated him to no end. But when he was with Piper he *felt* something rather than simply going through the motions of living.

When his horse shook itself and stamped impatiently beside him, Quinn surged to his feet. Sitting here, lost in bittersweet memories and wishing for something he would never have was a waste of his time. In a way, being out here alone at Phantom Springs—after years of avoiding the area—had helped him face his demons and make peace with his past.

Too bad that the prospect of an empty future was still giving him fits.

Quinn gathered the reins and led his horse along the winding footpath to the valley below. He should rejoin his battalion that was celebrating victory in town and keeping a close watch over the prisoners in jail. But he was compelled to ride to the garrison to make certain Piper had resolved her differences with her father.

According to Captain Duncan, Roarke had arrived on the scene and had bustled both his daughters into the coach to reach the fort. Quinn planned to be on hand to provide reinforcement for Piper—just in case Roarke tried to railroad her into returning to Galveston with him.

Or perhaps Piper had suffered through so many ordeals this week that she had lost her taste for excitement and independence. For all he knew she might have decided to head home and leave the memories of her misadventures behind.

The thought of never seeing Piper again left a dull ache in Quinn's chest. Sure, he knew she was better off without him around to complicate her life. He had very little to offer her. And certainly, her social status was so far beyond his that it was laughable to even picture them together.

But if she remained in this area he could at least check up on her occasionally. If she returned to Galveston she might as well be halfway around the world—completely lost to him forever.

Quinn muttered at his dismal thoughts as he mounted up, then reined his steed along the path. He *should* return to town. No sense torturing himself by seeing Piper one last time. But damn it, she was his *wife*. He *was* entitled to make sure she was all right, wasn't he?

Quinn looked back toward Catoosa Gulch, then trotted off, wishing he could sprout wings and fly to the garrison. If he quickened his pace he might outrun the rain that was a few minutes behind him.

Too bad he couldn't outrun this nagging feeling that he was about to lose someone who had become a little too vital and necessary to him.

Chapter Sixteen

Piper paced the confines of her room in the officers' quarters. Exhausted though she was from the kidnapping and the encounter with her father, she was having trouble settling down for the night. It didn't help that the approaching storm made the air fairly crackle around her and set her nerves on end.

Or was it simply her emotions that were making her so restless that she was wearing a rut in the planked floor?

Although Penny had convinced her that it would be better to defy their father's demands *after* they had enjoyed a good night's sleep, Piper wished she could march to Roarke's room right this minute. She wanted to tell him that she had no intention of heading east with him. Might as well get that fiery confrontation over with now instead of putting it off.

Piper smiled, thinking that as much as she dreaded the confrontation with Roarke, she dreaded the thought of never seeing Quinn again even more. In a short amount of time he had become a necessary part of her life. Forgetting him, she predicted, was going to take considerable time and effort.

She wheeled at the sound of the unexpected rap at the door. Roarke, no doubt, had come to make a few more demands. Piper mentally geared herself up to have it out with her father once and for all. She was spoiling for a fight and it seemed like the perfect time for one.

Mentally prepared to square off against Roarke, Piper whipped open the door. Her jaw dropped open when she saw Quinn smiling down at her. Reflexively she flung her arms around his neck and hugged him close.

"You greet everyone who knocks on your door like this, do you?" he teased.

Suddenly her world seemed a brighter place. Piper leaned back to grin mischievously at him. "No, just ruggedly handsome Rangers who keep saving me from disaster."

Quinn frowned as he brushed his forefinger over her bruised cheek. "I have something that will treat the sting and swelling. Come sit, Piper."

She sank down on the edge of her bed and watched him pull the saddlebags off his shoulder. He fished out a small tin then smoothed the soothing ointment over her bruised cheek, lips and neck.

"Indian remedy," he said, then grinned wryly. "Or would you prefer peyote buttons to relieve the pain?"

Piper wrinkled her nose at him. "This is fine. It has a cooling effect." When he came to his feet to tuck the poultice into his saddlebags, Piper stared curiously at him. "Did you round up the desperadoes and stuff them in jail?"

"Half of them," he reported as he looked around her small quarters. "The other half didn't make it out alive." His gaze darkened and his jaw clenched. "Roy and Sam Morrell left the canyon draped over the back of their horses. After six months of craving revenge for my friend's murder, I have honored Taylor Briggs's request to give those bastards what they deserve," he gritted out. "Taylor was trying to scout their trail into Dead Man's Canyon and they bushwhacked him. I didn't find him until it was too late to save him. *Now* he can rest in peace."

Piper didn't ask if Quinn had personally seen to their demise and he didn't elaborate. All that mattered was that the bandits who had terrorized the area, kidnapped Piper and Penny and had murdered Quinn's friend were no longer a threat. Justice had been served—Texas Ranger style. And that was that.

"What about the spies working for the stage line?"

"Commander Butler intends to round them up on his way back to Austin."

She smiled in satisfaction. "I don't think this is a good time to be wearing a red bandana tied on your left shoulder."

Quinn returned her wry smile. "No, it isn't." He stared curiously at her as he sank down on the edge of the bed. "I've been wondering what your father had to say about our marriage."

Piper chuckled. "He didn't say a thing because I haven't told him yet. And Penny hasn't announced that he will be a grandfather, come winter. She thinks we should grant him the night to recover from his arduous journey before we spring the news on him."

She cocked her head to the side and peered up at him. "Is that why you're here? To make sure I didn't get hauled back to Galveston against my will?"

"Partially."

"And the other reasons?" Foolish hope and anticipation swelled inside her.

"I came to say goodbye."

Deflated, Piper glanced the other way. Well, isn't that what she expected? Quinn wasn't going to get down on bended knee and beg her to make this a real marriage. He might feel *lust* for her occasionally, but he didn't *love* her. He didn't want or need her in his life. She knew that. She just couldn't convince her foolish heart to give Quinn up as a hopeless cause.

Piper cursed under her breath when she felt tears welling up in her eyes. She had ridden an emotional teeter-totter the whole livelong day. She had reunited with her sister, been abducted, rescued and overtaken by her father. She had held up without shedding a single tear. Now here she was, on the verge of blubbering because Quinn had arrived to voice his official fare-thee-well.

That, it seemed, was the last straw that crumbled her hard-won composure.

Turning her back, she blinked rapidly and muffled a sniff. She would not reduce herself to blubbering, she vowed vehemently. Quinn's last memory of her was *not* going to be of a weepy, whiny female who sat in a pool of her own tears.

Inhaling a cathartic breath, Piper squared her shoulders and heaved herself to her feet. "Well then, goodbye, Callahan." She thrust out her hand and manufactured a smile, disconcerted that he was studying her astutely. "I owe you my life and I will forever be indebted to you."

He smiled crookedly as his hand folded over hers. "It has been interesting knowing you, Piper."

When he rose to his feet she looked up into his amber-colored eyes, wanting to smear that unreadable expression all over his bronzed face, wanting to strangle him because he didn't return the feelings boiling up inside her like a geyser. Wanting to curse herself up one side and down the other for not being woman enough to make an unforgettable impression on him.

When he turned away to walk out of her life for good, everything inside her objected. The hell with it, she thought recklessly. She was not going to let him leave without knowing that he was taking her heart with him. Her *whole* heart, not just an insignificant piece of it that she could live without.

"One last thing," she said as he reached for the door latch.

He glanced over his shoulder at her. "What's that?"

Piper lifted her chin and stiffened her resolve to speak her piece before she broke down and humiliated herself. "You asked me not to fancy myself in love with you, but that's the one favor I can't grant you." She drew in a shaky breath and said, "I'm sorry, but I *do* love you. Don't waste your breath trying to talk me out of it, because I *know* what I feel."

His expression turned grim. Piper wheeled away because he was breaking her heart by keeping silent. If he didn't leave quickly she might do something unforgivable—like throw herself in his arms, beg him to give their marriage a chance, and then plead with him to take her with him wherever he went.

"I'm done talking so you can leave now," she murmured, swiping at the betraying tears that boiled down her cheeks.

But the door didn't creak open, indicating that he had left so she could fall apart in private. No, he was still there, watching her teeter on the edge of a mortifying emotional outburst.

In another few seconds that was exactly what was going to happen because Piper was already losing her tentative grasp on self-control and it was going to be straight downhill from here.

"Damn it, Callahan. When I want you to stay you won't. When I give you the chance to go, you won't do that, either. Just what does it take to get rid of you?"

"I'll go after you answer one question. Just *when* did you come to the conclusion that you loved me?"

Quinn stared at the rigid set of her shoulders and heard the tears in her voice. He ached to close the distance between them to hold her close and console her. But he didn't dare. He knew it would probably be his undoing.

He almost smiled when Piper lurched around and tilted her chin in that familiar expression of defiance. "*When?*" she said as tears bled down her flushed cheeks. "All you can say after I told you how I feel about you is *when?*"

He shrugged helplessly as she glared at him.

"If you must know I suspected it days ago. But I

knew for certain while I was staked out in that canyon and I saw you charging in, hanging off the side of that horse. I kept thinking that I would at least get to see you one last time…just in case the rescue attempt went sour," she blurted. "I know you don't want to hear it and I know you don't love me back, but I need to be able to tell you the truth and you need to accept it."

Her voice grew louder with each word as she shook her finger at him. "So do *not* annoy me by telling me that I'm mistaken about my feelings for you. I *know* what I *feel!* Guaranteed!"

Quinn was compelled toward her, though common sense shouted at him to bid her goodbye and walk out the door without looking back. "And what am I supposed to do with this confession?" he asked as he halted a few feet away from his forbidden fantasy. "Ask you to be my wife and live out here in the middle of nowhere? Ask you to follow me through this wild country and risk having you meet with another disaster that might turn out worse than the others you've encountered since you came here?" He sighed audibly. "Just what is it that you think should happen here, Piper?"

She stamped her foot in frustration and whacked him on the shoulder. "First off, don't test my temper because I'm not in the best of moods at the moment," she spouted. "All I said is that I love you. I did *not* ask you to give up your duties for me. I didn't ask you for *anything* but the acceptance of my feelings for you. Can't you just say, *Thank you. That's nice to know?*"

"Thank you," he repeated, biting back a grin while

he watched her silver-blue eyes flare in irritation. "That's nice to know."

She swatted him on the other shoulder.

"What's that for? I said exactly what you told me to say," he pointed out reasonably.

Her bewitching face flamed bloodred. "You are impossible!" Her arm shot toward the door. "Just get out! Go!"

"*I'm* impossible?" He threw up his hands in a gesture of futility. "One minute you are giving me hell and the next minute you're up to your lovely neck in trouble and scaring me half to death. And if that isn't enough to make a man *crazy* you suddenly tell me you love me. What am I supposed to do?"

"Leaving would be good. It's what you want, after all."

He saw another round of tears floating in her eyes and watched her Cupid's bow lips tremble. His heart twisted in his chest because somewhere along the way everything that affected Piper affected him. Watching her cry was killing him by inches. He had to get out before he caved in and gave her whatever she wanted, even if it was the last thing she needed.

He wheeled toward the door. "Fine. I'm gone."

He had taken two steps toward the door when she said, "It really would be easy to hate you, Quinn Callahan."

"I thought you said you loved me. This just proves that you don't know what you want and that we're better off without each other. Neither of us seems to be able to think rationally when we're together—"

When she broke down in tears completely and crumpled onto the edge of the bed he knew he should keep walking. But he was rushing to her side to enfold her in his arms before he even realized it. Then she flung her arms around his neck and kissed him blind, deaf and stupid.

The taste of Piper had been his first downfall and he was pretty sure it was going to be the last. His intimate knowledge of her luscious body and the forbidden emotion she summoned from him was his ultimate defeat. He wanted her so badly that he ached up to his eyelids.

If nothing else, he was going to lose himself in this impossible female and get her out of his system once and for all. Then he was going to say goodbye and tell her how he really felt about her—without voicing the words that he had never spoken to another woman.

And then he was going to do Piper the greatest favor a man could do for a woman who was too damn good for him.

"Make love with me one last time," Piper whispered brokenly as she fumbled with the buttons of his shirt. "I want to touch you, every solid, muscular inch of you. I want to feel you deep inside me—"

His mouth came down on hers with wild urgency. Her words and the images they evoked left him hard and needy in the space of a heartbeat. Quinn devoured her like a man who had been starved for days on end. All the while he battled the conflicting feelings of wanting her and wanting what was best for her.

The need to have her naked and yielding in his arms one last time won out over common sense. Plus, he wanted to know if the hazy memories of their wedding night were as fantastic as he thought they were. But he was very much afraid that the truth was going to come as a blessing as well as a curse. For then he would know for certain that she had touched him in every way possible and that leaving her behind was going to hurt every bit as much as he predicted it would.

Quinn was sure that when he took possession of her luscious body that she was going to take what was left of his shriveled soul in exchange. Then there would be nothing of him but an empty shell when he walked out of her life.

Quinn closed his eyes against the conflicting thoughts that chased each other around his head. He didn't want to think; he wanted to savor the feel of Piper's silky body beneath his fingertips. He wanted to hear those raspy whispers of love tumbling from her lips. And then he wanted to sink into the flames of her desire and burn alive this one last time—for all times.

"I need you," he murmured huskily as he caressed the curve of her neck and breathed in her alluring scent.

"That's all I will ever ask of you," she whispered back.

Piper wasn't sure how and when they had come to be naked on her bed. Didn't really care, either. But the one thing she did care passionately about was offering Quinn all the mind-bending pleasure he had introduced her to the previous night. She shifted away from his distracting kisses and caresses to focus her attention on pleasing him as much as he had satisfied her on their wedding night.

Her hands swept over the muscled wall of his chest and her lips skimmed his bronzed flesh. She heard him hiss out his breath when she flicked at his male nipples with her tongue and teeth. When her hand glided down his washboard belly she heard his rumbling groan. It inspired her to draw more sounds of pleasure from him.

He could flash that carefully neutral stare at her time and again, but tonight she would delve beneath that wall of self-discipline and seduce this man who had stolen her heart without even trying.

To that dedicated purpose Piper trailed a row of steamy kisses across his ribs and belly. Her caresses skimmed over his hair-roughed thighs and calves, marveling at the sinewy muscles and tendons beneath her fingertips. When her hand cupped his rigid length and she felt him flinch, battling for self-control, she smiled wickedly.

She had discovered that she held the same kind of sensual power over him that he held over her, and she was going to make use of that knowledge. She was going to brand the memory of their lovemaking on his mind. If she could be nothing more than an erotic memory, at least that was something. It was better than being another of the forgettable women who had come and gone from his life.

Just let him try to block out the feel of her hands and lips making a provocative feast of him. Let him try to forget his own helpless response and how she had made him ache, as she ached with the maddening want of him.

"Piper, stop!" He gasped as she stroked his erect flesh from base to tip. "You're driving me—"

"*Crazy.* I know," she murmured. "But I'm determined to make you love every moment of *crazy* before you go away."

She took him into her mouth and suckled him while

her hands skimmed his inner thighs. She heard him groan in tormented pleasure. Felt his big body tremble in helpless response. She flicked playfully at him with her tongue, traced him with her fingertips. She smiled in satisfaction when another rumbling moan slipped past his clenched teeth.

"Damn it, woman," he rasped. "You are playing absolute hell with my self-control!"

"Damn you for making me love you so much," she whispered against his softest flesh. "Why couldn't you have been like every other man that I turned away without the slightest regret? Why did you have to leave your mark on my heart and soul? I can never be free when your memory holds me captive."

She lifted her head and stared at him while she caressed him intimately. "Turnabout is fair play, Quinn. All I'm asking is for you to remember me, to remember this night."

As if he could ever forget the tantalizing feel of her warm lips skimming his throbbing length, the feel of her fingertips stroking him, teasing him, driving him insane with hungry need. And worse, he let her touch him in ways he had never allowed another woman to know him. He would never forget that she alone made him break every rule about becoming hopelessly attached to anyone who had the power to hurt him.

She was his weakness. *She* tangled up his thoughts, destroyed his willpower and left him burning with barely controllable desire. *She* reduced him to a quivering mass of sensations and emotions and *she* left him sinking into erotic oblivion.

And when he didn't think he could endure another instant of her evocative kisses and caresses she brought her lips back to his, letting him taste the desire she had called from him. Desperate, frantic, struggling to draw breath, Quinn clamped hold of her hips and settled her exactly upon him.

A sigh escaped his lips as he sank into her velvety warmth. He glanced up to see the smile of feminine satisfaction on her enchanting face. She knew she had the ability to make him a slave to her passion. She knew that whatever she asked of him he would give. If she wanted a handful of stars then he would find a way to pluck them from the sky. He would do anything for her if she would appease this wild ache that thrummed through him and left him burning like wildfire.

When she arched against him, driving him deeper, a holocaust of sensations blazed through him. He clenched his teeth against the onslaught of inexpressible pleasure. His body lifted off the bed, seeking ultimate depths of intimacy with her, craving her like a mindless addiction.

And when she rode him, setting a frantic pace that took him so close to the edge of restraint that his entire body shook, Quinn hooked his hand around her neck and brought her head down to his. He kissed her for all he was worth, conveying all the need and affection that bubbled inside him.

He felt her body respond to his urgent thrusts, felt her contracting around him, burning him up in all-consuming passion. He crushed her tightly to him and held on for dear life as shudder after shudder wracked his body.

He felt his strength and energy draining away, felt himself drifting on some far-flung plateau in a world rife with so many indefinable sensations that they overwhelmed him.

And then he heard the same sizzling sounds of lightning and crackles of thunder that had followed him to the fort. Rain pounded against the windowpane, consuming the world as he had been consumed by Piper's passion. It was a long moment before Quinn's heart rate returned to normal and he found the strength to shift away from her.

"Stay the night," she whispered as she snuggled up beside him.

He chuckled softly. "I'm not sure I could get up, even if someone held a gun to my head." He draped his arm around her waist, holding her chest to chest and heart to heart. He smiled drowsily as he inhaled the sweet scent that was unique to her alone. Then he pressed a kiss to her lush lips. "Good night, Piper."

She didn't respond for a moment, but he heard her whisper, "Goodbye, Quinn. I will love you…for always." And then he fell asleep.

Chapter Seventeen

❧❧❧

Piper was jolted awake when she heard the door to her room creak open. She was surprised to discover that Quinn was still nestled beside her. She had expected him to be long gone by dawn.

Bleary-eyed, she glanced toward the door, and then yelped in embarrassment when she saw her father looming in the doorway. He staggered back as if he had been shot, then a look of stunned outrage claimed his face.

"Who the hell are you and what are you doing in my daughter's bed?" Roarke roared at Quinn.

This was not the way Piper had envisioned the encounter with her father. Her face went up in flames as she clutched the sheet to her bare breasts and glanced wildly at Quinn who met Roarke's mutinous glower with that trademark stare that suggested nothing got to him.

Piper would have given anything if she could match that poker-face expression he had perfected into an art form.

"Roarke Sullivan, I presume," Quinn said, as calmly as you please.

"Yes, and I *repeat,* who the *hell* are *you?*" Roarke growled furiously.

"I'm Piper's husband."

Piper watched her father's jaw scrape his overinflated chest, saw his eyes pop as he staggered back another step to brace his arm against the doorjamb for support.

"Her *what?*" he howled in disbelief.

"My husband," Piper repeated. "Would you please step outside so we can dress?"

"No, I will not," Roarke snapped, then filleted Quinn with a glower. "You have miscalculated if you think you can attach yourself to my daughter and profit from it, you scoundrel. I will cut her off as surely as I disowned Penelope for marrying beneath her station!"

"Your money is the very last thing that interests me about Piper. I have twelve years of salary as a Texas Ranger stockpiled in a bank in Austin. Not to mention several thousand from bounties I've collected."

His gaze narrowed threateningly and his bronzed face took on a formidable expression. "Now you heard *my wife's* request. Leave the room so we can get dressed. Do *not* make me get up and forcefully remove you."

Roarke made a big production of slamming the door on his way out. Dust dribbled from the woodwork and a muffled curse resounded around the hallway.

"I'm sorry," Piper murmured as she scrambled from bed to gather her clothes. "I didn't want you to have to face Papa's wrath."

"Wouldn't have missed it," Quinn said as he pulled on his breeches. "That's why I'm still here."

Not because he was so attached to her that he couldn't bear to leave her behind, Piper mused as she wormed into a clean gown. Quinn had hung around for the inevitable fireworks, no doubt. She had told him she would deal with her father, but he obviously didn't think she could handle the task.

She started when she felt his hands working the buttons on the back of her gown. Her feelings of rejection and frustration multiplied when she realized this was the first and last time Quinn would be around to assist her in dressing. There would be no more of his considerate help, none of the everyday gestures and companionship that married couples probably took for granted.

"I said I will handle my father and I will. I'll divert his attention and you can climb out the window and be on your way. No sense hanging around for another round of the Sullivan family feud."

Quinn chuckled in amusement as he fastened the last button. "For a woman who insists that she's in love with me—the first woman to make any such claim, by the way—you sure are in an all-fired rush to get rid of me."

"I would like to keep you," she replied as she pivoted to face him. "But I know that's the last thing you want."

Before Piper could reach the door, Quinn surged past her. She watched her father rake Quinn up and down in blatant disapproval of his style of dress.

"What are you? A half-breed?" Roarke muttered disrespectfully.

"It wouldn't matter if he were," Piper interjected as

she stepped in front of Quinn to face her father toe to toe. "Quinn Callahan is the Texas Ranger who saved my life several times over. And most importantly, he is the man I love. You can disinherit me if you wish, but I intend to stay married to him. I'm not going back to Galveston with you."

"Neither am I."

Piper glanced sideways to see Penelope striding toward them. "Good morning, Papa." She breezed past him to pump Quinn's hand. "I'm your sister-in-law and I want to thank you for saving Pi yesterday." Spinning about, she smiled brightly at Roarke. "I have another surprise for you, Papa."

"I've had enough surprises for one day, thank you," he scowled, still glaring resentfully at Quinn. "I am your father and if I say you are coming back to Galveston, married or not, then you are. You belong in a place where the name Sullivan means something. I'm not sure *anything* means something out here in the middle of nowhere!"

"Long tiring trips aren't recommended for me right now. Your grandchild is due this winter. Furthermore, I am still very much in love with Matthew. I'm not leaving him. Ever."

"My grand—" Roarke's voice fizzled out as he stumbled back another step. When he recovered his power of speech he said, "That settles it. You and Piper are definitely coming home. I will not have my heir raised on this godforsaken frontier that is better suited for sidewinders and bandits."

He focused his stern expression on Piper. "As for you, young lady. Being married to a Texas Ranger is no better than being married to an army captain. Both of you were groomed to wed aristocrats and live in proper society. You have no business in this lawless country. Yesterday's calamity testifies to that!"

"Piper isn't going anywhere that she doesn't want to go," Quinn said ominously. "I'm here to see that she gets what she wants."

Roarke's gaze narrowed to match Quinn's foreboding stare. "And I'm here to see that she gets what she deserves and you are not it!"

"Regardless, you'll have to go through me to get to her," he insisted.

"This is none of your concern, Callahan," Roarke snapped. "I don't know what spell you cast over my daughter, but I intend to see that she is thinking with a clear head by the time she gets home."

Quinn took an intimidating step toward Roarke, looming dangerously over him as only Quinn could. Piper was pleased to note that Roarke shifted uneasily when Quinn bore down on him like the flapping angel of doom.

For once Roarke had met his match and he seemed to recognize that fact.

"You must not have heard me, Roarke," Quinn said in a voice that rumbled like thunder. "She wants to stay here. She wants the freedom to make her own choices instead of having you lord over her like you have for years."

Piper eased in front of Quinn again to confront Roarke. "I do not mean to sound ungrateful, Papa, because I am aware of all you have tried to do for me for years. But I'm old enough to make up my own mind about my future and to face the consequences of my decisions."

She inhaled a deep breath and plunged on. "I want a marriage to Quinn. He has earned my admiration, respect and affection. I never had the slightest interest in John Foster. He is nothing more than a puppet dancing on his father's string. But Quinn is his own man. He meets the world on his terms. That is a trait that I aspire to possess myself."

Penny stepped up beside Piper and tilted her chin to the same defiant angle. "Since I'm not leaving Matthew, either, you might as well save your breath, Papa. This is one argument you can't possibly win and you need to realize that. *Now.*"

When Matthew Duncan strode forward to stand at attention beside Quinn, Roarke stared over his daughters' blond heads at his sons-in-law. "I will pay you both very handsomely to walk away right now," he bargained. "Name your price. I'll see to it that you have more money than you can spend in a lifetime. I'll even buy your tickets west, all the way to the Pacific. I hear the climate in California is very nearly perfect."

Quinn smirked. "Can't say that I have a hankering to step beyond the Texas border. The weather here suits me just fine and I like having my wife an arm's reach away."

"Same goes for me," Matt chimed in. "All I ever wanted was Penny. Nothing is more important to me than she is."

"I'll loan you a horse if you want to ride north to catch the stage running from Van Horn to Austin," Quinn offered generously. "Wouldn't want you to have to hang around this *godforsaken wilderness* longer than necessary."

Roarke's rigid shoulders sagged as he glanced from one determined face to another. "You would deprive an old man of seeing his beloved daughters? Deprive him of watching his grandchild grow up?"

"You aren't that old," Quinn said frankly. "Besides, it won't be too long before the railroad reaches this part of the country. You can visit anytime you wish."

Roarke scowled. "You drive a hard bargain, Callahan. The least you could do is compromise a bit."

"He never compromises," Piper said, grinning impishly. "According to Quinn, if you start compromising then that's all you get done." She eased back a step to curl her hand around Quinn's elbow. "We are staying here. All of us. This is not negotiable." She stared ruefully at Roarke. "I'm sorry, but Penny and I are never going to be like Mamma. That's not who we are."

Quinn watched a look of defeat cross Roarke's face. He almost felt sorry for the older man who was accustomed to getting his way—and had run up against a brick wall today.

"Fine then," Roarke burst out, flinging his arms in a gesture of frustration. "Take my stubborn, rebellious daughters off my hands and we'll see if you have more luck controlling them than I did. But I *will* be back in time for the birth of my grandchild."

When Roarke stuck out his chin Quinn knew immediately where Piper and Penny had inherited the mannerism. Grinning, Quinn offered his hand in a gesture of truce. "Matt and I will be more than happy to take your rebellious but adorable daughters off your hands. Feel free to return for a visit whenever the mood strikes, Roarke."

"But if I decide to shower my daughters and my grandchild with gifts then I want to hear no complaints from my sons-in-law," he insisted. "It is *my* money, after all, and I will spend it where and how I wish."

He stared directly at Quinn. "And furthermore, I'm not accepting the use of your horse. I plan to spend the week with my daughters."

Piper inwardly winced at the announcement. Not that she objected to visiting with her father, now that he realized both of his daughters were determined to live their own lives. The problem was that Roarke would be suspicious when Quinn rode off—and didn't come back.

"Good," Penny said as she smiled at Roarke. "It will give me a chance to show you around the garrison and the surrounding area. This really is panoramic country, Papa. It might even begin to grow on you. Out here, there is no one to crowd your space."

Roarke snorted. "And that is about the only nice thing you can say about this last outpost on the edge of the frontier."

When the threesome ambled down the hall, Piper stared up at Quinn. "This is your chance to make a fast getaway," she murmured. "I'll dream up an excuse to explain your absence." She flung her hand dismissively. "Ranger duties or something."

"I've been thinking—"

Piper pressed her forefinger to his lips to silence him.

"You don't have to do any thinking on my account. I can handle Papa now that he has faced the inevitable."

"Piper—" he murmured against her fingertip.

She breezed back into the room to grab his saddlebags, then thrust them at him. "Just go. It's what you want."

Quinn huffed out his breath. "Woman, you need to understand that you can't boss me around any better than I've been able to boss you. Otherwise, this marriage isn't going to work."

She smirked caustically. "*Work?* It doesn't have to work. It's legal and that's all it has to be."

He took the saddlebags she thrust at him and dropped them beside his feet. "It *does* have to work. I have two Comanche recruits to replace me in the battalion. I have decided to reclaim my father's ranch at Phantom Springs."

Piper blinked in confusion. "You *lived* in the canyon where the showdown took place?"

"It's still my property. And with the Rangers stationed in Van Horn and this fort nearby, I can supply them with beef and horses. I'm tired of going where the wind blows me. If I want to put down roots then I'm entitled, aren't I? So…I was thinking…that I have a wife I want to keep and property to build on. I also have a new father-in-law who insists on checking up on me every six months."

He smiled crookedly when Piper stared up at him as if he had ivy sprouting from his ears.

"If you have your heart set on teaching at the fort you can stay here during the week, but I really must insist that you're home with me on weekends."

Quinn chuckled out loud when she choked on her breath. "You want me to live with you?" she finally chirped, astonished. "But *why?*"

Quinn shifted awkwardly from one moccasined foot to the other and looked away from that intense, silver-blue stare. "I think you know why, Piper," he mumbled self-consciously.

"No, I don't. Tell me *why,*" she demanded.

He sucked in a steadying breath to force out the words that he had never spoken to anyone since he couldn't remember when. "Because you make me happier than I have ever been. Because being with you feels right, natural, necessary. Because *I love you,* damn it. I tried not to, but I can't help myself."

"You love me?" she squeaked, staring at him in stupefied astonishment. "When did this happen?"

Quinn chuckled. "When I asked you the same question you practically jumped down my throat. I thought the correct response was, Thank you. That's nice to know."

She waved him off. "Just answer the question."

Irresistibly drawn to her, Quinn reached out to trace the lush curve of her mouth. "I'm not quite sure. I think it must have sneaked up on me when I wasn't looking. Or maybe it was when you got kidnapped and I was afraid I would never see you alive again. It felt like there was something I needed to tell you and I didn't know if I would have the chance.

"Or maybe it was last night when I walked in and felt like I had finally come home because you were here." He threw up his hands in frustration and said, "Oh, hell, if you want to know the honest truth I think I fell in over my head while you were dangling off the cliff in the overturned coach and Lucky knocked off that ridiculous veiled hat you were wearing as a disguise. I saw the bewitching face that went with that sassy mouth and fiery spirit and I—"

Quinn grunted uncomfortably when Piper leapt at him and sent him staggering backward. Her laughter was sweet music to his ears. The feel of her legs wrapping around his waist and her arms clenching around his neck reminded him of the magical, intimate moments they had shared.

And suddenly the resentment, grief and hardships he had battled more than half of his lifetime dissolved because Piper kissed him as if he were the center of her universe.

Quinn decided, right there and then, that he had finally found the missing half of his soul. He was tired of fighting his way through life, tired of denying that this fiery, adorable female was the one who made him *feel* again, made him hope and dream of a bright, promising future. With her.

"I will love you forever and ever, Quinn Callahan," Piper murmured as she cupped his face in both hands. "Guaranteed."

Quinn dropped a kiss to the tip of her nose. "I love you, too, sweetheart, but life has taught me that nothing is forever."

She smiled impishly up at him. Her love for him shone in those glorious blue eyes like the midday sun. "Maybe *nothing* lasts forever," she whispered, "but *this* will."

When she led him to bed and made wild sweet love

with him, she murmured that *he* was the most precious gift her heart desired. And when they were body to body and soul to soul Quinn felt himself soaring to delirious heights of the most incredible passion he had ever known, experiencing emotions that came bubbling up from nowhere like the pure, clear water in Phantom Springs.

"All I need is to see you every morning for the rest of my life and to lie in your arms every night," she assured him. "*That* is the truth. *You* are my *forever,* Quinn."

And suddenly he believed in happily ever after.

Because Piper said it was so…and she always told him the truth.

* * * * *

Harlequin Historicals®
Historical Romantic Adventure!

FOR RIVETING TALES OF RUGGED MEN AND THE WOMEN WHO LOVE THEM CHECK OUT HARLEQUIN HISTORICALS!

ON SALE MARCH 2005

THE BACHELOR
by Kate Bridges

At the town harvest festival, dashing bachelor Mitchell Reid is raffled off for charity—and lands in the unlikely arms of no-nonsense, hardworking Diana Campbell. Ever since the Canadian Mountie mistakenly tried to arrest her brothers, she's attempted to deny her attraction to the roguish Mitch. Twenty-four hours spent in his company just might change her mind....

TURNER'S WOMAN
by Jenna Kernan

Rugged mountain man Jake Turner rescues Emma Lancing, the sole survivor of an Indian massacre. Burned by love in the past, he's vowed to steer clear of women. But the young woman in his care is strong and capable—and oh, so beautiful. Can this lonely trapper survive a journey west with his heart intact?

www.eHarlequin.com

HHWEST36